Are You My Mother?

A NOVEL

C.H. Avosa

avosa books

Avosa Books
Baltimore, Maryland, USA
avosabooks.com

Discussion questions © 2021 by C. H. Avosa.
Author photo copyright © Chandra Guglik.
Cover and interior design by Avosa Books.

Cover fiber artwork copyright © Julie Shackson. Used by permission. julieshackson.com

First paperback edition March 2021

Publisher's Cataloging-in-Publication data

Names: Avosa, C.H., author.
Title: Are you my mother ? A novel / C. H. Avosa.
Description: Baltimore, MD: Avosa Books, 2021.
Identifiers: Library of Congress Control Number: 2021904558 | ISBN: 978-1-7365799-0-9 (paperback) | 978-1-7365799-1-6 (ebook) | 978-1-7365799-2-3 (Kindle) | 978-1-7365799-3-0 (audiobook)
Subjects: LCSH Adopted children--Fiction. | Birthparents--Fiction. | Family--Fiction. | African Americans--Race identity--Fiction. | Donation of organs, tissues, etc.--Fiction. | BISAC FICTION / African American & Black / Women | FICTION / Family Life / General | FICTION / Medical
Classification: LCC PS3601.V645 A74 2021 | DDC 813.6--dc23

chavosabooks.com

- 1 -

Dear God,

I don't even know what to say. I got an email last night saying that Mom isn't my mother and my real mother needs a kidney transplant and that's the only reason they're telling me and this person is my sister? I thought it was just a scam phishing email thing but she knew info about Dad and how could she possibly know? Help. I don't know what to do or who to talk to or what to think. Of course Mom is my mom. How could she not be my mom? Is that even possible? Help me, please. Give me wisdom on what to do and what to think. Thank you that you are my father and that's one thing I know for sure. Amen.

- 2 -

Sol reluctantly leaves her prayer journal on her overstuffed couch and groans as she forces herself to hurry. Knowing she's already late for work, she unsuccessfully tries to fix her red eyes in the mirror while concentrating on not spilling coffee on her yellow striped shirt. She doesn't know how she's supposed to work with this email on her mind, but she knows these kids are counting on her, and she's counting on them. They always make her feel better anyway, but she doesn't know how she's supposed to concentrate.

"Good morning, Sunshine!" her friend Faye sings out when Sol walks into their office at the renovated warehouse in the middle of Baltimore. Their literacy program, Read-Imagine, is one of the many nonprofits that sit side-by-side in the building, all committed to loving and serving the city that's synonymous with despair for those who only know it by reputation. Their program partners with the city's public schools, coordinating volunteers to work one-on-one with children who need a little extra help. They also give the children books to take home each week to read with their families and build their at-home libraries.

The chill in the building from the AC blasting the old warehouse's exposed brick gives Sol a much-needed jolt, and her eyes widen a bit. Faye's role is recruiting new volunteers, but her desk is also right inside the door, so she takes it upon herself to act as the unofficial greeter when the mood suits her. Usually, Sol loves to see her first thing and chat for a few minutes, but today, she knows she doesn't have time even if she wasn't trying to hide her red eyes.

"Hi, Faye! Sorry, I'm running late... I'll stop by later!" Sol calls out as she rushes past.

When Faye met Sol, she remembered from her high school Spanish class that "sol" is the Spanish word for "sun," and so she loves using all kinds of sunny nicknames that make Sol smile. Faye was also proud of herself for pronouncing it correctly. If anyone is unsure, Sol just tells them it's pronounced like "heart and soul."

Of course, Sol's not Spanish, Latina, or even a fluent Spanish speaker herself. Her parents are what she and her two sisters, Willow and Dove, describe as "crunchy granola." They are not quite hippies, but idealists. Or, in the case of her dad, he was an idealist. He died in a car accident when she was only five, and she had mostly grown up with her stepfather, Mike. They have all called him Mickey since he came into their lives when they were little kids obsessed with Mickey Mouse. Plus his ears kind of stick out.

Just as Sol gets to her desk, she hears, "Hey, Sol Food, I brought you some real soul food for lunch," and catches a glimpse of her sister Willow's blond hair out of the corner of her eye. Years ago, she recruited her to work there in marketing. Willow is a vegan and always working on new recipes that she likes to try on Sol. Some are delicious and some…not so much. Living in Baltimore, a city inextricably linked with Chesapeake Bay blue crabs, her vegan crab cakes are always a favorite with vegans and nonvegans alike. It must be the Old Bay seasoning. Today, when Willow sees Sol's face, she stops in her tracks, and all chatter about lunch halts instantly.

"What?" Sol says, distracted and trying to get herself settled. "Sorry."

"Are you okay?" Willow asks as she peers into Sol's face, her green eyes filled with worry. She's so close that Sol can smell her mint shampoo.

"Oh yeah, just had trouble sleeping last night. Are my eyes super puffy?" Sol tries to play it off but escapes to the restroom on the floor above them as quickly as she can. She goes into a stall and tries to take deep breaths without inhaling the strong vapor of disinfectant that hangs in the air. She comes up here when she needs to get away or a little privacy. It's not ideal, but where else can she go?

Just don't think about it, Sol. You have to get through the day. Pretend it never happened. You can think about it later. Sol's a master at talking herself off a ledge. Falling apart is just so inconvenient sometimes. She can have a meltdown when she gets home from work. That's when she remembers she's supposed to be having a first date with a guy from her dating app tonight. Ughhh…between that and realizing she's due at a school in twenty minutes, Sol doesn't even have time to think about the email again until later that night.

- 3 -

Sol texts her best friend, Thea:

Hey, I'm going out with this new guy, Franklin, tonight. Can you be my safety person? 💀

Thea: *Of course. Send me the details. Which one is he again?*

Sol: *The one with the eyebrows. Okay, we're meeting at that coffee shop on Thames St down in Fells Point at 7 tonight. Should be done by 8:30 AT THE LATEST. You know what to do. Thanks, girl! Pray for me!*

She puts on her favorite orange sweater with the polka dots that hugs her in the right places and is loose where she keeps thinking she should lose a few pounds. She wears her long, wavy brown hair down and freshens up her makeup. She doesn't want to overdo it. Her favorite jeans and orange wedge heels complete the look.

Sol is thirty-six, has never married, and knows that dating in real life is a lot different from in the movies. This is one reason she stopped watching rom-coms. They just lead her to have expectations that are out-of-touch with reality. For one thing, these safety texts. In the movies, it seems like the people meet up with a new guy and fall in love on the first date. In reality, Sol knows that as a single woman living alone, her personal safety has to come before any potential romance. That's not to say she doesn't believe in falling in love and living happily ever after. It just hasn't happened for her yet. She dates on and off. Franklin is the first guy she's meeting after taking a few months off the dating scene.

"Hi, nice to meet you," Sol says as she stretches to hug the guy with the prominent eyebrows, Franklin. *Does he get them waxed?* she wonders as she looks at his face. "Should we get coffee?" Sol walks confidently over to the counter, knowing Franklin is watching her and that she looks good.

Thankfully, Franklin likes coffee and doesn't seem too high maintenance about it. Then again, he could just be on his best behavior for their first date. Sol has learned a lot from being on the dating scene so long, like not judging too much by the first date. And for the first date, keep it brief and inexpensive. There can always be a second date, but you can't get back those hours or dollars you spent on a bad first date. She loves coffee and even took a barista class to learn how to make all the fancy espresso drinks, so coffee on a first date is usually a good call. She orders a latte and decides against getting anything to eat, even though that chocolate cupcake in the case looks amazing.

"So, Franklin…or do you have a nickname? Do people call you Frank? Or what's your middle name?" Sol jumps right in with easy questions to get the conversation started. She's gotten good at small talk after so many first dates.

"Well, my middle name is Lyndon, so no one calls me that. No, everyone pretty much calls me Franklin. My last name…Campbell…you probably know my father ran for city council last year, so my last name was on every yard sign...so that really belongs to my father."

"Oh, so what happened in the election? I'm in a different district, so I didn't really follow that one. He didn't win?" Sol asks.

"No, this lady won. I don't know, I think she knew someone who pulled some strings. Girl power." Franklin rolls his eyes at this last statement and then must remember he is on a first date and stops talking and stops rolling.

Sol just looks at him. *Is this guy for real?* she thinks. *Well, it is his dad; maybe he's just hurt he didn't win.*

"Okay, so I'll call you Franklin then," Sol continues.

"What about you? Sol means 'sun,' right? Are you Spanish?" Franklin asks.

Sol has been getting these kinds of questions all her life: What was she? She was white, but with her olive skin, dark hair, brown eyes, and Spanish name, she either blended in or confused people. Spanish, Hispanic, Latina, black, mixed, light-skinned, Italian, Greek, Jewish. Sometimes she just introduced herself as Sunny to spare herself that conversation.

"No, I'm white," she says simply.

"Oh," he says. Sol can't tell what he thinks about her answer. She presses on, attempting to steer the conversation in a different direction. "So, what do you do for work?"

Franklin proceeds to tell her about his job as an insurance broker. She finds it a little hard to come up with follow-up questions besides trying to understand his role in the larger insurance process. But she's happy he has what seems to be a stable job. She tells him a little about her job, but he doesn't seem to have many follow-up questions about that either.

Sol knows from his profile that Franklin is divorced and has children. She thinks it's a little too much to ask about that on their first date, even though she's curious to know what happened. He doesn't bring it up either, but she figures they can talk about it in the future if there's another date.

After an hour of chatting, Sol says goodbye with another quick hug. Franklin holds the hug for a couple seconds longer than Sol expects. She takes another look at him as she's leaving. She thinks he's attractive and the date wasn't bad. *Well, maybe,* she decides.

She texts Thea: *On my way home. Thanks for looking out!*

Thea: *How was it?*

Sol: *It was okay. He asked me out for dinner next week, so I guess we'll see.*

Thea: 👀

Sol: *What does that mean?*

Thea: *Just okay?? We're not going for just okay!*

Sol: *I know, I know. But I want to give him a chance.*

Thea: *The eyebrows?*

Sol: *They're kind of cute. In a BIG way.*

Thea: *SMH! Good night!*

- 4 -

Sol walks into her second-floor apartment in the shared rowhouse and right on the table in front of her is her laptop. It immediately reminds her of the previous night's email. Thinking about Franklin and whether she even wanted to go out with him again had distracted her. Now here she is, wired from the supposedly decaf coffee she had on her date, and she reads the email again.

Dear Sol,

My name is Shyla Broward. I know this is out of the blue, and I'm sorry, but there's just no easy way to do this. Please keep reading because this is important. My mom's name is Janice Broward, and she knew your dad, Patrick Garnett, in Baltimore in the early 80s when she was at University of Maryland Law School. We live outside of Boston. My mom has chronic kidney disease, and now her kidneys have failed. She's on dialysis but needs a kidney transplant. She's on the transplant list, but the wait can be five years, and they say she's hard to match. I don't think there's any way her body can wait that long.

She's only 64 years old. We're asking all of our family and friends to at least find out if there's a chance they could be a match and would be willing to donate. We don't know what else to do. I'm an only child. I don't match, and I put my name on a list to do an exchange if someone else matches. I feel helpless. I was talking to my mom's sister last week, and she said she had something to tell me. My mom tried to stop her, but she told me about you. She told me you're my sister. You're my mom's daughter. She had you with your dad, Patrick, but she couldn't keep you. She asked your dad to take you, and your mom raised you as her own, and they all promised to never tell. That's all I know. But now my mom needs a kidney, and we're desperate to find someone who matches. A family member may be less likely to get rejected. I don't know what I can tell you to even make you believe me, but please, please, I'm begging you to at least talk to me.

Here's all my contact info. You can write me back at this email address or text me or call me. I'll come to Baltimore or wherever you are.

Sincerely,
Your sister,
Shyla Broward

Her adorable mixed-breed rescue dog, Jericho, gets up from his giant dog bed and stares at her. "What?" she asks. He always knows when something's wrong with her. He leans his head on her knee, and she scratches him behind his ear. "Thanks for being a girl's best friend. Let's go for a walk and get some air, huh?"

She trades her heels for tennis shoes, then lets him pick which way they walk. Their neighborhood is located in midtown Baltimore City near Johns Hopkins University, and they both have their favorite routes. He's pretty big and protective of her, and there are usually lots of students around. The school has its own security guards out on the sidewalks too. Even though Sol loves Baltimore, she's not naïve about the crime, and she stays on her guard when she's out, especially at night. The late spring night air has a chill, but it feels refreshing to be outside.

When they get back, she starts searching the internet intently, starting with her "new sister" Shyla Broward. She finds a lawyer in Boston with that name, but she looks black, so that doesn't seem to match. There are a few others scattered around the country. Does she have a married name? She didn't mention a husband. Social media yields nothing. No mutual friends. "Janice Broward" is not exactly blowing up the internet either. She never had this much trouble when she was looking up her online dating guys. Now *that* yielded a lot of information.

She starts looking up basic information about kidney disease and kidney transplants. What the email said is true, but she had never given it much thought. She knew there was a waiting list but didn't know so many people were dying while waiting on that list. The amount of information she finds is overwhelming, and she's not even sure which things to read. She finds a sample letter for how to ask people to donate an organ to you. *Did Shyla read that same page?* She gets lost in the #kidneytransplant hashtag on Instagram for an hour before she asks herself what she's doing.

"You don't even know if this is real," she says out loud. Jericho looks at her with anxious eyebrows, as if to say *I'm worried about you—is everything okay?* She looks back at him and says, "I know, Coco. Our lives may be about to change."

Meanwhile Sol asks herself why she doesn't just ask her mom. Sol's relationship with her mom is good. They're not super close like some of her friends are with their moms, but they get along well. Maybe it's just that with the three girls, she had to spread her love around more. Anyway, she doesn't want to hurt her mom if it's not true, but if it is true… If it is true, what does that say about her mom? That she kept the truth from her all these years? Does that mean she loves her less because she's not really hers? Or more because she chose her when she wasn't really hers? Or maybe either way, she is really hers because she has raised her as her own? Did her mom adopt her? She has to talk to someone about this. Going around and around in her own head about it is getting her nowhere.

- 5 -

Hey, Thea, I know it's getting late, but any chance you're free?
I need to talk. Sol texts Thea. She knows her best friend can
keep things confidential.

Thea calls her two minutes later and cuts right to the
chase: "Are you okay? What's this about? I'm worried about
you. Don't tell me it's about that guy."

Thea and Sol have been friends since high school, and
Thea can read Sol better than anyone. They stayed close
even though they went away to different colleges and then
were reunited when they both ended up back in Baltimore.
Thea married her high school boyfriend, Quentin, and they
now have two daughters. The girls are both in elementary
school now, and Thea is recently back to work full-time as a
project manager at one of the big financial firms downtown.

"I'm okay," Sol replies, halfheartedly.

"Phew. Well, what is going on?"

"It's complicated." Sol catches her up on the email and
everything she's thinking so far. Thea listens and doesn't
make a sound until she's done.

Then she says, "Holy crap."

"I know."

"Is it true?

"I don't know."

"You have to talk to your mom. Even if you're afraid of the truth, you have to find out the truth. You're never going to be settled until you figure this out. This is crazy. This is about the fundamentals of your life."

"I know."

"Do you want me to come with you?" Thea offers.

"Let me think about it." Sol doesn't know if she even wants to talk to her mom. She doesn't know anything right now. Everything she thought she knew wasn't real. Or was it? She's questioning everything.

Thea breaks into her thoughts. "Okay, well you can't stop me from praying. Heavenly Father, please help Sol right now. Give her wisdom and courage to do what she has to do. Help her to know that she's held by you no matter what. In Jesus's name, amen."

"Amen."

Sol loves that Thea prays for her like this. She thinks she needs all the prayers she can get right now. Thea is the one who invited her to her church's serving day all those years ago, where Sol decided to become a Christian, so they have had a lot of years of practice praying for one another.

"Thank you, Thea." Sol hangs up and collapses on her bed.

- 6 -

Dear God,
I don't know what to do. I'm so confused. Thea says I should talk to Mom. And say what? "Are you my mother?" Seriously? Ugh. Help me to know what to do! I can't think about anything else, and Thea's right, now I'm going to be thinking about this until I know the truth. I can't go back. And if Janice really is my mom, she could be dying right now! This is so much pressure. If she is my mom, would I even want to give her a kidney anyway? She's a stranger! Would I do that for a stranger? So many questions, and I have no answers. Help!

- 7 -

JERICHO22? SUNNYDAZE83? What password did she last use? Her work email has decided to prompt her for a password today for some reason. She's anxious to check her email to see if they're going to get a grant she helped write the application for. It would make such a difference for this special advocacy project they're trying to get started.

When she finally just resets it to LATTE21218, she doesn't even have an email about that. She does have a new message through her professional profile online, though. It's Shyla, the lawyer she found, who saw that Sol had visited her page. Sol still hasn't replied to the email from the week before.

"Sol, since you visited my business profile page, you must've gotten my email about mom. I know it must be a shock. It's a shock to me too. But this is urgent. Please get in touch. We need to talk. Your sister, Shyla."

Sol still doesn't know what she wants to do, so she just shuts down her laptop and heads out to her first school visit of the day. She tells herself she'll figure it out later. As she drives, she quizzes herself with the practice track from her adult Spanish class to keep herself from thinking about lawyers named Shyla, kidneys, and unexpected emails. She figures the Spanish class will be more useful than the barista class, at least until she gets her own espresso machine. "Un cafe con leche, por favor."

- 8 -

That Sunday, Sol's family gets together for Mickey's birthday. Her mom cooks a ton of homemade Polish sausage, potato pancakes, and sauerkraut, his favorite meal. Patricia Thompson is originally Patty Sipinski from a big Polish family in Baltimore and has recipes that have been passed down in her family for generations. Mickey always talks about how blessed he is to have found her—and not just because of the cooking. It's a bittersweet story, since the reason they met and eventually married was because Sol's dad, Patrick, had died.

Mickey is Mike Thompson, the owner of Mike's Moving. Everyone in Baltimore knows his company's jingle: "Make your move go right, move with Mike..." All these years later, people still sing it to him. That jingle was the best money he could have ever spent on his business. Mike's Moving is who moved Sol's family into the house they bought with Sol's dad's insurance money. Mickey and Patty became friends, and he always seemed to be there when she needed help with something. They got married about five years after Patrick died.

Today Mickey is turning sixty-eight, and the timing

helps Sol figure out her next move. Her mom has always kept a row of photo albums on a bookcase in the living room. Sol decides to look for a picture of her mom when she was pregnant with her. Willow sits beside her as they look through the old pictures and talk about their memories. Memories of their dad too, though she wonders whether she really remembers him at all or if the memories are conjured from the stories people have told her over the years and the old pictures like this. Dove was a little older when he died, eight years old, and so she definitely has real memories of him. She's living in California now, working with a high-profile commercial real estate development company, so Sol can't tap into her memories now. Dove did a quick video call to say happy birthday to Mickey, but that was hours ago.

"Oh, here's a picture of mom pregnant with me! And you and Dove are just swarming her legs!" Willow shouts out.

"Oh, here's one of mom when she was pregnant with Dove. Looking super crunchy granola! I love your hair parted down the middle like that, Mom!" Sol yells to the kitchen.

"Aww, here I am at my first birthday! Aren't I cute?" Sol says. "No preggo mom, though! Hey Mom, do you have a picture when you were pregnant with me?"

"I don't know—isn't there one in there?" Patty answers.

"Hmm, I don't see one," Sol says, but she decides not to push it. They keep looking through the albums and especially crack up about their old prom pictures.

The Polish food has her thinking about her Grandma and Grandpa Sipinski. They both died when the girls were in high school, but before that, the family had all spent a lot of time together. Patty's younger sister lived in the Sipinski family house now. Sol looks through the older pictures to find one of her grandparents and asks her mom if she can take it home with her.

She doesn't really remember her dad's parents much. After Patrick died, they pretty much disappeared. Patrick was an only child, and his death completely devastated them. Her mom had once told them that shortly after Patrick died, his dad developed dementia. They used to send checks for the girls' birthdays, but she can't remember when that stopped either. She didn't think about them much because they weren't really there in the years she remembered. But now that she's looking through these old pictures, she realizes that it's another missing part of her family tree.

When she gets home that night, Sol starts looking through her papers for her birth certificate. *Where did I put it? When did I last even look at it?* She searches for two hours before she finds it wedged in the back of a drawer.

When she looks at the certificate, it says just what it has always said:

State of Maryland Certificate of Live Birth

Child's name: Sol Surya Garnett

Date of Birth: June 22, 1983

Hour: 7:39 AM

City or Town of Birth: Baltimore City

Hospital Name: Harbor Hospital

Father's Name: Patrick Gant Garnett

Mother's Full Maiden Name: Patricia Liliana Sipinski

I certify that this child was born alive on the date and hour stated above.

Certifier's Signature

Date Signed: June 22, 1983

She's so confused but decides that's enough detective work for one day. She leaves the papers strewn all over her bed and takes her journal to the couch with Jericho to try to at least get a couple of thoughts out.

- 9 -

Dear God,

Things are just more confusing now. I didn't find a picture with Mom pregnant and she seemed kind of vague about it. I found my birth certificate and it says she's my mom. Could my birth certificate be fake? Who fakes a birth certificate? Should I have said yes to doing a DNA test when Willow was thinking about giving them to the whole family for Christmas gifts last year? Would finding out through a DNA test make this easier or harder? Because who knows what it would say? I have to talk to Mom. I know I do. Please help me to figure out how to do it.

- 10 -

After texting her friend Faye the details of where she'd be and perusing the menu online, Sol meets Franklin for dinner that Thursday at Mesa Mexican Restaurant in a suburban shopping plaza. She figures that even if the date isn't great, at least she knows the food will be delicious! She arrives straight from work and is wearing a red shirtdress and flowered ballet flats. He also comes straight from work and is wearing khakis and a red polo shirt. She laughs when she realizes they're matching.

She gives him a quick hug hello and tries to focus her attention on the present moment. She wants to give him a chance, but it would be a stretch to say she's excited about him right now. She doesn't have enough information yet, so she'll see how the night goes. It's times like this that she wonders if or how things would be different if she were already married. It's not like she can talk to Franklin about whether her mom is her real mom and what she should do about the email from Shyla when it's only their second date. She hopes that if she did have a husband, he would provide emotional support and advice in this situation, but she also knows that relationships don't always go the way you'd think.

Sol and Franklin are seated in a booth next to a round table with a couple and three young children. The children are coloring on their kids' placemats, and the couple seem at peace, chatting intermittently. Sol had kind of thought that she would have that life by now. She wonders if she's any closer to it in her thirties than in her twenties. She gives herself credit for being out on a date. She knows she has to meet new men somehow.

The restaurant isn't overly crowded, but there are enough people there to create a buzz. Sol looks over the menu and tries to find something without beans and that won't be too messy to eat. Two dates is definitely not long enough to be comfortable having gas around the other person! Even though she had already looked at the menu, she hadn't narrowed down her choices yet. She looks longingly at the margaritas but thinks it's probably better to skip the alcohol until she has a better sense of who he is. She decides on chicken enchiladas with the green sauce instead of the red. Franklin goes all in for steak and seafood fajitas with a jalapeño margarita. Sol knows the smell from his sizzling fajita pan will be in her hair before the meal is over.

"So how is your week going?" Sol asks Franklin after they've ordered from the waitress.

He loads a chip with salsa, stuffs it in his mouth. "Ugh," he says. "It was supposed to be my weekend to have the kids, and I had planned to take them to this family party at my parents' house, but my ex is acting completely psycho and doesn't want me to take them now. So I've been going back and forth with her all week."

"Oh, that sounds frustrating. Why doesn't she want you

to take them?" Sol asks, careful to sound neutral. This is the first time he's talking about his ex-wife and children, and she wants to know everything. She wonders what caused their marriage to break up and how that bodes for her possible relationship with him. And could she see herself as a stepmom to his children?

"She says my parents feed them too much sugar, and she wants them to eat this whole all-natural diet. Blah blah," Franklin says as he eats two more chips. "Anyway, I definitely want to have more kids and can't wait until I can make all the decisions without having to ask her opinion. Do you want to have kids? Wait, you don't have any, do you?"

"Um," Sol is taken aback by the question and is trying not to look at the chip piece that has fallen out of his mouth. "No, I don't have any yet, but I've always wanted—"

"Hey, babe, can I get some more water?" Franklin waves down the waitress who had taken their order. He turns back to Sol. "This jalapeño margarita is hot!"

Sol stares at him in shock. "Did you just call her 'babe'?"

"Yeah, what's wrong with that?" Franklin asks, surprised, slurping at his ice.

"Uh, that's not the right thing to call a grown woman who's not your wife or girlfriend. Anyway, yes, I would like to have kids."

"Oh, okay, who knew? Don't call a woman, 'babe.' Haha. So what if you can't get pregnant?"

"Well, I've always thought about adoption. I'm already what they call 'advanced maternal age,' so I don't know what my chances are. What about you—would you want to adopt?"

"No, I don't want to have someone else's kids. I want them to look like me. And like my other kids." He seems completely oblivious to the look on her face.

"Oh." Sol knows it's his right to not want to adopt. But she is a little taken aback by his answer, especially since she had just said she has always thought about adopting. But she has heard that same view from others before. Some people do feel strongly about it. She wonders what kind of a father he is. She decides to just dive right in with more uncomfortable questions since things are already a little uncomfortable—for her, at least.

"So do you want to tell me a little about your marriage or what led to your divorce?" she says.

"Haha, I knew that question was coming. All women are the same and want to know that," he says laughing, then takes a drink of his margarita.

"Well, I wouldn't say we're all the same, but it is kind of an important question when we're getting to know you and thinking about a romantic relationship." Sol thinks this is obvious but tries to be patient and not get distracted by his offhand comments.

"Sure, I'll tell you what happened. She thought I was cheating on her. She could never get used to me talking to other women or having female friends."

"But you weren't?" Sol has to ask just to be sure.

"No, of course not. I mean, she started talking about emotional affairs or something, and I was just like, no, I don't even care about them," he says, waving his margarita in the air for emphasis.

"Oh, and you couldn't work it out?"

"I'm here, aren't I?"

Sol is thankful when the food comes, and the bartender turns on the Orioles game in the bar area. Franklin focuses on assembling his fajitas, and they both kind of watch the game as they chat. Sol decides she's collected enough information for her to ponder for now, and Franklin doesn't ask very many questions.

As expected, the food is delicious and neither of them has leftovers. Sol confirms in the bathroom that the fajita smell has indeed gotten into her hair. She takes an extra minute to pull herself together, then returns to the table to split the check with him.

In the parking lot, Franklin takes her hand as he walks her to her car. Sol has to admit that it's nice to hold hands and be out on a date. Sometimes she has to remind herself that she can be a "leading lady," not just a "supportive friend."

When Sol gets home, she texts Faye to let her know, then checks her dating app and sets up a coffee date with another guy, Raymond, she's been messaging with. She doesn't want to overreact to the conversation with Franklin at dinner, but she's definitely questioning whether there's any hope for their relationship.

The phone rings shortly thereafter, and it's Thea wanting to know about her date. Thea wants her to find a great guy and get married, so she's always asking about Sol's dating life and trying to find guys to set her up with. Sol appreciates it, but she has to admit sometimes it's annoying to be grilled by someone who doesn't really understand what it's like to be out on the dating scene in your late thirties, patiently (or impatiently) trying and hoping, over and over again.

"Sooooo???" Thea opens.

"Hi, Thea!"

"Spill the beans, Sol."

"Well, I don't know."

"What do you mean you don't know? Did you get to know him any better on this date?"

"I did. I think there are some red flags. We talked about his marriage and kids a little. Um, and one other thing."

"What, Sol? Why are you beating around the bush?!"

Sol lets out a huge sigh. "He called the waitress 'babe.'"

"He what?!"

"Yeah. I mean, I corrected him and everything, and he acted like he didn't know it was inappropriate."

"Seriously?! This guy is a piece of work."

"So anyway, I set up a date with another guy from the app."

"Thank goodness! Sol, I told you it's a numbers game. The more guys you go out with, the more chances you have to find a good one."

"Uh-huh."

"You know I'm right. You're amazing—you just need to go out with more guys."

"Thea, you're not the one who has to go out with all these 'roughs' to find the 'diamond.'"

"I know, I know, haha. But I know what I'm talking about!"

"How do you know? Did you read an article about it? You married your high school boyfriend! You didn't have to go through all this."

"I know, but this is how it is these days. I just want you

to find someone great!"

Sol decides it's no use having this conversation right now. "I know, Thea. Okay, I'm tired, I'll talk to you later."

"Night, Sun."

Sol rolls her eyes at Jericho, then grabs his leash to take him out back before they go to bed.

- 11 -

The stack of folded laundry on her bed is growing. Sol tackles the pile of unmatched socks next and thinks she may need to rearrange the sock drawer too. She's supposed to be leaving to meet with her mom, but she's stalling. There's a bundle of unopened mail that looks inviting. Anything looks more inviting than having this conversation with her mom about Shyla's email. Sol has so many conflicting emotions. She's afraid of finding out that the story is true, what it will mean for her, and how it will change things, but she feels like she has to know. There's no going back now.

She pulls up to the arboretum, one of her favorite spots in the city, where Patty is scheduled to meet her. She loves to come here and get lost in the trees and plants, especially now in the spring when the flowers are all in bloom. She made up a story—okay, she lied—about Read-Imagine planning an event and wanting to check out the arboretum as a possible venue. Her mom is great at event planning and loves everything natural and sustainable, so Sol asked her to consult on how the fictional event could be organized here.

"Hi, Mom!" Sol tries to force some cheer into her voice as she sees Patty walking up with her notepad and pen in hand, ready to plan. Her mom looks energized by the space's possibilities, and her shoulder-length gray hair is blowing in the breeze, giving her a bit of a mad scientist look. Sol feels almost bad when she sees her mom is wearing her clunky sneakers and has a camping water bottle strapped onto her waist.

"Hey, hon! It's so fun to meet you in the middle of the week! Do you want to tell me what you're thinking for the event, and we can talk about the logistics while we walk around?" her mom says, jumping right in.

Sol freezes for a second, forgetting that the event is a cover story, then quickly snaps out of it. She clears her throat and tries to keep her voice neutral. "Actually...can we go sit on that bench over there and talk about a few things first?"

"Sure, whatever you think is best," her mom says, as she follows her to a bench that's set back a little from the paved path. The bench has a gold-colored plaque on it that says *In loving memory of Iris.*

Sol makes sure to leave several inches between them on the bench, and when they're both seated, she tries to talk, but promptly bursts into tears.

Patty fumbles to put her things down quickly and puts her arm around Sol's shoulders. "Hey, what's going on? Is this event stressing you out?"

Through sobs, Sol tries to explain, "Mom, sorry, there actually is no event." She wipes her nose on the front of her shirt, then continues. "I just told you that to get you to come here. I have to ask you about something. Or some*one*, I guess I should say."

"What? Okay, what's going on? Now I'm worried!"

Patty's eyes get a panicked look.

Sol takes a deep breath, then another, trying to stop crying and steady herself. Finally, she croaks out, "I got an email."

Patty patiently waits for her to continue. They both watch a robin alight at their feet, take five steps, and then fly away.

"It said that someone named Janice Broward is really my mom."

Patty's head snaps back. "What?!"

"Is it true?" Sol whispers without looking at her.

Her mom cries out, "Sunshine, I'm so sorry!" and tries to hug her. Sol pushes quickly away from her until she's on the very edge of the bench.

"So it is true?" Sol follows up glumly. She can't look at her mom. She keeps her eyes focused on scratching off her peeling fingernail polish.

"Oh, Sol, I should have told you everything before. I told myself over and over again that I would. But I was afraid— that you would leave me or hate me or think I wasn't really your mom. I didn't want to mess things up. And then, the more time that passed, the harder it was to tell you. I love you so much. You know that, right?" Now Patty starts to cry too. Sol hadn't thought to bring tissues, so she wipes her nose on the front of her wet shirt again. Soon, they're both covered with snot and tears and streaked makeup.

Finally, Sol says, "Mom, I don't understand. What in the world is going on? Are you my mother??"

Patty sighs deeply and takes a minute. "Sol, I love you. I'm your mom. I'll always be your mom. Forever and ever. You are the most precious thing to me. You and your sisters. But, no, I didn't give birth to you. The email is true. Janice Broward is your biological mother. I knew you would find out sooner or later. I just wish I could have been the one to tell you."

"So tell me now. What happened? How did this happen?!" Sol urgently pleads, searching her mother's face.

Patty clenches and unclenches her hands, then slowly picks up her camping canteen and takes a sip of water. "The year before you were born, your dad and I decided to separate. We had gotten pregnant with a second baby when Dove was about one year old. We wanted to have this big family, and we were so excited. We told everyone; everything was perfect. But then, when I was just about eleven weeks along, I lost the baby. And then everything fell apart. I cried every day; I just couldn't stop. Your dad cried too. But, after a while, he wanted to move on. He said, 'Come on, let's try again. We'll have another, we'll have five more.' He thought the best thing to do was to try to get back to 'normal' and get pregnant again. Things are a little different now—people are grieving their lost babies a little more— but then I just knew I couldn't get back to normal. So we had a lot of arguments. We couldn't agree on what to do to move forward. So after this went on for a while—and don't forget, Dove was still a toddler—we decided to spend some time apart. Your dad moved in with his friend who lived down in Pigtown, and he would bike to work downtown. We weren't really talking at all then, just trying to get some breathing room. But I didn't think we'd get a divorce or anything. We just…took a break. It was hard to know what to do."

Sol sits as still as a statue, listening to Patty talk. In her head, she knows that her mom is talking about her own father, Patrick, who had tragically died when she was five years old and who she has grown up loving and missing. In her heart, though, it's like her mom is just talking about some other family. She has seen her friends go through some complicated situations like this and knows that things happen all the time. She just never thought it could happen to her, in her own family.

Her mom continues, "We had been separated almost a year, and then, I got a call from your dad one day. We did still talk, but this was a day that changed my life. He said he had gotten someone pregnant in the fall, that they had broken up before she even found out she was pregnant, but she had just given birth. It turns out that he had met her at the café where he stopped for coffee every morning. I mean, I didn't even know he was seeing anyone. He was crying and so upset I almost couldn't make sense of what he was saying. And I was so shocked that it didn't make sense anyway. He hadn't told the woman—Janice—that he was married before they started dating, and when she found out, she broke things off with him right away, but then she discovered she was pregnant just a few weeks later. She was planning to have the baby—you—on her own even though she was in law school. But then I think there was some other stuff going on, and she didn't see any way that she could take care of you. So she asked your dad if we would take you. So that's how everything happened."

What the heck? Sol thinks. *This is how I came into the world??*

Now that Patty had gotten started, the story comes

flooding out. "I was so sad and angry. I felt betrayed by your dad. I couldn't believe he had started a relationship with someone else, much less gotten her pregnant. I thought we were going to work things out. I just hung up on him because I was so upset. But my mind would not stop thinking about you. I cried and cried. Your dad called me again a few hours later and said, 'Patty, I think we should raise this baby together. I love you. I know I haven't been the best husband, but we can do this. We may have lost our baby, but here's another baby that needs us.' I told him I'd think about it, but I knew I wanted you from the very beginning. From that first phone call. My heart was already joined with yours. A couple hours later, I called and told him. The next day, your dad brought you home and moved back in. And from that day, we worked to rebuild our family."

"But wait," Sol interrupts. "I just looked at my birth certificate, and it said you were my birth mother at the hospital. Harbor Hospital. I looked for it the other day after I got the email. Remember, I was at the house looking for pictures of you when you were pregnant with me?"

"Yes, I know. The birth certificate is confusing, but that's just what they did back then. When a child was adopted, they issued a new birth certificate so no one would ever know. It wasn't like it is now with open adoptions." Patty's replies are coming out so smoothly now, like she has been rehearsing the answers to these questions for years.

"Are you kidding me?!" Sol wonders how that's even legal.

"Yes, that's just what they did. They thought it was best. I mean, that's what we thought was best too, to let you think that I was your birth mother," Patty shrugs. "Wait, you never told me who sent you the email."

"Shyla sent it," Sol replies.

Patty's brow wrinkles. "Who is Shyla?!"

"Janice … my biological mom, I guess … needs a kidney transplant. Her daughter Shyla emailed me and asked me about donating a kidney! *She* just found out about *me* because they're trying to find anyone who might be a kidney match, and Janice's sister told her!" Sol blurts out.

Patty tries to hug her again, and Sol lets her this time. "I'm so sorry you had to find out like this. I should have told you years ago." Patty sits there, deep in thought. After a few minutes, she murmurs, "A kidney transplant."

Even though Patty has gone off in her thoughts some-where, Sol is still hoping her mom can provide some answers. She feels like there's so much she still doesn't know. She shifts uncomfortably on the bench and jiggles her leg impatiently. "Mom, what am I supposed to do? I haven't even written her back yet."

Patty snaps out of her reverie. "I'm sorry, hon, but I don't know what you should do. You're going to have to decide what you want. I know Janice loved you and was just doing what she thought would give you a good chance at life. And you have it. You have a great life. We named you Sol because you brought light into our family at a really dark time. I would never go back and change that. But you're a grown woman now. This is your life." Her mom starts crying all over again.

Sol just leans her head back on the bench and watches the clouds move slowly across the sky.

- 12 -

Dear God, wow, this is a lot. But I'm glad I know the truth now. Nothing has changed, but everything has changed. I still need to figure out what to do. What do you want me to do in this situation? I'm so confused.

- 13 -

When Sol sees the woman with the giant white flower behind her ear, flowered dress, and natural hair pinned up in vintage rolls a la Billie Holiday, she knows Thea has beat her to their favorite pizza place, Ledo's. The conservative dress code at Thea's job and her love of music are some of the reasons her friend loves to experiment with different styles—especially those of iconic black performers—when she's not at work.

When Thea waves to her, Sol flies into her arms for a big hug, and immediately the tears well up in her eyes. Thea hugs her tight and then looks into her face.

"There's nothing that pizza and beer can't fix," Thea says, and they both laugh, then find a booth. Sol is once again in the situation of trying to fix her makeup with the napkins on the table. Even though Sol and Thea always order their same favorite things every time, they both carefully study the menu. Sol thinks maybe they just need to come here more often to try some different dishes. They both put their beer orders in too.

Once their pizza arrives—meat lovers for Thea and chicken parmesan for Sol—Sol fills her in on everything that happened with her mom—well, both of her moms. "Are you kidding me?" "What?!" "Wow!" are the only words that escape from Thea as she listens with rapt attention, even ignoring her pizza until the end of the story. She doesn't even flinch when Sol pauses for a sip of her drink.

When Sol finally finishes the story, Thea just says, "So what are you going to do?"

"I guess I have to write Shyla back. One way or the other. I can't imagine what she's going through either. She just found out about me, not to mention her mom needs a kidney!"

Thea nods. "I agree. Do you want me to help? Let's do it now!"

Sol is exhausted just from telling the story. "Nah...I think tomorrow will be better. Right now, let's just focus on the pizza! I need a break from thinking about it. Plus, I want to see what you think about these guys from the dating apps..." Sol pulls her phone from her purse.

"Okay, girl, I'm here for whatever you need, but I'm not going to let you off the hook. I'm checking in tomorrow on this email." Thea gives her the serious look that's usually reserved for her two daughters when they're acting up. "So what's going on with the guys? You know I'm not a fan of Mr. Eyebrows. Why do you keep seeing him?"

They order another round of beer and settle in to talk about guys, a good distraction for Sol, even though it can be a tough topic sometimes too.

"Ugh, I don't know. I keep thinking these bad moments with him are one-offs. Hope springs eternal, right? Anyway, you'll be happy to know I set up a date with a new guy,

Raymond, this coming Sunday." Sol smiles sneakily and wiggles her eyebrows.

"Yay! I want to see him!" Thea grabs Sol's phone and starts looking through Raymond's profile. "Okay, he looks good! Ooo, six feet, three inches—nice and tall. Government job; sounds stable. You have to let me know how it goes!"

"I know. I'm cautiously optimistic. I'll let you know! I mean, sometimes I think you got the last good guy. I bought a new red dress too—so pretty! I mean, I don't want to overwhelm the guy on our first date or anything, but I just love this dress. Your outfit today looks amazing, by the way. I meant to tell you, but you know…tears."

"Thanks, Sol. Okay, you seriously need to send me a picture on Sunday! I hope this guy's a good one."

"Cheers to that," Sol says, and they raise their glasses for a toast.

- 14 -

When Sol gets home from work the next day, she snuggles up with Jericho and gets her laptop situated on a tray in front of her. "Alright, buddy, you've got to help me with this email," she says to him. He looks back as though he under-stands and is saying *I'll be here.*

Dear Shyla,

I'm sorry it took me so long to respond. I just needed some time to digest everything. I know this is urgent, but you can imagine how shocked I was to get your message. I don't know how I feel about the transplant yet or getting tested. Can you tell me what the next steps would be so I can think about it some more?

I do want to know more about you and your life and Janice. I talked to my mom (Patty), and she told me the whole story. I still can't believe it, but I know I don't have all of the time in the world to get used to this news. You said you're an only child. Who else is there in your family, and who is getting tested?

Sol

- 15 -

Sol doesn't know why, but this situation is making her appreciate her family even more. When she sees her sister sitting at her desk the next day, she comes up behind her and hugs her shoulders. "Sunshine on my shoulders..." Willow belts out, singing the old John Denver song Patty used to play all the time.

Sol laughs, then whispers, "Hey, Will, I have to talk to you about something but it's kind of serious. I know it's not the best time, but it's weighing on me."

"Okay, meet me out by my car in ten minutes and we'll talk," Willow says immediately.

Even though it's early on the West Coast, Sol texts her older sister, Dove, to see if she can join them. Dove texts back to say she has a big meeting this morning, and she'll have to catch up with her another time. Sol knew it was a long shot that she'd be available.

Once they're in Willow's car, Willow asks, "What's going on?!"

Sol looks out the car window and realizes that people they know are intermittently walking by. "Can you drive around the corner?" she asks. Sol doesn't know how the conversation is going to go and whether she'll be able to keep her emotions in check, much less how Willow will respond. Once again, she realizes she's forgotten to bring tissues.

"Seriously, Sol? Okay, but tell me what's happening. You said it was serious." Willow drives out of the parking lot and parallel parks in a space down the block.

Sol makes sure Willow is in park before she speaks again. "It is," she says. "Now I've talked to Mom, and I found out it's true. I got this email the other day saying she wasn't my mom."

"What?!" Willow exclaims. Her shocked face tells Sol she can probably skip the next question, but she asks anyway.

"So you didn't know?"

"No! Are you kidding me?" Willow's eyes are wide.

"I talked to Mom on Tuesday. She told me how it all happened. I just didn't know if I was the last one to find out," Sol says. She fills Willow in on everything that's been happening, including how Patrick and Janice got together. She's not as emotional as she had been over the past couple of weeks since she's had a little time to get used to the idea. She manages to get through the story without crying, but now Willow looks like she's tearing up.

When Sol finishes the story, Willow hugs her across the front seat of the car. "Wow, Sol, I can't believe this. I guess that means technically you're our half sister or adopted sister? Ugh, I want to talk more, but I have a meeting in two minutes! Thank you for telling me, though. I'm sorry you've been carrying this around alone for weeks!"

"Thanks, Will! It feels good to talk about it even though

I'm so confused. I love you, and I'm so happy to have you as my sister. I'll let you know what happens!"

"You better! And you know I'm here for you if you need me." She drives them back into the parking lot, and Willow rushes off to her meeting.

- 16 -

Sol checks her email that night and sees that Shyla has written her back:

Dear Sol,

Thank you so much for responding. I know it's a lot to take in. I was so shocked to find out, but I'm so happy too. I've always wanted a sister. I know it's not the same, but we still have time to get to know each other if you want to. Some of the other people in the family knew about you and some of them didn't. It was a complicated situation, and my grandmother didn't want it to be even more complicated by bringing a lot of people into it. Gran knew about you and of course Pops, our grandfather, did too. They helped Mom while she was pregnant with you. I don't think they approved of her getting involved with your father, but they accepted the situation and tried to help Mom get through it. As I told you, my Aunt Jackie knew about you because she was there. I have a lot of aunts and uncles! Gran and Pops believed that children were a gift from God, and it shows! I wish you could have met them. Gran lived to be 90 but died just a few years ago, and Pops—we say he couldn't go on without her since they had been married so long; he died just a few months later. My dad's parents are still alive and retired to Florida, so we try to go visit every year. Have you heard of the Villages? It's like a whole city down there, but really, it's a retirement community. They actually had twins two times, plus other kids—if you can believe it—so I have a lot of cousins. I don't know if my dad's parents know about you yet, but I think my mom is telling everyone now little by little. With her health, things that seemed like such a big deal are coming into better perspective. I think she's afraid that you will hate her, but she says she has been thinking about you all these years. She took a break from law school after the pregnancy and left Baltimore as soon as she could after you were born. I think it was a really hard decision for her to give you up, and she didn't want to be reminded of you everywhere she turned. She always planned to go back to finish school. Your dad sent her letters every now and then just to let her know how you were doing. It sounds like he was crazy about you by the way he talked about you! He said he was sorry that things had happened the way they did, but he would never change anything because he just adored you. My mom showed me some of the letters the other day, and I even saw your baby picture. You were such a cute baby!!!! She kept them and would read them over and over, despite wanting to forget to make it easier. When your dad died, her friend from the coffee shop called to tell her. She was so sad that he had died, but she was even more sad that you had lost your father. Your mom did write to her once after that, but my mom knew she was grieving, and it was hard just to get through the day. Our mom (sorry, I don't know what to call her) met my dad when she came back here, and they got married, and I was born in 1986. I wanted to fulfill Mom's dream of becoming a lawyer, and now I am one. You probably already saw this online. Mom did become a paralegal, and she instilled a passion for a law career in me. What about you? Can you tell me about your family? I would like to get to know you if that is okay with you.

Your sister,

Shyla

- 17 -

The new red dress looks amazing paired with her light brown wedges and clutch, even though the neutral accessories make her feel so conservative. She got lots of compliments on it at church. Sol gives herself a wink in the mirror, then texts Willow with the details of her first date with the new guy, Raymond. *Hope springs eternal*, she says to herself. Franklin has been asking her to meet again, but she's been too distracted to make room in her schedule for him. She picked a coffee shop in a Baltimore suburb to meet Raymond for their date today. She's hoping that means she doesn't run into anyone she knows. The locals call Baltimore "Small-timore" for a reason!

When Sol sees Raymond, she smiles and gives him a quick hug. "Nice to meet you!" They do the normal small talk, and Sol thinks he's pretty cute. She likes how he asks questions and seems interested in learning about her too. She knows it's a little hard to tell on the first date—people tend to be on their best behavior and looking their most attractive—but it's a good start. She asks about his living situation and he says, "Well, I usually stay at my parents' house during the week because they live near my job."

"Oh, really?" Sol says, surprised but trying not to show it. "I thought you said you just bought a house." She can't believe how many guys she's met who live with their parents!

"I did," Raymond replies. "But it's in Rock Hall on the Eastern Shore. Of course my realtor sold it to me like, 'It's only about twenty-five miles away from here.' But he didn't tell me that was if I had wings or a boat! It's a new build, so it's not like I was driving there to look at an existing house. I was looking at plans and picking all my options. The place is amazing! And the price was so good! I mean, maybe I was a little starry-eyed. But turns out my commute over the Bay Bridge ends up being almost two hours to get to work. I should have known it was too good to be true. So I usually stay at my parents' house and then go home on the weekend. What about you?"

"Oh, that makes sense," Sol answers, trying not to show her disappointment that he is a grown man living with his parents and looking for a wife. "Yeah, I'm thankful my commute isn't bad. I have an apartment in a rowhouse in Baltimore City near Johns Hopkins University. The best thing is there's a shared backyard that I can use to take my dog out. So tell me about your job."

They continue chatting, and he seems nice, but all Sol can think about is how can she consider dating someone who lives with his parents. Even though he does have his own house. Once again, she's thankful she's learned to keep her first dates to an hour. When they say goodbye, Sol makes sure not to make any promises about seeing him again.

She texts Willow to let her know she's back home and

then texts Thea: *Another one bites the dust. I'll tell you every-thing tomorrow. SMH!*

Thea texts back, *Oh no, not another one.* 😵 *That dress though!*

- 18 -

The next day, all the stress of thinking through the truth of how she came into this world finally catches up with Sol. She wakes up in the morning and immediately realizes there's no way she can function at work. She takes a rare sick day and gets back in bed after quickly taking Jericho out in the backyard.

She sleeps for a couple more hours, decides to make herself some French toast, and then once she's sufficiently fortified, spends the afternoon on her laptop looking up everything on her mind. Even just typing in "I just found out I'm adopted" in her search bar brings up a whole unexpected community of people called "late-discovery adoptees." Evidently, the explosion of DNA testing, sold as "find your roots," has led to a lot of unexpected consequences, which are not all happy. Some people are finding out their dad isn't really their dad. Some people are finding out they were adopted as a baby. She hasn't seen anyone yet who finds out their mom isn't their mom, but she feels a little better knowing she's not the only one who received shocking news like this in her late thirties.

The way people handle it varies. Some of them want to

reconnect with their birth families. Some feel betrayed by family members who knew the truth but never told them. Some of them feel blessed when they realize they were rescued from a hard life. Some are excited to connect with family members they never knew they had. Most people say they feel confused and a mix of all these things. Sol definitely does.

Since the sun sets so much later this time of year, Sol is still looking things up into the evening and starts investigating the kidney donor and transplant process. She had only read the basics the other day, and already, that was so much information to understand. She remembers that she never talked to Dove after their texts the other day. She calls her now since she figures Dove should be out of work, despite the three-hour time difference. The call goes to voicemail after one ring, and then Sol gets a text, *Can't talk now. Call you later.*

Sol wonders how she can communicate to Dove how important this is without telling her everything over a text or voicemail. She tells herself to be patient and that the world doesn't revolve around her. She knows Dove is working hard to advance in a male-dominated field. Dove mentioned that she started going by her middle name, Emerson, at work, and Sol can read between the lines to guess that's why Dove wears glasses with no prescription in them, walks the line between looking nice without being too pretty, dyes her hair darker, and always wears heels so she's taller.

Sol finally texts back, *Okay, please call me when you're free this week!* 💜

She continues reading about which blood types match

each other, how the transplant process works and how they leave the old kidney in there, how many people are on the waiting list, and what the recovery is like.

Sol wonders if she's warming up to the idea of donating a kidney. She tells herself she's just educating herself so she can make an informed decision. She makes herself an ice-cream sundae to finish off her day, gives Jericho a squirt of whipped cream for being a good boy, and climbs into bed with her journal.

- 19 -

Dear God,

Seriously, what are you doing with this situation? I've connected with Shyla and she seems nice. But the whole kidney thing? I don't know. I think I want to meet my biological mom. Does she want to meet me or does she just want my kidney? Would I have ever found out about her if she didn't need a transplant? I know you know all about adoption and complicated family lines because they are everywhere in the Bible. Even Jesus was adopted by Joseph! Help me get through this. Thank you so much for my family. I feel closer to them but also further from them, knowing my story. Mom and I aren't even biologically connected! At least I know I have the same bio dad as Dove and Willow. This is so weird.

- 20 -

The next morning when she wakes up, Sol know she wants to meet Shyla. Before she can chicken out, she texts her for the first time ever. *Hi, Shyla, it's Sol. Can you meet this weekend? We can meet in the middle in NYC.*

Shyla texts her right back: *Yes, Saturday at 1 p.m.?*

Perfect! Meet me at the fountain at Pier 84.

Sol texts her friend Thea: *Road trip to NYC Saturday. Meeting Shyla!!!*

Thea texts her immediately: *Perfect, Quentin is taking the girls to a playdate Saturday. Let's do this!*

- 21 -

A couple of days later, Sol has agreed to meet Franklin at the park downtown by the harbor. There's a free concert, and thousands of people are putting down their blankets and sprawling on the grass. Franklin has brought a cooler and snacks. Sol sets up their chairs. *Maybe he's not so bad,* she thinks. *Either way, I need a distraction!*

"Have you ever heard this band?" Franklin asks as he starts pulling drinks out of the cooler. They lean back as the music starts to play. The people-watching is always the best part of these outdoor concerts, and this one does not disappoint. The concerts attract all types of different people you wouldn't normally see together, from high schoolers on dates to young parents with their children to friend groups of Baby Boomers. Sol just hopes Franklin doesn't say anything inappropriate and ruin the moment. He has his arm around her, and it feels kind of nice to be there with him.

The first set goes perfectly. They can't really hear the music clearly, but it's really the atmosphere that matters. Sol finds herself relaxing a little after all the drama in her life lately. At the break, they stand up to stretch their legs, and Sol tells Franklin she's going to New York that weekend.

"Oh really? Why? I thought you were going with me to look at that boat I might buy," he replies, brows furrowing a little.

"Sorry," Sol answers. "I remember you mentioned it a couple weeks ago, but we didn't actually make plans, right? Anyway, this is kind of an emergency."

Should I tell him? she asks herself.

"It's a long story, but I just found out I have a sister I've never met!" Sol blurts out.

"Ok, so your dad was a player?" Franklin says flatly. "But why is that an emergency?"

Tears immediately spring to Sol's eyes. "You don't know anything about my dad!" she cries out and walks away before she does or says something she'll regret.

Thankfully, Franklin lets her go, and Sol loses herself in the crowd. She squeezes down by the water's edge and tries to regain her composure. *First the comment about the female candidate who beat his dad and now this. Ugh. Why am I even here with him? This is the last time I'm going to see him.* Sol stays down by the water for what seems like an hour. She feels her red face start to cool down. What he said made her so angry, but she knows she's been asking herself the same thing—if her dad really was a player. Franklin keeps texting her, and she eventually goes back to get her stuff. "I've got to go," she says as she avoids eye contact.

"I don't know why you're so upset," Franklin says. "What is going on? You still didn't even tell me about the emergency. Do you want me to go with you?"

"I'll talk to you later," Sol throws back as she walks away.

- 22 -

"Try to sound that word out. You can break it down into smaller parts." The next day, Sol is spending the day at one of the fifteen public city schools their program partners with. As she looks all around the room at the students concentrating on reading books with the program volunteers, Sol thinks about their stories. Of course, most of their information is confidential from the volunteers, but Sol knows more about them since she helps to run the program and do assessments.

She knows that the idea of a nuclear family with a mom, dad, and siblings at home is just a fairy tale for most of them. But on the other hand, most of their lives are full of grandparents, aunts, uncles, neighbors, coaches, pastors, teachers, and friends who love them. Sol has always thought there's room for more love no matter what your circumstance and has tried to be one of those bonus people in their lives. She gets a chance to meet their relatives sometimes as they pick the children up from school. She loves to hear their stories about the families noticing the improvement in their reading skills. One student's grandmother told her she was shocked when her grandson sounded out "SA-VINGS" on a billboard! She asked how he knew that word, and he proudly told her he read it.

Now that Sol has found out more about her own situation, she looks at them and wonders, *Are their lives really that different from mine? I just found out that I'm the "bastard" child of an affair. But I'm surrounded by a family that loves me. Did I think I was better off than them? I know a lot of them don't have dads at home, and I had lost my dad too, but I always remember Mickey being around. How can I learn from them instead of just thinking I'm "saving" them? How can I serve and understand them better?*

After the session ends, one of the students comes up to her. "Hi, Ms. Sunny!" she says, with a big smile on her face. Sol hugs her around her shoulders and says, "Hi, Jalin! What did you read today?"

"We read *Ada Twist, Scientist.* The girl was just like me! She asked sooo many questions!"

"Oh, I love that book! Ada Twist *is* just like you—she's curious and doesn't give up even when she hits a roadblock!"

"Plus her hair looks like mine too—so cute! See you next time!" Jalin calls as she returns to class.

No, I don't think we are that different, Sol thinks as she packs up for the day.

- 23 -

Jericho does his "happy dance" when he sees Willow's dog, Granola, and they run to the back door to be let out to play in the yard. Saturday has arrived quickly, and Sol drops Jericho off at Willow's house before she goes to pick up Thea. After Thea gets in Sol's orange hatchback, squeezing to fit her Erykah Badu-inspired headwrap, she connects her phone to the car's sound system. "I made a playlist," she says. "The ultimate 'meet-your-sister-you-didn't-know-you-had-because-your-biological-mom-you-didn't-know-you-had-needs-a-kidney playlist!" They both laugh. "Let's start with 'Family Affair' by Sly and the Family Stone!"*

"Once a DJ, always a DJ!" Sol says.

The whole ride, they sing along or chat about lighthearted things like movies or the antics of Thea's kids and Jericho. As her long-time friend, Thea knows now is a time to distract Sol from the stress and anticipation of the situation.

After about three and a half hours, they make it through the Lincoln Tunnel into Manhattan, and Sol texts Shyla, *Be there in 5 minutes.* There was a time when Sol came to

---

*See the appendix for the playlist or search "C.H. Avosa" on Spotify.

Manhattan several times a year for work or to meet up with friends who lived there, so she knows the city a little. She even dated a guy there briefly, but that didn't go anywhere.

"How are you feeling?" Thea asks as they get close to the meeting point.

"I'm nervous but excited—I think." Sol quickly checks herself in the rearview mirror at a red light.

"Let me pray for you real quick while we're at this light. You know they're not going to let us double-park for long when I drop you off. Lord, please bless Sol and Shyla's meeting right now. Hold them in your hand. No matter what happens. Amen." They drive around the corner and see the fountain Sol has picked to meet at with tons of people and dogs walking around.

"Amen! Thank you, Thea! Okay, meet me back here at 2:00. I'll text you if anything changes! Love you!" Sol calls as she tries to quickly get out of the car while Thea runs around to jump in the driver's seat.

She looks at the picture on her phone that Shyla sent her. Yes, she's the black lawyer from Boston that Sol originally found when she Googled her. Sol takes a couple of deep breaths and closes her eyes. When she opens them again, she thinks she spots Shyla behind a group of kids by the fountain. It's hard to tell with the sunglasses. She's dressed in jeans and boots and her curly, natural hair is in a pretty up-do created by an intricate pattern of twists. She looks like she should be on the cover of a magazine for "stylish lawyers you want to hang out with."

"Shyla?" Sol tentatively asks as she approaches the woman.

"Oh my gosh, Sol! It's you!" Shyla exclaims as she

rushes to give her a big hug. "I can't believe this. You do look like her. Look at you. Oh my gosh, I can't believe this is happening. How did you get here? What do you want to do? Should we go by the water? Or do you want to get a coffee? Honestly, I could use a glass of wine! I've been so nervous with anticipation. What do you think?"

As Shyla takes a breath, Sol jumps in, "Let's go by the water! I think there's a coffee stand over there too."

"Okay, great idea! Let's go. Good thing I wore these low heels. I wasn't sure what to wear. What do you wear when you're going to meet your sister for the first time? You're so cute! I love your bag! Did it take you long to drive up? My drive wasn't too bad. I have to come here for work sometimes, so I'm used to it. I like to drive, and if you can believe it, the New York drivers aren't as bad as the Boston drivers. The only issue is where to park. I parked in a garage over here, but it's going to cost me like $40. But don't take that the wrong way—you're worth it, of course. I would pay anything to be here with you. Oh, here's the coffee stand. Do you like coffee? I can't live without it! But I did have to cut back last year because I was having serious withdrawal issues when I didn't have like ten cups a day! But that's the lawyer life for you!"

Sol's worries about their meeting being awkward are quickly fading away as she sees—or hears—that Shyla is a talker. After they get their coffee, they find a bench near the water. "Oh my gosh, do you want to see pictures? I have so many to show you. I'm like the family photographer. I'm always up in people's faces taking pictures! But maybe you don't want to see? I don't know what you're thinking or feeling. Do you think we look alike? I see you got Mom's nose. I look a lot more like my dad. His side of the family has such strong features."

"Yes, I'd love to see pictures. You can tell me about everyone. I was wondering about your dad. I can show you my family too." They both settle on the bench and put their purses next to them.

Shyla gets out her phone and starts swiping through. "Okay, here's one of Mom. This is from last year before she started getting really sick. We were having a birthday party for one of my dad's sets of twin siblings. We call them 'Salt and Pepper.' I'm not sure where that came from, but it was from their childhood. Like I said, the families are huge, and I have tons of cousins. I don't even know them all! But no sisters. You're my only one! Okay, here's Dad and two of his brothers. There are my oldest cousins, their sons. Oh my gosh, I bet you want to see Mom's parents. Okay, let me see if I can find a picture."

While Shyla searches for a picture of her grandparents, Sol says, "Oh wow, the family really is huge! I can't believe I had all these relatives and didn't even know! I guess I would have shown up on your tree if I did the DNA test. This is just so weird that we didn't know for so long."

Sol tries to put a finger on what she's feeling, but she finds that she can't. Shyla's chattiness puts her at ease since she doesn't have to come up with things to say—not that she could get a word in edgewise. All the relatives make her feel a little overwhelmed, but there's also a strange sense of relief.

Shyla nods. "You're right," she says, "but with this big

family, you would probably just pop up as a cousin somewhere and no one would look into it further. Anyway, here are Mom's parents, Pops and Gran. Mm, I think this was Gran's eighty-fifth birthday. They got out there on the dance floor!"

Sol stares at the picture. "Can I look at that?"

"Of course," Shyla says as she hands her phone over.

Sol zooms in to the picture and scrutinizes the faces of the people she now knows as Pops and Gran.

Shyla digs in her large satchel purse for lip gloss while Sol looks at the picture, but after a minute, she notices Sol is still not talking. "Are you okay? Is this all too much for you? I mean, I meet one new person, and you're finding out about like forty new people."

"Um," Sol stalls. She takes a sip of coffee.

"What?"

"I don't know how to ask this without it coming out wrong." Sol continues to peer deep into Shyla's phone.

"What? You can ask me anything! I'm sure you have a million questions!"

"Uh."

"Just ask me!"

"Is Pops black?" Sol blurts out.

"Oh my gosh, Sol. You didn't know? Yes, he's black. So is Gran. But they are so light-skinned that Mom can pass for white with her wavy hair. Of course, my dad is black so that's what makes me darker. But you are pretty light. You actually look so much like her. Your skin tone, that is. Did anyone ever ask you if you were black? I guess they would just see your parents and think you were white. I'm so sorry no one told you. Are you okay? Wow, that is a lot to find out! I wasn't even thinking about that."

Sol keeps looking at Shyla's phone and flips back to the picture of Janice. "Yes. I mean, I just found out that my mom isn't even my mom. So I guess I'm as okay as I can be. This makes a lot of sense, actually. You do look like her too. But I can see what you're saying about your dad's family's strong features. They all really look alike!" Sol tries to keep her tone lighthearted, and thankfully there are a lot of people walking through the park creating distractions.

Sol takes another sip of coffee and tries to digest the latest revelation. *Her biological mother is black?*

Shyla jumps back in to allow Sol to compose herself. "Yes, something about those eyes and cheekbones! Let me show you some pictures of the Salt and Pepper twins! They are identical, and sometimes even people in the family can't tell them apart! Sometimes they dress alike just to mess with our heads! Especially when the Patriots are playing and they're wearing their matching jerseys! Let me see if I have a picture. Oh my gosh, look at them here! They crack me up! They are older, but they have so much spunk. They keep us all on our toes!"

Sol forces a smile and tries for an easy question that won't bring up more emotion. "So how did you all end up in Massachusetts?"

"Oh, the family has been living there forever it seems. I guess since Pops' dad got a job there back in the day working as a Pullman porter on the railroad. You know, the Great Migration, a lot of blacks were moving out of the South if they could—looking for jobs and to get away from that slave legacy there. Of course, that's how he met his wife—right there at South Station. The rest is history! They made a life there. Of course, their family probably make up 10 percent of the whole black population in Boston! You know, New England isn't exactly known for its diversity, though Boston has changed a lot over my lifetime. Mom ended up going to Baltimore for law school, and that's when she met your dad. Once she gave birth to you, she moved back home. Is your family from Baltimore?"

"My family... oh, it feels weird to say that now that I'm finding out all this. I mean, the two parents I have at home right now—I'm not biologically related to either one!" Sol sinks down a little on the bench.

"But they're still your family," Shyla says softly. "Family isn't just about biology."

Sol doesn't answer right away, and this time, Shyla lets the silence continue. Finally, Sol clears her throat. "Yeah, you're right. I'm still adjusting to everything. I mean, I am officially adopted by both of them, so they are my family. Anyway, my mom, Patty, my dad, Patrick, and my stepdad, Mickey, all come from Baltimore families. People don't leave there! I guess that's why it ends up being 'Small-ti-more'! Everyone is one step removed from everyone else. A lot of people do come for school or work and some of them stay too."

"Did you ever live anywhere else?"

"Well, I went away for college to Charleston Southern University. I wanted to experience living in a different place for a while, but I didn't want to stay down South. I wanted to come back in Baltimore. I mean, you know the reputation. People love to bash it or avoid it. But that's my home. It's a special place. But why not me and each of us to do something to make it even better?"

"That's great that you could do that, Sol. I will have to ask Mom what her experience was like there. This is bringing up questions I never thought about." Shyla gets up to throw her coffee cup in the trash can.

Sol does the same, then says, "Yeah, sometimes I feel like the problems are too big to make a difference. But what choice do we have? Just give up and let it fall apart? Anyway, what kinds of lawyer things do you do? Sorry, I don't know the right way to ask that!"

Shyla laughs. "That's okay, people ask me that all the time! Some lawyers don't even specialize and try to help their clients with whatever they need, and in the big firms, some specialties are very, very narrow and you spend all day doing the same type of thing. I guess I'm kind of in the middle. My firm works with mostly medium-sized companies, and we help them with a variety of needs, everything from intellectual property to real estate to employee rights. Now tell me about what you do. I mean, I already scoped you out online, of course!"

"Oh, that makes sense," Sol replies. "I guess every company has legal needs. As for my job, we have a program that partners up with the city schools to bring volunteers in so the students can get more one-on-one help with their reading. I manage the program at four of the schools, working with the administration and supporting the on-site staff. But, Shyla, I'm kind of nervous, but I do want to know more about your mom. I mean, our mom. Is she in the hospital now?"

"No, it's okay. She's not in the hospital now. She's on dialysis and doing pretty well. I mean, some days are better than others. But we have to find a donor because she can't stay on dialysis forever."

All of a sudden, Sol cries out, "Why could she keep you but not me?" Then she breaks down sobbing. Shyla puts her arms around her shoulders, and they sit in silence for a few minutes. Sol blows her nose with her napkins from the coffee stand.

"I don't know," Shyla answers. "She met my dad and they got married. But just because she gave you up doesn't mean she didn't care. I mean, your dad was still married to your mom when she was pregnant. She told me she never stopped thinking about you. I think you should meet her. Then you can ask her all the questions you want to ask her. What do you think?"

Sol thinks to herself, *it's too late to turn back now. You have to get your questions answered. What if she dies and you never have a chance to meet her?*

"Okay," Sol whispers.

Shyla hugs her. "Let me call her right now! Be right back!" She walks a little bit away, and Sol sees her talking on the phone.

Shyla rushes back over. "She wants to know if you can come tomorrow."

"Tomorrow?" Sol never thought this would happen so fast.

"She says, please. If you can."

Sol closes her eyes and prays, *Lord, help me. I'm scared to meet her, but I want to meet her.* Sol takes deep breaths and texts Thea: *Hey hon, there may be a change of plans. I'll let you know ASAP. When do you have to get back?*

"Okay, let me see if I can make it happen. Can I ride with you?" Sol says.

She texts her boss, Zakirah, apologizing for bothering her on the weekend, but Zakirah says she's happy to cover for her on Monday since Sol rarely takes time off. Sol then calls Willow to ask her if she can keep Jericho. Then she calls Thea and explains the situation, and they agree that Thea will drive her car back to Baltimore.

"I guess we will have a lot more time to talk," Sol says, still not believing she's doing this. She never considered herself a very impulsive person.

They quickly grab some snacks and pick up Shyla's car from the expensive garage. They spend the four-hour ride talking and getting to know each other. Once they get to Massachusetts, they stop at Target to get some clothes, deodorant, and a toothbrush for Sol. Shyla drops Sol off at the hotel she found on a last-minute deal site for her. "Are you sure you don't want to stay with me?" Shyla asks as Sol gets out.

"Yes, I'm sure, but thanks. I just need some time to myself to prepare for this. See you tomorrow!" Sol says as she goes to check in.

- 24 -

When Sol gets to her hotel room, she flops down on the bed. *I can't believe this is happening. I can't believe I'm here,* she thinks. After lying there for thirty minutes immobilized, she reaches for her phone. Three missed calls from her mom. She calls Thea.

"Hey, did you make it back okay?" Sol asks when Thea picks up.

"Yes, I'm back, no problem. But Sol, what is going on? Tell me everything! Are you really going to meet her? What did Shyla say?" Sol can hear a door close in the background.

"I'm still trying to take everything in. But Janice asked if I could come tomorrow, and I figured I have to jump on it while I have momentum. Otherwise, I might chicken out. And what if she dies?! I do want to meet her while I can!" Sol sits up on the bed, realizing how much she needs her friend right now.

"Okay, the biggest thing on my mind—I didn't expect more major surprises—but I was looking at all the pictures on Shyla's phone and...she's black. My biological mom. I mean, really light but still. What does this even mean? I find this out when I'm thirty-six?! Does this change anything?

I mean, obviously, I haven't been treated like I'm black because I look white and have a white family, and I guess people just assume they're all my biological family. And I'm light enough. I mean, on dates, the guys would always ask about my ethnicity, but I never thought twice about it. Why would I?" Sol realizes she's thinking aloud.

"Wait, what?" Thea sounds as surprised as Sol feels. "Okay, wow, Sol. You're right, that is a lot to find out now after you've just found out your mom adopted you. Why don't you tell me what happened?"

Sol fills her in on her meeting with Shyla, including the photos and stories—what she can remember, anyway. She knows she's not exactly thinking straight right now.

"I'm just so confused on how I'm supposed to feel," Sol says after she tells Thea everything she can think of. She lets out a big sigh and closes her eyes.

"I don't think there is a 'supposed to,'" Thea says. And I don't know if it will make you feel better or worse, but you're not the only one going through this. I was just reading an article the other day about how people are finding out all kinds of things about themselves with all the DNA testing going on. Like some of the DNA stuff is good, but they don't really prepare you for finding out stuff that's shocking like this. They even have these social media groups forming called like 'That was not the parent I expected,' or that they were conceived by donor sperm or something."

Sol groans. "Ugh, that's so wild! I guess it's good I'm not the only one. Maybe I can find a group. I have to do something to work through all of this! Thanks for being there for me! Mom keeps trying to call me, but I don't know what to say.

I can't believe she never told me. I wonder if she knows that Janice is black. I don't think she ever met her. And thank God I haven't gotten married and had children yet because can you imagine if I had without even knowing my own history? I could be passing on kidney disease or who knows what else! I have so much to learn about this whole new family I have."

Thea takes a deep breath. "Sol, I know you're so mad at your mom. And you have every right to be. She should have told you for sure. But she's still your mom. She loves you. You have talked about adopting children yourself. What if your adoptive child cut you off like that after you had raised them since they were a baby?"

Sol thinks for a second. "Yeah, you're right. I guess I'm still in shock. I feel like I want to keep this to myself right now."

"Well, maybe just text her and let her know you're okay. Can I pray for you?"

"Please do. I need all the help I can get. Thank you so much for going with me today. I really need the moral support." Sol closes her eyes.

"Of course, I'm glad I could go. Plus, you know I wouldn't pass up an opportunity to get a peek at Shyla! Lord, I pray that you would comfort Sol right now in the midst of all these revelations about her identity. Help her to have peace knowing that even though everything has changed, nothing has changed, and you still hold her in your hand. Help her as she goes to meet her biological mom tomorrow. I pray for her biological mom, Janice, right now. Heal her in the name of Jesus. Give her grace to know how to talk with Sol tomorrow, and let it be a sweet time for both of them. In the name of Jesus, amen."

"Thanks, Thea! Love you! I'll let you know what happens tomorrow. Let me go text Mom real quick. You know Franklin has been texting me too, but ugh, I don't know what to do about him. He doesn't seem to get it."

After they hang up, Sol texts her mom to let her know what's going on and then calls Willow to check on Jericho. Before they hang up, Sol asks Willow if she's talked to Dove lately. "I haven't even told her about any of this because I can't get her on the phone."

"No, I haven't talked to her either. But didn't she say she was trying to finish up a big contract or something?" Willow replies.

"Oh, yeah, that must be it," Sol says, trying to force herself to not be hurt. "Good night, Will!"

Normally when she stays in a hotel, Sol would catch up on all the cable shows she doesn't get at home, but tonight she feels like that's too frivolous. This is a life-changing moment. She's also completely exhausted from all the excitement and driving. She sits in silence for a long while replaying everything over and over in her head. Then she pulls out her journal from her purse.

- 25 -

Dear God,

I don't know where to begin. Well, I don't need to recap anything for you because you knew all of this before I did. But how I'm feeling... I know you know that too but maybe it will help me to write it out.

1. I have a different mother from my sisters and my mom is not my biological mother. How do I feel about that?

Hmm, Thea is right. I have talked about adoption too and I would want my adopted children to see me as their real mom. But that is all hypothetical! This is real! I guess the thing that really hurts is that they didn't tell me the truth. They lied to me! My birth certificate is a lie! Mom had years and years to tell me. Did she think I couldn't handle it? Well, maybe I can't! But here we are—made worse from her waiting so long! And what if there are medical things I needed to know? And what if I wanted to have kids? And what if I found this out from DNA testing? I am so not ready to talk to her. I'm just so angry at her keeping the truth from me. Am I now supposed to be grateful she decided to take me?!

2. My biological mother is black. How do I feel about that?

I guess I'm not as surprised as I could be. Maybe just because my whole life people have been confused about me. But it's different for people to question whether I'm mixed or bira-cial and for me to know that I am. Of course I have a million black friends and coworkers and students who I love, and this doesn't change anything about that. Maybe it was just meant to be? Or they knew before I did? I don't know. I think this will take a while to process. It's so complicated, especially with the history in this country.

3. I met my biological sister/half sister today and I'm going to meet my biological mother tomorrow. How do I feel about that?

Everything has happened so fast that it's hard to know how I feel. It was not even a month ago that I got Shyla's first email, and now here I am. I'm so thankful that Shyla is easy to talk to. She seems so excited to meet me and have me in her life. I guess it's different for me because I already have two sisters, and she's an only child. But I want to know the truth. I have a whole family that I've never met. I'm scared, but I feel like I have to do it. What is Janice going to be like? I don't know what to expect at all. Will she look sick? Will that change how I feel about her? What will we say? What do you say when you're meeting your biological mother for the first time? Will she like me? Will she be proud of how I turned out? What will happen after this? Is she going to ask me to my face whether I'll give her one of my kidneys?! What will I say if she does? I don't know about this whole kidney thing!

Lord, I just really need you to help me. I mean, you made this whole thing happen, right? I know that you'll be with us tomorrow. Help me to not freak out. Help me to be honest. Help me to trust you. In Jesus's name, amen.

- 26 -

When she closes her journal, Sol puts on the dog-patterned pajamas she bought at Target and lays out the yellow-and-orange shift dress on the other bed for tomorrow. She rips off the tags and thinks, *So this is the outfit I'll meet my biological mother in.*

She texts Franklin and Raymond, whose texts she has been ignoring the whole day: *Hey, I'll be busy all day tomorrow, but I'll get in touch when I'm back in town.* She doesn't have the space in her head to think about whether she wants to see either of them again.

She's feeling drained from the long and emotional day, but when she gets in bed, she can't sleep. She knows she needs to get some rest, but her mind is racing through all her questions and wondering what will happen the next day. She sets her alarm plus a backup alarm so she doesn't oversleep. After lying there for twenty minutes, she gets her phone back out and starts scrolling through the #kidneytransplant and #kidneydisease hashtags on social media. So many people have shared their stories. She's crying over these strangers' stories. Most of them are hopeful, but not all of them. One woman ended up marrying her donor.

Some of them talk about the day of the surgery. Some of them talk about what it's like after. Some of them have pictures of their scars, and they're smiling. *Could I ever do this? Would I want to?* Sol wonders.

She looks into the steps of how they figure out if you're a match. A million half-baked pieces of information float up in her mind from different movies, news, and conversations she's had over the years. She knows the recipient's body will sometimes reject a donor organ, but maybe not if you're a family member?

Sol still hasn't heard from Dove, and when she remembers that it's earlier in California, she tries texting her again: *Hey, I have important news! When can you talk?*

Before she can even wait for a reply, Sol falls asleep with the phone in her hand.

- 27 -

The next morning, both alarms go off for ten minutes before Sol cracks one eye open and remembers where she is. Then she starts freaking out. *Am I seriously doing this today?* she asks herself. She looks in the mirror. "Yes, you are doing this. It's going to be okay. You're going to get through this. The truth will set you free, right?" she says out loud to herself, feeling less than convinced.

Sol puts on the livestream from her church as she gets dressed and ready the best she can with her purchases from the previous day. She wishes she had more time to prepare, but she knows that if she didn't do it like this, she would probably keep putting it off. She's glad she keeps a little makeup in her purse, and that helps her to feel a bit more confident in her last-minute look. She twists her hair up into a knot and pins it in place. She figures simple will be best today.

She rushes down to the hotel lobby for coffee and a yogurt to tide her over until lunch. She sticks a breakfast bar in her purse too, just in case. She doesn't want to end up hangry.

She texts Thea: *Please pray for me. I can't believe I'm meeting my biological mom today.* 😳 *Help me, Lord!*

Thea texts back right away: *Yes, I've been praying already this morning!* 🙏 *I got you! Let me know how it goes!* 💜

At 10:30 a.m., Shyla picks her up in front of the hotel, and they drive to Beverly, a nearby town on the "North Shore," where Janice lives and Shyla grew up. As they drive, Sol looks out the window. *I guess I would have grown up here too*, she thinks. It's a well-kept residential area once they get off the highway. So far, she hasn't seen any black faces. She remembers what Shyla said about the demographics here and wonders what it was like for her. She files that question away in her mind for later.

"Ugh, the Red Sox!" she can't help but say out loud as she sees someone wearing a jersey. As a life-long Baltimore Orioles fan, it's an automatic reaction to one of their biggest baseball rivals. Shyla just laughs.

"So tell me again what to expect," Sol says, as they get closer to the house.

"Okay, we're going to Mom and Dad's house. They will both be there. Mom has been calling and texting me nonstop. She sounds really excited to meet you. Dad is being his normal stoic self, but he's a good host. Sometimes he can come off as gruff. Don't pay him any attention; that's just the retired military in him. He would do anything for Mom, but sometimes he forgets we're his family, not his junior officers," Shyla responds.

"Okay," Sol answers as she looks back out the window. She wishes Shyla hadn't told her that about her dad. She was hoping for a friendly, laid-back guy. *God, please help me! I'm so nervous!* she prays silently.

"Are you okay?" Shyla asks. "Thanks for doing this. I

know it's a lot. When she asked if you could come today, I almost didn't tell you because I thought it may be too much. But I'm so glad you agreed. Plus, I get to spend more time with you. I want to know everything about you. But I'm trying to talk a little bit less than normal to give you a break! I know I can talk a lot! But you know if you need chatter, I'm your girl. Just give me the look!"

"Thanks, Shyla. I seriously might need to give you the look. Will you stay there with me when I meet her?" Sol is trying her best to remain calm, and she's thankful she doesn't have to do this alone.

"Yes, I can if that's what you want," Shyla says as they pull up in front of a small house that has the entire front yard filled with small trees, bushes, and flowers. There's a birdbath on one side of the front walk and a rustic bench on the other. Paving stones make curved paths through the abundance of plants. Sol can name only a few—brilliant white dogwoods, pink peonies, and magenta roses—but she also wonders how the colder weather affects what they can plant up here.

"Mom loves her flowers, as you can see! She got Dad into them too, and they both work in the yard all the time! Well, her not as much anymore, but she still supervises and does a lot of the planning!"

"Wow, it looks so nice!" Sol replies as she takes a deep breath and forces herself to open the car door. She does love flowers and has been trying to grow them in pots in her apartment. Could that be hereditary? As soon as the thought crosses her mind, she shakes it off. Growing flowers is pretty common, she tells herself. This situation has her mind a little confused.

As they walk up to the house, the front door opens before they reach it, and Sol sees a man who must be Shyla's dad. Their faces look almost identical—besides his mustache, of course. They both have café au lait-colored skin and high cheekbones. He is tall, maybe six feet, three inches, standing ramrod straight, and not smiling. His pressed polo shirt is tucked into his pressed khakis, which end at the perfect length to show his spotless loafers.

"Hey, Dad," Shyla says and hugs him. At the hug, his lips break into a smile. Calvin Broward offers his hand to Sol for a firm handshake, and she's reassured but also a little intimidated by his grip. "Welcome, Sol. You can call me Calvin. Janice is out on the patio. Why don't you come on back?"

As they walk through the house, Sol scans the pictures on display. Most of them are of Shyla, but there are others that she's sure are family members since she can now recognize the telltale cheekbones. Mixed in with the family photos are closeups of flowers she doesn't know the names of. She has a strange feeling in the pit of her stomach that's something like nostalgia, but she doesn't have time to examine it. She knows she needs to stay focused on the one task in front of her—meeting her biological mother. She feels like she might throw up and takes deep breaths to try to calm herself.

As they enter the patio area, with flowers spilling over every available surface, Shyla links her arm in Sol's. It's just in time to catch Sol from falling because, as soon as she sees Janice, she goes weak in the knees and just stares at her. Janice must be reacting in the same way because she almost spills her water as she struggles to set it down on the table next to her. They both seem to be in shock. Shyla helps Sol sit down on a garden chair across from Janice. Calvin places sweating glasses of ice water with lemon wedges in front of Shyla and Sol and quickly retreats into the house.

Minutes pass.

"You're beautiful!" Janice finally blurts out, as her eyes fill up with tears.

Sol just stares at her.

"I look just like you, don't I?" Sol finally manages to whisper. "I always wondered why I looked so different from my sisters, and now I know…"

Janice nods. "I can't believe I finally get to meet you. After all these years. I never stopped thinking about you, but I never thought I'd see you. You know, your dad used to send me pictures…before he died," Janice says as she starts to get choked up.

They are silent again, drinking each other in. Sol feels like she uploaded her photo to one of those retirement-planning websites that "age" you in your picture to show you what you might look like in the future. She and Janice have that same extreme arch in their eyebrows. Their eyes are set a little far apart, and their brown eyes sparkle. Their noses are rounded, and their lips are full with a little cupid's bow in the middle. Janice wears her dark hair in a pixie cut, and it's mostly silver. Her face and body have a puffy look, like someone blew up a balloon a little too far. She wears a loose-fitting, flowy moss green tunic and pants. Sol spies a bright green Crocs gardening shoe poking out from under the table.

After a few minutes of staring at each other, Janice shakes her head a little as if to break out of a trance. She pulls some envelopes from her lap and sets them on the table. She slowly opens the top one and pushes the contents over to Sol. "I thought you might want to see the letters."

Sol doesn't know what she was expecting, but it wasn't this. She looks down at the folded paper, a letter from her dad. Did she ever know his handwriting? Here it is. He touched this piece of paper. Inside the letter are three small pictures. They are all of her. On the back of each is written "Sol Surya Garnett" with her ages. *Same dad, just not the mom I thought,* she says in her head. One picture is her as a baby in her crib—the same crib that's in Dove and Willow's baby pictures. One is her with Dove holding a stuffed bunny up to her. She doesn't remember that bunny or this picture. The last is a close-up of her fast asleep.

"I don't know how much you already know about what happened," Janice begins hesitantly.

Sol doesn't respond and keeps her head down. She's entranced by seeing the letter her father sent Janice all those years ago. It's short and to the point: "I hope you are feeling better. Sol is growing well and eating some baby food now. She smiles a lot and makes us smile. —Patrick"

Janice tries again. "Thank you for coming today, Sol. I know it was a shock to find out about me. I didn't want Jackie to tell Shyla, but my sister has a mind of her own. They think you may be able to help me. I just wanted you to just be able to live your life without any extra burden from me. I don't know if that was right or not, but that's what Patrick and I agreed to all those years ago. Have you had a happy life?"

Janice toys with a napkin as she waits for Sol to respond. Sol continues to flip through the pictures and look at the letter, thinking about her father, who she doesn't even know if she remembers. Janice pushes the other letters over to her. "Do you want to look at these other ones?" she asks.

Sol doesn't respond but begins to open the old envelopes, careful not to tear the contents. The return address is unfamiliar. It must be somewhere they were renting when she was a baby. Postage was only twenty cents. She takes in every detail.

In the next letter, she's a little older. This one is from 1985. Her dad reports on her getting into everything and all the words she knows. Her first word is "Dove," her sister's name, except she says it like "Duff." Her favorite food was bananas, which she still loves now. Sol's mom Patty has told her these stories too. Patrick congratulates Janice on her marriage.

Sol remains silent as she examines the letters. It's not like she hasn't seen baby pictures of herself before. But this connection and her dad reporting on her to someone else puts a new spin on everything. It's like a piece is falling into place where there has been only blank space. But she didn't know there was blank space until this moment sitting here and seeing the face of someone that looks like her.

In the next letter, Sol has a new baby sister, Willow, and Patrick sends best wishes for Janice's new baby too. When Sol reads this, it's as if she just remembered that Shyla is sitting next to her. She looks over and says, "You were born the same year as Willow. We were living parallel lives." Shyla just nods, uncharacteristically silent.

In the fourth letter, Sol has begun preschool and loves to run around the house singing the ABC song over and over again. Her hair is dark and curly in the pictures, and she wears it in pigtails.

The last letter is addressed in Patty's handwriting. Sol knows what's coming, but she can't stop herself. There are no pictures in this envelope—just one small piece of paper torn off a notepad from the First National Bank of Maryland. "Janice, I just wanted to let you know that Patrick died in a car accident last week. Patty"

Sol puts down the stack of envelopes and takes a deep breath. She stares at the top of the table. The silence seems to go on forever. Birds continue to chirp in the yard, and a breeze tugs at the napkin Janice had put down on the table, but inside of Sol, everything seems frozen. How will she ever unfreeze from this moment? Everything was fine—she had a good life. But now these revelations have knocked her off balance. Sol tries to stabilize her thoughts.

"Were you in love with my dad?" she asks suddenly, jerking her head up. She doesn't know why this is the first question she chooses to ask, but at this moment, it seems imperative to know. That she wasn't just a bastard child of an affair. That she came from something real and not a fling. That she was born out of love and not out of sin. She's sick thinking about the alternatives. She's sick thinking about her mom Patty being hurt and then having to see her every day. Does her mom hate her? Does she just remind her of what her dad did to her? Does her mom know what Janice looks like, and does Sol remind her every time she looks at her? Sol forces herself to look at Janice. She's feeling angry. Not only did she lose her dad when she was young, but now it's like she's losing her mom. The only mom she's ever known. She stares at Janice with hatred in her eyes. She didn't expect to feel this way, not after meeting Shyla. But now, she can't stop. "How did this happen? How did I happen? It's not supposed to be like this!"

Janice steadily looks back at Sol with softness in her eyes. "You're right, it's not. I never would have written your story like this. But I don't regret having you. I could never regret that. I'm sorry we never told you the truth, and you had to find out like this. I'll tell you anything you want to know."

Sol is reminded of her conversation with her mom, Patty. *Didn't she say the exact same things?*

Janice continues slowly. "In terms of love, I don't know if I was in love with your dad. Honestly, we didn't know each other very well. I didn't have much experience with men because I had been so focused on my studies all those years. Patrick and I chatted as I got his order ready every morning at the café, and then one day, he asked me out. I had no idea he was married, Sol. He didn't tell me; he didn't wear a ring. I said yes because I thought it would be nice to have a break from my studies every now and then.

"I did enjoy going out with him, but when I found out he and your mom were still married and had Dove, I ended things right away. I didn't want to break up a family. I had no idea it would be a big deal for me to go out with him. I mean, I don't think he was even looking for anything. Maybe he just thought it would help him feel better for a little while. I don't think he was even thinking straight. After that, I asked him to please find somewhere else to get his coffee and he did.

"I never saw him again, but after only a few weeks, I found out I was pregnant. I called him right away and told him about you, but I also told him I didn't want anything from him—just thought it was the right thing to tell him. We never talked about ending the pregnancy; we both always wanted you. You know, he was still staying there at his friend's house downtown. My plan was that I could have you and raise you myself while I finished school— somehow—and then we could move back to Boston."

Sol abruptly looks up from where she had been tracing the condensation on her glass. She had never heard some of these things.

Janice doesn't miss a beat and the story continues flowing out. "For a while, everything was going well. I kept up with school and work. My belly was getting bigger, and eventually, I told my family and school and the people at the café. I got more and more confident that everything was going to work out. I started thinking about names and planning how I could move stuff around in the apartment to make a little nursery for you. My family was supportive, but they were also caught up in everything going on up there, and no one at school or work questioned it. I had health insurance through school and started going for prenatal visits. I really want you to know what happened next so you can understand a little more why I wasn't able to keep you and raise you on my own like I wanted to."

Sol looks up and says, "Okay," even though in her head she doesn't think there's really anything that Janice can say that would be a reason she could understand.

Janice nods and continues. "I got to thirty-three

weeks in my pregnancy—it was May 23rd—and went for a checkup. The nurse took my blood pressure, which they did every time, and which had been completely normal up until then. Like I said, everything had been going great. But this time, the nurse rushed out of the room and came back with the doctor just a few seconds later. It turns out that my blood pressure was dangerously high, and they admitted me to the hospital that day with preeclampsia.

"After a couple days, they sent me home but told me I was going to be on bed rest for the rest of the pregnancy to try to prevent an emergency and keep you developing as long as possible. And they would be checking me frequently. I wasn't able to work or do much of anything besides lay in bed and read my law textbooks. This is before the internet, of course. Thankfully, classes were already over for the semester."

Sol is listening intently now, staring at Janice and waiting to hear what happened next.

"I called my parents—what else could I do? They were really worried but also thankful that I was getting checked often in case something went wrong. After I called, my sister Jackie borrowed a friend's car to come down for a few days, but she couldn't stay too long that first visit because she had to get back to work. My parents couldn't get away from their responsibilities with work and my brothers and sisters. When she came, Jackie brought an envelope of cash she had collected from the family to help out. She begged me to give her Patrick's number, but I refused. I didn't want to get further entangled with him. I hadn't spoken with him aside from that one call to tell him about you.

"My friends from school and work pitched in to help take care of me when they could. But mostly, I was alone at home with you. I sang to you, read to you from my books, told you stories. My mom called when she could to try to encourage me to hang in there. She apologized for not being able to help more with the bills but said they would try to get some more money together for me. You know, they were so proud of me when I went off to law school, and I couldn't believe that now here I was pregnant and alone on bed rest in Baltimore.

"The doctors wanted me to get to at least thirty-seven weeks in the pregnancy for you to be as healthy as possible, but my blood pressure was hard to control. They were continually monitoring me. I was swelling up all over—my feet, then legs, even my face. I went to the hospital a week after they let me out for them to check everything. Then the next week when I went, they told me I would need to stay. Jackie was able to get just a little time off work—she was working at the courthouse by then, so her life was really determined by case schedules—and she came back down just when I got to thirty-seven weeks. Thank God she did, because they had to induce labor a day after she arrived.

"To be honest, I don't remember a lot from those days. I think Jackie went to my apartment to get my mail or something, and there was a bill from when I was first admitted to the hospital. Thankfully, I had the school's health insurance plan, but that plan wasn't designed for anything like what I was going through. The hospital bills and out-of-pocket costs started piling up quickly.

"She must have talked to the hospital billing department multiple times about my situation but didn't want to worry me. Finally, she told me that I already owed more than $43,000. You were born perfectly healthy, thank God, but they wouldn't let me see you. I was in the ICU, and the doctors were still trying to get my blood pressure under control. I didn't know what I was going to do. All my plans and confidence of raising you on my own were now drowned out by the thought of the bills. By the time I was released, I think I owed $78,000. I felt hopeless. I was making like $3 an hour. My family didn't have a lot of extra money. Plus I had debt from law school, and I didn't know if I would even be able to finish and graduate. How did I think I would go to class with a newborn baby? How did I think I would have money to pay someone to take care of you?"

Janice finally takes a break to sip some water. She is starting to look tired. Sol takes the moment to say, "Wow, I didn't know any of this." Shyla had been so silent that Sol had forgotten she was there, but she also whispers, "I didn't know either."

"Honestly, I don't know if your mom ever knew or what your dad told her," Janice replies. "But I would hate for you to think I didn't care about you. Jackie offered to move down and help me raise you while I finished school. She said she could work at the courthouse down here. But then that would just have made two of us with full-time responsibilities and a newborn. Every day she asked me for Patrick's phone number. She said he needed to know what was going on.

"The longer I laid there in the hospital, the more the costs added up, and the more I thought about what would be best for you. I wanted so badly to keep you, but after a while, I thought that would be selfish because I couldn't really provide a good home for you. Finally, I told Jackie I would give her Patrick's phone number. I told her I wanted him to take you and raise you. But only if he got back together with his wife. She was shocked. She begged me to keep you and let her help me raise you. But I had no idea how we would pay off this huge debt. I was looking into whether I could declare bankruptcy or what I could do. I wanted you to have a stable home, a chance, not starting off in poverty and debt and uncertainty. I mean, we were still just trying to stabilize my blood pressure. I told her I wouldn't give her the number if she didn't agree. So finally she did. I mean, I didn't know what he would say, but I was just hoping he would say yes."

The thought that her dad could have said no to taking Sol is a horrifying prospect. Sol finds that she has been listening to the story like she doesn't know how it ends. She feels her body tensing back up. Her jaw and hands are clenched. She also starts feeling guilty for putting Janice through all of that. She knows it isn't anything she had control over, but she feels terrible that Janice ended up in the hospital and in all that debt just because she decided to keep Sol.

"Jackie came back to see me after she talked to him," Janice continues. "Her face was like stone. I had no idea what had happened. She said Patrick was really upset that I had been in the hospital and hadn't told him. That he asked a million times if I was okay and if you were okay. She said she wanted to tell him off for taking advantage of me like that, but she knew this was a time to hold her tongue. She said she told him what I said, and he wanted to talk to Patty about it.

"The next day, Jackie called him again and he said he and Patty wanted to take you and they were coming to pick you up that very day. I never even saw you when you were born, I never gave you a name. Jackie saw you through the nursery window, but I didn't want to change my mind. I didn't think I could give you a good life. I didn't see how we could make it work. And you would be with your biological father. I knew your mom would love you like her own. I just knew it. Have you had a happy life, Sol? That's what I wanted for you."

"She did love me. And still does," Sol answered testily. "But she lied to me too. My dad is dead and both my mothers lied to me all my life. I'm glad to know the truth finally, but is this supposed to make everything okay?!" Sol stares at two yellow butterflies in the yard. *How will this conversation end?* she thinks. *Where does she want it to go?*

Janice lets the silence sit for a few minutes and turns her attention to the yard too.

"You have every right to be angry," Janice finally says. "We should have told you. Despite the circumstances, I'm glad I have a chance to tell you the truth now. When I look back, I'm ashamed of how we handled it, agreeing to keep it a secret forever. I don't know how long my kidney will hold out, but I'm glad I'm getting to see you in this moment. Seeing you for the first time. I don't want anything from you, but thank you for giving me the gift of coming to see me. You didn't have to do it." She turns to her other daughter. "Thank you, Shyla. I know you're trying to help."

Sol feels conflicted but doesn't want meeting her biological mother for the first time to be a bad memory. She takes a deep breath. "I'm glad I got to meet you too. I mean, that's why I came. And to meet Shyla too. It's just...complicated. But I guess it explains a lot. You keep asking me if I've had a happy life. I guess you want to know if you did the right thing. Well, no one could have known that my dad would die like that. My mom does love me as her own and so do my sisters and my stepdad Mickey. I never thought to question whether I belonged. I just laughed sometimes when on first dates guys would ask if I was black or Latina or something. My life has been hard sometimes, but yes, I have a good life. My faith in God has been an anchor."

Calvin comes out at that moment with a plate of apple slices and puts them on the table between Janice and Sol. "How are you all doing out here?" he asks. "Sol, if you want to stay for lunch, I have chicken salad for sandwiches."

Sol looks over at Shyla. Shyla raises her eyebrows. Sol looks at Janice. Janice says, "Sol, I'd love for you to stay as long you can, but you have already done my spirit good by coming this morning. It's up to you."

"Chicken salad sounds great, thank you," Sol says to Calvin, forcing a smile.

"Okay, I'll get lunch going," he responds. "It should be ready in about fifteen minutes."

Sol grabs an apple slice. "I didn't realize it's already been so long since my little breakfast snack!" she says to Shyla. "Actually, may I use the restroom?"

"Let me show you where it is," Shyla says and leads Sol inside.

"Thanks for staying with me, Shyla. I need the support," Sol whispers as they walk through the house.

"Of course! Although you know I wanted to jump into that conversation so many times! She's so happy you're here, I can tell."

In the bathroom, Sol checks her phone. There are texts from her mom, Franklin, Willow, and Thea. She texts her sister and mom back and responds to Thea with, *Keep praying for me! I'm still here. I'll fill you in later! We're going to have lunch in a few minutes.* Franklin apologized for what he said about her dad at the concert, but it was hard to resolve things via text with all this other stuff going on.

Sol uses the bathroom and then checks her face in the mirror. Not horrible, but she does think she looks a little pale. She adds a little makeup from the pouch in her purse, takes a deep breath, and rejoins the Broward family at the kitchen table. Mr. Broward—Calvin—has made them all plates with chicken salad sandwiches, and there's a big green salad and fresh fruit. "We grow lots of vegetables in our garden out back and are regulars at the farmers' market too. Our greens are doing really well this year, so we're eating salad every day."

Now that "the worst" is over—the shock of seeing each other face-to-face for the first time—Sol finds she can almost pretend she is just chatting with the parents of a friend.

"I hope we don't get sick of salad! We've been trying to make different homemade dressings that have less salt, but you all have all these choices," Janice adds as she points to a long line of store-bought dressings. "So tell me more about what you're doing for work, Sol."

Sol excitedly responds, thankful to talk about something else for a bit. "I don't know what Shyla already told you, but I work with a literacy program in Baltimore City. It's great! We partner with the public schools and have volunteers to work one-on-one with students that need a little extra help. I started volunteering with them when I was still in college to get credit for one of my classes. After I graduated and moved back, I started doing it with the Baltimore chapter.

"One day I was talking with one of the coordinators after my session, and she told me about a job that was open helping manage the program at some of the schools. I wasn't sure about it because my degree was actually in public policy, but I went and met with them, and I took the job on the spot. So I've been doing it about fifteen years now, and I recruited my younger sister, Willow, too! She does more of the marketing and social media stuff, and we are actually teaming up on some of the new initiatives to get our volunteers involved in lobbying for educational policy change."

Talking about her work gives Sol a little break from thinking so much about the implications of these newly discovered relationships. Everyone at the table avoids heavy topics, and they chat about the garden and Shyla's job and baseball for the rest of the meal.

After lunch, Sol asks if Janice has pictures from when she was younger. "It's weird to finally meet someone that looks like me."

"You know," Janice replies, "I have a few framed in the house, but the rest are in a box in the basement somewhere. I didn't think to pull them out. I kept those letters from your dad in a drawer and let myself look at them once a year—on your birthday. Which is in just a couple weeks! But let me show you these. And I have some really cute ones of Shyla!

"Here's me and Calvin at our wedding in 1985. This was just a couple years after you were born. I was twenty-nine then, so younger than you are now," Janice explains. Sol peers into the picture for signs of recognition. There's no doubt that she looks like Janice.

Shyla jumps in, "Look at her hair! That eighties feathering! But I bet you were in style with it back then. Just kidding, you look great, Mom! This picture always makes me laugh, though! I asked Mom if I could borrow her dress when I get married. Look at those shoulder pads! I didn't even know wedding dresses could have shoulder pads! Not that I could fit into this dress anyway. You know my shape is a little different, thanks to Dad's side of the family! Anyway, we'll figure it out when the time comes! Maybe I can just borrow the veil—that should fit!" Shyla bursts forth with commentary after being silent so long.

"I do love the shoulder pads!" Sol plays along.

"Ooo, look at this one of me!" Shyla continues. "Wasn't I the cutest? You see how big this doll is? That's because I would pretend the doll was my sister, not a baby! This could have been you! It's not always easy being an only child, believe me! Especially when you like to talk! I talked the ears off this doll! And my imaginary friends too!"

"And your parents too!" Janice says, laughing.

"Definitely your parents too!" Calvin chimes in from the kitchen.

"You know it! You had to pay for not giving me a sibling!" Shyla shoots back. "Oh, here's my graduation picture! Do you have one like this? Did we all share the same string of pearls or what?! Do you have any pictures on your phone you can show us? We want to know everything! Not to overwhelm you, but since you're here, it would be great. I can't believe I didn't know you growing up. Oh, can I take a picture of you and Mom? I want to remember this day. Let's go back outside, and we can take pictures with the flowers."

"Yes, my Target outfit will be immortalized! Good thing we found something cute in my size!" Sol agrees.

They grab Calvin on the way out and start taking pictures. Sol finds that if she stays in the moment, she's okay. If she starts thinking about how she ended up in a Boston suburb on this very day, she starts to get upset. So she keeps telling herself, *Focus. Just focus. Stay in the present.*

After the pictures, they sit back down outside. Sol is glad she had scheduled her flight for the next morning instead of tonight, even if she had just done it because it was much less expensive. The time is going so fast. Even though Janice had told Sol she didn't want to burden her, Sol thought it would be wrong to not even ask about the kidney situation. "Janice, tell me more about what's going on with your kidneys."

"Are you sure you want to talk about this?" Janice replies.

"I am."

"Okay, well, after you were born, my health stabilized. I moved back in with my mom and dad, thinking I could go back and finish law school as soon as I could. Then I met Calvin, and we got married and had Shyla. We put as much money as possible toward the debt, and things were looking up, even though I never did make it back to law school. But then in my mid-forties, some routine tests showed that there were some issues with my kidneys. The doctor said that it could be from the preeclampsia—which didn't recur during my pregnancy with Shyla, thankfully—because the preeclampsia can damage your other organs. So I changed my diet and started exercising, and I was doing okay. But my kidney function was still declining a little bit every year, and when I turned fifty-eight, it finally got bad enough that my nephrologist started talking about dialysis or a transplant.

"A few years later, my kidneys did fail, and I started going to a center for dialysis two days a week. At first it was okay, but the way I felt was so up and down depending on whether I had just had my treatment, or it was the day before my treatment, or what. So Shyla did a lot of research into the options, and she thought we could try this other kind of dialysis I could do at home every day. Thankfully, I have Calvin because it's a lot of work with all the supplies and everything—they have their own room! I had to have surgery for them to put in my catheter where they hook up the machine. Anyway, it's a pain, but it's going okay. But really it's a temporary solution. I need a transplant.

"So Jackie and Shyla started mounting a campaign to find a match, starting with our family. And Shyla probably already told you our family is big. I don't have the energy to do it myself, but I can't stop those two. Maybe it will work, and maybe it won't. Unfortunately, we do have a few things that run in our family that automatically disqualify people, like high blood pressure and type 2 diabetes. So that's how

Jackie ended up telling Shyla about you. She thought you might be a match.

"I'm trying to be practical too if we can't find someone. Meeting you was one thing I did really want to do before I die, and I didn't know if I would ever have the chance. And now here you are. So thank you again for that."

Sol doesn't want to make any promises about the kidney donation, so she switches to interview mode. "What are some of the other things still on your list that you want to do?" she asks.

"Well, of course I'd love to see my grandbabies," Janice begins.

"No pressure!" shouts out Shyla.

"You know I'm not pressuring you, Shyla," Janice laughs. "Plus I have enough great-nieces and -nephews to keep me busy! One other thing I'd love to do would be to visit the Chelsea Flower Show in London. It's been going on since 1913! It sounds amazing! When you're waiting for a kidney, you can't travel much because you have to be ready for surgery at any time. So that would be so nice to be able to travel more, and that is one place I've always wanted to go."

"Oh, wow, that sounds amazing!" Sol exclaims.

At this point, Janice looks like she's feeling tired, and Shyla gives Sol a look and tells her mom they need to get going.

Sol begins to say her goodbyes. "I didn't know what to expect coming here today. And yes, I was angry and confused. But I'm glad I got to meet you, and I hope we can stay in touch. I will think about the kidney thing, but I can't make any promises right now. This is really a lot to think through."

"Sol, I don't want you to feel any pressure at all. But I would love to stay in touch if you want to. But again, I will leave that up to you. Thank you so much for visiting me. It does my heart good to see you are well. I'm sure Shyla wants to stay in touch too, but I'll try to encourage her not to overwhelm you either."

Shyla purses her lips but doesn't say anything as she looks at her mother out of the corner of her eye. "I'll drive you back to your hotel, Sol."

Sol says goodbye to Calvin and thanks him for the lunch, then gets back in Shyla's car.

"So what did you think?" Shyla says immediately as soon as Sol sits down.

Sol lets out a huge breath. "Do you mind if we stop at McDonald's on the way back to the hotel? I could use some fries."

"You've got it! We could even go out to my favorite sports bar to watch the game. Didn't you say the Orioles and Red Sox are playing? Whoever's team wins buys! And you know we're going to win so I got you, Sol!" Shyla teases.

"Oh, you're on, Shyla! I can't believe you started trash talking already! You must really have been waiting for a sister all this time!"

"You have no idea!" Shyla laughs. "I mean, you met my parents, so you know they're pretty nice, but it's a lot of pressure being the only child. Not only that, carrying on my mom's dream to become a lawyer. And who could I talk to about normal sibling stuff or share clothes and shoes with?!"

- 28 -

The Orioles are up 2-1 when they arrive and get seats at the bar with good views of the TVs. Once they both have drinks in hand and nachos in front of them, Sol asks, "So what has dealing with your mom's health been like for you, Shyla? You know this whole situation has been a lot for me to digest, but how have you been doing with it? You kind of laughed it off before, but it must be hard being the only child in this situation."

Having the game on and a room full of people is a welcome distraction from sitting face-to-face with her newly discovered mother. Even being here with her newly discovered sister is easier when there are other people to fill the space.

"You know, the hardest thing is not being able to just donate to her," Shyla answers. "Because, of course, I would give her a kidney in a second. And Dad has some other issues, so he's not able to donate. I'm on the list to do a paired exchange if someone else is a match for her and I'm a match for their recipient, but Mom's immune system is so complicated that it's really hard to match her. So now the challenge is finding someone who's a match and is also willing to undergo surgery and lose time at work for this woman they may not be close to. With her immune system, it's unlikely that someone is going to come up on the list in time for her. Plus, a kidney from a living donor has a higher chance of success and lasts longer, so we're trying to find someone that will do that.

"Oh, she needs someone who is blood type O. Did I mention that? I'm A negative, unfortunately, even though Os are the most common and are the universal donor! Do you even know your blood type? Just curious if there's even a chance! I don't want to pressure you. Thankfully we have a big family, so I'm hoping one of my cousins can do it.

"Other than trying to find a match for her, work has been keeping me really busy, so I haven't been able to be as involved as I'd like to. My dad is great, though, and the rest of the family. It is a little hard being her only child through all this. It's a lot! Well, I guess I can't say that anymore now that I know about you! But you know what I mean. It's times like this I really wish I were married so at least I would have someone to help me with everything. Well, at least I hope my husband would be helping me!

"I don't think I told you, but I was in a serious relationship with a guy at my law firm for three years, and I thought it was headed toward marriage, but it didn't end up working out. Ugh, he's white, I'm black—it's complicated. So now I'm not only trying to get over him, I have to see him every day at work! That's why they tell you to steer clear of workplace romance! I'm at the point where I'd like to just go out for fun and to take my mind off of so many serious things! I would love to hear your dating stories based on your mention of the kinds of questions your dates ask.

"Anyway, I'm kind of used to dealing with Mom's illness and our life since she's been dealing with it for so long. But this is another level. Well, I'm not used to you, of course! You were an unexpected piece of news! But such an exciting one! I hope you feel the same way. I know it's deeper than that—I'm not that naïve! But I really like you, and even if we weren't related by blood, I would want to be friends! I feel frustrated that they kept us separated for so long, but better late than never, right?!"

Sol responds when Shyla stops for a sip of her drink. "Well, next you'll have to come to Baltimore, and I can show you around. I'd love for you to meet my family there too. Like any regular friends would. I know my family is so interested to meet you too. It's actually been a little hard with my mom because she hid the truth from me for so long. I understand, but I also don't understand. I mean, I'm thirty-six years old. Don't you think she could have told me when I became old enough to understand? And now with all the DNA testing, of course I would eventually find out."

"Yes, I would love to visit and meet everyone!" Shyla squeals. "I've never been to Baltimore. Maybe we could go by the law school too so I could see where Mom went to school. Sorry things have been hard with your mom, though. I can't believe that I was the one to drop this news on you."

They talk like old friends through the end of the game, and then Shyla drops Sol back off at the hotel with plans to take her to the airport in the morning. Sol doesn't even rub it in that the Orioles won.

- 29 -

Dear God,

I can't believe I met my biological mom today. Even though it's not quite a fairy tale, thank you that she decided to go through with the pregnancy and made sure I had a good home to go to. Help me to forgive all of them for the choices they made. Even Dad. I'm sure if he were here, I would be mad at him too. Thank you that the truth is coming out now. Help me to know what to do about the kidney stuff. I don't even know where to begin. Is this why you had me meet her now—to give her a kidney? I'm going to have a lot of thinking to do after this. Thank you that Shyla is friendly and has become a support through all this. I want to document it for posterity: Today is The First Time I Met My Birth Mother.

- 30 -

These pages sound like they're a good start to a movie script, Sol thinks as she closes her journal. She then texts her family and friends, promising to tell them everything that has happened when she gets back. She's way too tired to relive everything now. She makes a date with Franklin for that upcoming Friday. She figures she has to have something on the calendar that's not so serious. They decide to go to an improv comedy show, and Sol prays that the performers are funny.

She decides to spend the rest of the night turning off her brain and catching up on the cable shows she has been missing.

She must have started to doze off, because in that hazy time between wakefulness and sleep, Sol's phone rings, and she thinks it's in her dream before she actually wakes up and answers it. She doesn't even look at the screen, but then she hears a voice she's been waiting for—it's Dove.

"Hey, Sunny," Dove says nonchalantly, as though Sol hasn't been trying to reach her for over a week.

"Oh! It's you!" Sol reacts sleepily. She's happy to finally hear from Dove, but she wishes she had been more ready.

"Of course it's me. Were you asleep? Oh yeah, it's later there."

"Yeah, but I'm glad you called. I've been wanting to talk to you." Sol runs her hand over her face as if trying to wipe off the sleepiness.

"I got your message, but I've been so tied up trying to finish this big contract. It's a huge opportunity for my career. I knew you would understand. I mean, if something happened to Mom or Willow, you would have called me, right? So do you want to tell me your news?" Dove sounds like she's still in a rush.

"Yeah, well, things have been happening so fast. I'm actually in Boston right now." Sol's now in the bathroom splashing water on her face.

"What are you doing in Boston?" Sol hears the click of a keyboard in the background.

"It's a long story, but I'll try to tell you the short version."

"Good, because I have to finish up some work tonight."

Sol tries not to get thrown off track by her sister's hurry to get off the call. "About a month ago, I got an email saying that Mom wasn't really my mom and that my real mom needed a kidney transplant."

"What?! What a scam!" Dove scoffs.

"I know, that's what I thought at first too. But the person that wrote the email knew things about Dad," Sol says evenly.

"About Dad? That's ridiculous." The keyboard sounds continue.

"I know, this is why I really wanted to talk to you. I was kind of trying to figure it out on my own—why was this woman saying this? But I finally asked Mom, and she said it's true. She told me everything and said she and Dad were separated for a little while, and he got someone else pregnant, and that I'm that baby." Sol talks slowly, remembering that even though she has gotten used to the news a little, this is the first time that Dove is hearing it.

"Why would she say that? I can't believe you fell for this, Sol. Is Mom having mental issues?"

Sol takes a deep breath. "I met her today. My biological mother."

"Don't tell me that's why you're in Boston! This is crazy! What are you doing? These people are running a huge scam!" Dove's keyboard sounds have stopped, and her voice is angry and getting louder.

"I don't think it's a scam. I look just like her, Dove."

"I think they just brainwashed you into believing this unbelievable story! I was there, remember?!" Dove is practically screaming at her.

"I know you were, Dove. But you were just a little girl," Sol whispers.

"Okay, Sol, whatever. Listen, I have to go do some work. If this is what you want to do, then do it. Maybe you're having a mid-life crisis or something. You want to be in a different family?! But I don't believe it for one second. I'm going to call Mom too when I get a chance because I can't believe she would let you believe something like this either. Bye, Sol." Dove hangs up before Sol can even say goodbye. Sol didn't know what she expected, but that was definitely not it. She feels confused, but she's also so tired she figures maybe she's not thinking straight. *Could this really be a scam? Why would Mom tell me it was true then?*

In the morning, Sol decides not to think about her call with Dove as Shyla drives her to the airport. She's looking forward to getting back to her own house after her impromptu trip to Boston. Sol had no idea when she left two days prior all that would happen that weekend, but she doesn't regret doing it. If she had had all the time in the world to plan, she can't think of another plan that would be better. She has met her biological sister and mom. In the airport, she looks at the business travelers headed to their Monday meetings. She looks down at her semi-rumpled clothes and knows that she's the same person, but it will take a while to understand what to do with all this new information.

She sleeps the whole flight home. She feels like she may never get enough sleep to recover from all the drama of the past few days and weeks. She gets an Uber home from the airport since everyone is now at work and then goes to pick up Jericho from Willow's house. He gives her his usual excited greeting, and it's just what she needs to feel some sense of normalcy. She takes him for an extra-long walk around the art museum in her neighborhood and gives him some special-occasion salmon skin treats. "I missed you, Coco. You'll never believe what happened. You have a new grandmother," she says as she snuggles deep in bed to continue her day of sleep. Jericho pulls his bed next to hers, and soon they are both snoring.

- 31 -

The next day, Sol's back to work as usual, and she's busy the whole day with school visits. The pace of work takes her mind off everything that has happened in the last three days, but she takes a break to text Willow and Thea to come over to her place that night so she can debrief everyone on the reunion meetings: *Pad Thai and drunken noodles on me!* Sol knows that will entice them even if their curiosity doesn't. She stops by her favorite Thai food place on the way home and picks up twice as much as she needs.

That evening, the three women talk and catch up on everything that has happened. Jericho strategically lays under the table to catch any crumbs that may fall in the midst of the mayhem. They are all talking over one another, shouting out questions and laughing in some places. "So does she really look like you?" "Did you see her, Thea?" "But why didn't she tell you?" "So your new sister is nice? When do we meet her?" "I can't believe you had a black mom your whole life and didn't know it!" "How do you feel now?" "What will happen next?" "What made you go that same day?" "How long is she supposed to live?" "Shyla's not a match?" "Tell me what she looked like again. Did you get pictures?"

On that question, Sol remembers the pictures they took in the garden and passes her phone around.

"Oh wow, look at them!" "So how old is Shyla?" "She's a lawyer?" "You do look like your bio-mom, Sol!" "Well, she is super light-skinned, you wouldn't necessarily know she's black anyway." "But Shyla looks more like her dad? Did you meet him too?" "What did you have for lunch?"

This last question is from Willow, and Sol and Thea stop talking.

"Seriously, Willow? That's what you want to know?" Sol asks, incredulously.

"Well, food says a lot about people!" Willow defends herself.

Sol tells them about the chicken salad sandwiches and the vegetables from the garden, then about eating more at the sports bar.

"Were the Boston guys cute?" Willow asks.

"Seriously, Willow?!" Sol and Thea say in unison.

"Hey, just asking!" Willow says, laughing.

Once the initial recap is over, Sol continues, "I don't know what to do about the kidney situation. Did you know that people are dying on the waiting list every day? I had no idea. Shyla told me the blood type they need is O. I don't even know what blood type I am. So I'm thinking about at least finding that out. I did a little research, and it looks like a kidney center here is connected to hers in Boston, so I would be able to do the initial testing here. When you get a transplant from a live person, there's a lot more flexibility on scheduling and everything. When someone dies, you just have to be ready to go into surgery right away."

"Are you really thinking of doing this, Sol?" Thea asks. "You just met them. Do you want to take some time to think about it? I mean, does this cost you anything? Who pays for it? And what do you get out of it?"

"I don't know if I'll do it. I'm just thinking about it. She went through a lot to give birth to me. I mean, she could have had an abortion, given that whole situation, but she didn't. I kind of feel like I should at least look into it. Now that I've met them, it's different, like it's not just an abstract idea. Janice was telling me about her bucket list and how she wants to be practical if it doesn't happen. I mean, if you could give someone ten extra years of life, wouldn't you do it? I mean, I know it's not that simple. But I'm thinking about it. Would any of you all consider donating a kidney, or are you signed up to be organ donors after you die?"

Thea lets out a long breath. "Wow, big topic to think about. I would definitely want to talk to Quentin about it. But you know I'll go with you to get tested!"

"Me too!" says Willow.

"Thanks, you all. I really appreciate your support. I don't know how I could get through this whole situation without you. I mean, I want her to live. You won't believe it, but they actually have these things you can do if you don't match with the person you want to donate to. They can sometimes find another person that you match, and their donor matches your person. Like a crisscross thing, if that makes sense. You donate to each other's person. Or sometimes they can even make a chain where everyone is getting the right match, just not from their own donor. It's amazing the creativity that's keeping people alive!" Sol says.

"Of course we support you! We love you, Sol! We just don't want you to get hurt," Thea replies.

"I know, thank you, Thea. But I wonder maybe if I already got hurt and this would be part of my healing," Sol says.

"Yeah, maybe," Thea adds.

"Oh, speaking of hurt, I talked to Dove last night. I had never gotten a chance to tell her anything since the beginning of all this, so I was kind of giving her a recap of the whole story. She doesn't believe any of it. She thinks it's a scam!"

"Oh wow!" Willow says.

"She'll come around," Thea says.

"Yeah, I guess I wasn't really thinking about it from her point of view, but I guess the whole thing is a shock. Well, I'll talk to Shyla about what I would actually have to do to get tested, and I'll let you all know. It would be great if you can go with me. Good night, you two!" Sol says.

- 32 -

With everything going on, Sol has been putting Franklin off. He had been in full relationship mode, texting her *Good morning, beautiful* and sending messages throughout the day.

Meanwhile, she had been in arms-length mode, giving him the minimum of responses. She just didn't have the emotional and mental energy to do more as she was navigating through all the revelations and everything going on in her life. But she also didn't like handling things this way either. It seemed false. He deserved true communication too, even if she didn't intend to be in a relationship with him. He didn't seem to mind the way she was handling it, except the not seeing him part. She figured maybe he enjoyed a challenge, or maybe he just didn't pick up on any of it.

After the others leave that night, she calls him and give him the bullet-point version of what's been happening over the last few days and tries to give him her full attention for a bit as he describes his days.

"I had the kids this weekend and took them up to that amusement park I was telling you about, Dutch Wonderland. I wish you could have come with us."

Sol is surprised and says, "Oh, wow, do you think it's time for me to meet your kids?"

"Well, it was hard to get on some of the rides with just me and two kids, you know?" he says.

"Oh, yeah, that would be hard," she says, wondering again why she is still seeing him. They don't seem to be on the same wavelength at all, but he is pursuing her.

"Anyway, the kids love it there. There were so many other kids, and some of the lines were really long, but I just bought them cotton candy whenever they started to get cranky, and that did the trick! Some of those other parents are aggressive, though! This one mom said something to me about my son cutting in front of her kid in line. I was like, 'I don't know what you're talking about, lady.'"

"Oh, what are their favorite rides there? Is it mostly rides, or do they have performances too? I think my friend told me she went there one time. Is there a train?"

"Oh, yeah, the train is kind of lame, but the kids love it, so we rode on it like five times. I mean, we could just get on a train here and skip going to the park if that's what they want to do! What are you doing this weekend? Do you want to go to Six Flags? I won't have the kids, so we can go on the big roller coasters."

"Oh, I thought we were going to the improv show this weekend," she replies.

"You still want to do that? Sure, I just thought this might be more fun."

"Yes, I do still want to do that. I told you my friend Faye is in the show," Sol says, annoyed but too tired to respond to him. "I gotta go. I'll call you tomorrow."

"Okay, got it. Good night, babe," he says. She wonders how he made the leap to calling her "babe," but she falls asleep before she has time to figure it out.

- 33 -

The next morning, Sol is awakened by her phone ringing. It's her mom. Sol hasn't been communicating with her, except for short texts to let her know she's okay. Sol doesn't really know how she feels about everything, and it's too much to deal with everything and everyone all at once. She figures her mom will be there when she's ready to deal with that part of things—the fact that her mom lied to her.

"Sol, I'm sorry to call you so early, but I really want to catch up. I know you're upset with me, but I love you, and I want to talk." Sol is surprised that she's happy to hear her voice even though she's still angry.

"Hey, Mom," Sol says, yawning. "I've just been really busy with the trip and meeting everyone and coming back and trying to catch up on work."

"I know, I understand. Do you have time to come over for dinner? Bring Jericho. I'll have special treats for him too." Her mom knows the way to her heart is through her dog.

"Okay, sure, Mom, I'll see you later, but I've got to go." She decides she might as well get up since her alarm clock would be going off in seven minutes anyway.

It's another busy day at work for her, and Sol is doubly

motivated to help the kids in her program. She feels bad about even taking that one day off, and the kids have been telling her how much they missed her on Monday. She looks at them and thinks about carrying on her mom's and dad's hopes for a better world. Sometimes the needs here seem overwhelming, but every day, she sees progress in these kids' reading, and she knows it's worth it. Working with them always give her perspective on her own problems too.

After work, she quickly picks up Jericho and heads to her mom's house. She's hoping her mom or Mickey made one of her favorite meals, but she didn't want to be bratty about asking for it.

"Willow told me you're going to get tested to donate a kidney to Janice," Patty says as soon as she arrives.

"Hi, Mom, you don't beat around the bush, huh? Okay, give me a minute, and I'll tell you everything," Sol responds as she lets Jericho out into the yard. She stops in the kitchen on the way back to see what's cooking. Lasagna, one of Mickey's specialties, greets her there. "Oooo!" she says as she sees the garlic bread.

"Sol, I'm glad you came. I know I messed up, and it will maybe take you a while to forgive me. But I'm your mother for better or worse. Through everything. Blood or not. I lost your father, and I don't want to lose you too. I'm here, and I'm going to be in your life!" Patty says.

"Me too," says Mickey as he walks up behind Patty.

Sol gives them a three-way hug. "Of course you're always going to be in my life. But it's hard. I'm just trying to take it all in and wrap my head around it. Can you imagine finding something out like this in your thirties? I still don't understand why you didn't tell me. It's like the whole foundation of my life has shifted. That doesn't take anything away from you all, but I'm glad I got to meet my sister and my biological mom. Do you want to see pictures?"

Sol walks them through the pictures she took with Shyla and Janice. "So Shyla says her dad's genes took over everything. I wish I had gotten a picture of him because it's true. The family resemblance is really strong. But I do think I look like Janice. It's weird after all this time meeting someone that looks like me. Mom, did you ever meet her in person?"

"No, I never did. I never wanted to then. I was so shattered during that time. I never wanted to see her. I didn't want to even remember that she existed. I would just imagine that she was an unknown mom that couldn't keep her baby. That's the only way I got through it. After some years had passed, I didn't really have the opportunity, but I was terrified that you would find out and want to meet her and the whole story would come out. Like it is now. I did write to her just one time to let her know that Patrick had died."

"Oh yeah, Mom, she showed me the letters! She had that one—it was just a few lines—and the pictures that Dad had sent her of me when I was little."

"I do think you look like her," Patty says after she looks at the photos.

"Yeah, I agree," Mickey chimes in.

"I asked her to show me some pictures from when she was younger. I mean, I guess now I know what I'll look like when I get to be sixty-four years old. She didn't have a lot out in the house, but she said she would look through some old boxes to see what she can find.

"But you guys, I did find out more about what's going on with her disease. Her kidneys have failed. She's on dialysis, but the life expectancy on that is only like five years! I mean, I know she's basically a stranger to me, but if I'm a match for her, I could give her maybe ten extra years of life. She did choose to have me when she was pregnant with me, even though she was still in school and everything. Did you know she was $78,000 in debt by the time she left the hospital because of all the complications?!

"So I'm starting to feel—not like I owe her something—but more like asking myself whether this is actually part of the bigger plan for my life. I talked to Willow and Thea about it last night. If I make it through the initial phone screening, they said they'd go to the testing center with me and support me through everything."

"Oh wow, I had no idea about any of that. Tell me more about how the donation process works," Patty says.

"I have been learning so much about it. You get tested to see if you're a match. They do an initial screen, and then that determines if you get the full testing, which includes physical tests but also psychological tests and financial consultations, and I don't even know what else. The better physical match you are, the more likely her body won't reject the kidney and it can do its thing. Shyla was saying her immune system is really complicated, so it's hard to match. But if I did happen to match and were going to donate, we would schedule a day to both go in. They can do a laparoscopic procedure for me, so it's just a small incision and heals pretty quickly. And they don't even take her kidneys out—they just add the new one! The biggest thing is just being out of work for a little while and recovering. They have some independent funds that can help, but maybe I could do short-term disability or something. I have to do a little more research and get in touch with the center to get the process going," Sol says.

"Okay, I'll get tested too," Patty immediately responds.

"What? Mom, no. You hate hospitals and needles and all that stuff."

"Yes, I'm sure. I'm your mother. I want to be there for you. I know this doesn't change anything about the decisions I made, but the only thing I can do now is make good decisions going forward. You're right, I hate needles and I might pass out like that one time, but I want to do this with you."

"Mom, you don't have to do that. I don't want you to do it out of guilt."

"No, I made up my mind. We'll do this together," Patty says firmly.

"Okay! Thanks, Mom! That means a lot!" Sol says and hugs her. "Now, what about that lasagna and garlic bread?"

Over dinner, they chat about lighter things like the Mediterranean cruise Patty and Mickey are planning next spring and how in the world Sol is going to create a dress out of aluminum foil for Thea's annual World UFO Day party next month.

When she leaves that night, her mom gives her a long hug. "You'll always be the sunshine in my life, my baby girl," Patty says.

"Thanks, Mom. And you'll always be my mom," Sol says as she hugs her back. "I'll let you know when I get the testing scheduled."

She makes sure to grab some lasagna before she leaves.

- 34 -

The happy hour specials at Minato Sushi are legendary, not just for the drinks but for the sushi rolls too. Sol puts in some extra effort getting ready for her date there with Franklin. She's wearing her yellow sundress with the full skirt that makes her feel like a 1950s movie star. She had picked the perfect day that week to wash her hair so her waves would be defined but not too puffy.

She meets him on Friday before the improv show, and he greets her with an extra-long hug and a kiss on the lips. Their first kiss. It's just a peck, but it does tell her that he's trying to take the relationship somewhere. Sol is glad to be out on a date and hopes it goes well. Her life as a single person is great and full and fulfilling, but she does long for a romantic relationship too. She doesn't feel like she *needs* it, but she definitely wants it. Even after years of dating different people, she still has hope at the beginning of each new relationship. She has an idea in her head of her ideal man, but she also tries to be realistic that each of these men are actual people who are more complicated than an ideal.

As they eat their edamame appetizer, Franklin gives her a play-by-play of a complex work situation, and finally asks for more details about her trip. She tells him about how Shyla is so happy to have a sister and how she has such an outgoing and chatty personality. Sol tells him about how Shyla looks like her dad because his family has such a strong family resemblance, but that she looks like Janice. She pulls out her phone and starts showing him the pictures from when they first met and were taking pictures in the garden.

"Wait, is that her?" he says. "Your biological mom?"

"Yes, that's her. Don't you think I look like her? I even saw some pictures from when she was younger, and it's like I'm her twin!"

Sol looks over at him excitedly and is surprised to see the puzzled look on his face and hear him say, "Wait a second, is your mom black?"

"Yeah, she is. I was surprised, but you know people are always asking me if I'm mixed or Latina or whatever, so I guess it makes sense."

Franklin just stares at her.

"What?"

"So my girlfriend is black?"

"Um, first of all, I wouldn't say that I'm your girlfriend, and second of all, I would say 'biracial' but yes, I just told you that." Sol can feel herself starting to get upset, but she tries to keep her voice level. She eats a sushi roll and drinks some water.

"You know, there's a reason that those dating apps ask you what your race is," Franklin says.

Sol looks up, hoping he's not going where she thinks he might be going with this. "Oh yeah, what reason is that?"

"So you know what you're getting."

Sol hears his words, and it's one of those situations she knows she will look back on and think of a better answer. But she can't just leave that out there. She stares at him for a few seconds before she can respond. "Franklin, I'm not a product in an online store. I'm a person. I've been updating you on what's been happening with finding out about my biological mom. So do you have a problem with my mom being black? Does that change what you think of me and how you feel about me?"

Other people in the restaurant glance over, and Sol tries to keep her emotions in check. But inside, it's a storm. She can feel her face getting hot, and her heart starts beating faster. She hasn't even really processed the new information about her identity yet, and now here is this guy she's been dating telling her that it changes things for their relationship.

"Yes, actually, it does. I put 'white' for the ethnicity I wanted on my profile because that's the ethnicity I wanted."

"Okay, then I guess we're done here," Sol says as she pulls some cash out of her purse, leaves it on the table and walks out as calmly as possible while inside she's blowing up. Franklin doesn't follow her, and she manages to make it outside with only knocking one chopstick off someone's table with her purse.

On the drive home, Sol goes over and over the conversation in her head. On the one hand, she's glad she doesn't have to wonder whether she should continue dating him. She knows. She's reminded of that quote from Maya Angelou—something like "When someone shows you who they are, believe them." Franklin had said several little offensive things over the one month they had been dating, but she kept giving him the benefit of the doubt. She feels rising frustration at herself for doing that. *Why don't you trust your own judgment? Why can't you believe that there can be a good guy out there for you instead of putting up with things like that?*

Sol calls Thea and tells her what happened. Thea tells her to come right over. Sol makes a U-turn and heads to Thea's house.

- 35 -

When Thea opens the door, Sol sees she's wearing her nineties Brandy-style overalls and three-foot-long braids. Thea gives Sol a huge hug and pulls her into the house. She then holds her out and looks at her.

"Oh, excuse me, you look fierce! I bet you looked soooo good walking out of that restaurant on him too! He does not deserve you at all. I didn't want to tell you what to do, but I'm glad it came to this because he was not the one."

Quentin pokes his head around the corner. "Hey, Sol! Great to see you! What can I get you to drink?" he asks.

Thea responds for both of them: "Two gin and tonics, please! Thanks, hon!"

Then she turns to Sol. "I'm sorry this happened. What a jerk. But now that you're here, we can talk. I know you debriefed us on Monday, but I didn't really get a sense of what you're thinking and feeling. We can talk about it if you want to. I know it's been a tough night."

"Ugh, seriously. Good thing I didn't tell Faye we were planning to come to the show tonight. Honestly, I haven't processed much myself. I've just been going from one thing to the next and trying to keep my head above water. I mean, this whole thing with Franklin was ugly, but it does remind me that I haven't really thought through what it means for me that my biological mom is black. If anything."

Thea gives her a hug. "Sol, I always knew you were my 'sister sister'!"

Sols laughs and shakes her head. Just then two little voices call out, "Auntie Sunny!" and Thea's girls run in.

"Hey, I thought you two rascals were in bed!" Thea playfully scolds them.

"We were, but we heard Auntie Sunny's voice," Thea's adorable five-year-old answers. "It's been soooo long since we've seen her, and we wanted to get a sunshine hug from her and see if she wants to see our new paint in our rooms. The star machine makes it look so dreamy." She doesn't look sleepy at all.

"I'd love to see it! How about you show me, and then I can tuck you back into bed nice and tight?" Sol answers. She loves these kids, and honestly, feels like she could use all the hugs she can get.

After she has suitably admired the new paint colors in the girls' room and gotten at least fifteen hugs, she tucks them both in and returns to the living room. Her gin and tonic is ready, and she raises a glass to toast. "What should we toast to?"

"We are toasting to you in all your glory, Sol Garnett! Black and white, double adopted, awesome leader and friend, heart of service and glass-half-full eyes, the best dog mom and auntie to my kids! Here's to you!"

"Cheers to that!" Quentin says as he raises his glass.

"So tell me everything. Or anything you want. Good

thing your date ended early so you have time to spend with me!" Thea jokes. "But seriously, I'm sorry that happened."

"I guess I was wondering if this new information would change anything for me. And I found out the answer, at least a little bit. Franklin said he 'liked me so much,' he 'missed me,' it was like 'baby' this and 'sweetie' that, but as soon as he found out my biological mother is black, he completely changed his tune. So he didn't really like me as a person? Only when I was a white woman he was attracted to! Oh, and he kissed me tonight for the first time! Anyway, it's not like I have to tell you any of this. You've already been living it. Although, I don't think you can really pass for white!"

Thea laughs. "Yeah, on the one hand, you're the same person you always were. But on the other hand, the world may not think that."

"And it's like what level of responsibility do I have to let people know my bio mom is black? It's kind of like I'm undercover. I mean, I barely even correct people when they say my name wrong, but I guess that's totally different."

"Well, it's not like you need to start proclaiming your African heritage or something. But it does give you a unique position. I mean, to Franklin's point, if you plan to keep using the dating apps, you should definitely update it on there. As he showed you so clearly tonight, some people have strong feelings about their dates' ethnicity. I know you have always been open about dating different ethnicities, but not everyone is like that."

"Yeah, and I think even in terms of my job, it will help save me from dating someone who's not on board with my commitment there." Sol is thoughtful and stirs her drink.

"So has he texted you or anything? Or was that just the end? Did he even try to apologize?" Thea gives her a concerned look.

Sol pulls her phone out of her purse to see if she has any new messages. "Nope, no texts. And he didn't say anything after I left. He didn't even get up. He might still be there eating sushi! You know, I kind of blame myself because I have seen flashes of his character from the beginning and kept thinking it was a one-time thing or he didn't really mean it. Why did I do that? It had to take this big thing to make me take action."

"Don't beat yourself up. Now you know. Remember what I just said about your 'glass-half-full' eyes? We need you to keep those eyes! But next time I want you to give me more details because you know I will give you the real, non-emotionally involved assessment! 'Bye, guy! You didn't make the cut!'" Thea acts the last part out as though Franklin is standing right there in front of them.

Sol shakes her head in disbelief. "Thanks, Thea. I appreciate you. Were you saying something before about their being support groups for people who find surprising stuff out from their DNA tests?"

"Of course, there is a group for everything! I think the one I mentioned before was the people who had found out when they were older that they were adopted."

Thea pulls her own phone out of her back pocket and looks around for a few seconds before saying, "Oh here, I just found it. It's called 'late-discovery adoptees' and then there was the DNA test one called 'not parent expected.' I'll text it to you. But yeah, finding out about a different ethnicity, I don't know if there's one specifically for that. I'm sure you're not the only one. I told you I was reading that article about how people are finding out all kinds of things from their DNA tests. Whoops, sorry to the people that just wanted to find out that they were descended from royalty or something!"

"Phew, so complicated. Thanks for all your support. And for showing me to how to be an awesome black woman all these years! This is definitely a journey."

"I got you, sister!" Thea says and hugs her. Sol lets herself be hugged and knows she's blessed in so many ways.

- 36 -

The following week, the Baltimore Museum of Art is hosting a special event, and Jericho must smell the caterers' food from blocks away because he leads Sol directly there on his evening walk. After they've suitably people-watched and -sniffed for a good twenty minutes, the two head back home for a "normal" night of catching up on laundry, vacuuming dog hair, and working through the pile of mail that has accumulated while Sol has been distracted by other things.

At the bottom of the pile is a large, padded yellow envelope. She thinks maybe it's printer ink or something she forgot she ordered online, but she forces herself to deal with the top of the pile first. Thankfully, most of it can go directly into the recycling bin, but she does pull out a few bills and a wedding invitation for her cousin who lives on the other side of town.

When she gets to the padded envelope, she discovers that it's hand-addressed from Janice, postmarked about a week after Sol's visit. Sol quickly opens the envelope and starts pulling out the contents. She sees it's full of letters and pictures and recognizes some of the ones Janice had shown her when she visited. On top of everything is another sealed envelope that says "Sol" in large letters on the front. She opens it and pulls out some dried lavender sprigs and several sheets of paper filled with a long, handwritten letter that's signed by Janice. Sol puts everything else aside, sits down on the couch next to Jericho, and starts to read:

Dear Sol,

I can't tell you how much it means to me that you came to visit. There is so much to say after all these years, but we only had a little time. I hope we get to talk again. I'll leave it up to you, but I just want you to know that I want to get to know you if you are open to the idea.

I thought you might like to have these letters from your father since you didn't have a long time to know him. They give you a little window into what he thought and felt about you. I do also want to tell you more of the story. I was thinking about how you asked whether I loved him. Honestly, I have not thought about him and our relationship in so long. I tried to forget.

It was so painful to think that you were out there somewhere, and I didn't know you. I had never held you, my own baby. So I tried to push it out of my mind. That was the only way I could make it through. Jackie would sometimes mention a bit of news about you since she was keeping track of you, but I finally had to ask her to stop because it upset me so much.

But these last few years have made me think about things a little differently, and I knew I wanted to meet you before I died. Seeing you and going through these old letters has brought up so many things I thought I had forgotten. I also went through the old boxes of pictures like I promised and came across some of my old journals too. I took a whole afternoon to read through everything. I'm including a few pictures of myself from when I was younger so you can know me a little more too.

I can't make up for all these years of withholding your own story from you. But I want to tell you as much as I can. You deserve that and so much more. I have so many regrets, so many years that we lost. But all I can do now is try to make things right as much as I can.

First, I will tell you a little bit about myself. I grew up not too far from here, and we had a big family. My sister, Jackie, is two years older than me but we also had four other brothers and sisters who were older and younger than us. When I was around 11 years old, Thurgood Marshall was confirmed as a Supreme Court Justice. This was big—the first black Justice! I remember watching it on the news on our little TV. It really captivated me and from then on, I decided I was going to be a lawyer. I don't think I really even knew what a lawyer was then, but that's the path I followed, and I learned as I went. I worked hard, and my parents tried to help as best as they could. I took a few years after I graduated from undergrad to work and save up money for law school. When it came time to apply, I knew just where I wanted to go—The University of Maryland School of Law in Baltimore. Thurgood Marshall, my role model, hadn't been able to go there because it was segregated at the time, but later he successfully won the case against the school's segregation law on behalf of one of his clients. I was so happy when I got in! That's how I ended up in Baltimore.

Sol stops at the end of the second page to text Thea: *Hey, are you free? I want to show you what came in the mail.*

Thea responds in seconds: *What is it? I can't come over, but can we video chat?*

Sol gets Thea on video chat and shows her the pile of letters and pictures. She then rereads the beginning of the letter out loud for Thea and then continues on:

Law school was hard! I had no idea. I thought it would be like UMass, where I went for undergrad, just a little harder. But it was completely different, a whole new way of learning. Baltimore was also a bit of a culture shock. There I was, a light-skinned black woman from mostly white Boston showing up with my dreams of following in Thurgood Marshall's footsteps and in his majority-black hometown, but in a school that was still mostly white. Thankfully, there were a good number of other women in the program, so at least I didn't feel too out-of-place because of my gender. I was a few years older than most of the other students, but no one really noticed. I hadn't thought about any of that, only had my head in my books concentrating on getting in. I didn't think about what it would be like when I got there.

In the middle of my second year, I thought I was getting the hang of it a little bit. I was also working at a café nearby and had made some friends there and at school. It was nice to know that I could do well away from home and family. When your father started coming to the café, I didn't notice him at first, but I was always friendly with all the customers. One day he asked my name. Then he would linger to chat with me. But I honestly did not think twice about him until he asked me out one day. You know, you do look like him too. Well, I'm sure you've seen pictures, but he had that dimpled chin that made him look like a superhero. I thought he was nice, and so I said yes. The first time we went out, we just walked down to the Inner Harbor and got sandwiches. He told me about the work he was doing with the city planning department. He was so passionate about it. I told him about law school and the things I was learning. He asked where I was from since he could hear I had a different accent. He had a sadness to him, but I didn't know why then.

After that, we started seeing each other a couple times a week, but I never took it seriously. I wasn't thinking about being in a relationship or marriage or having kids. I was so busy with school and work that I didn't have time to think about anything else but going out with your dad was a nice break when I could. I have to credit working at a café and getting free coffee for keeping me awake through those days—

Thea cuts in just then, "Sol, how do you feel learning about their relationship? Is this weird for you?"

Sol thinks for a second, then says, "You know, it's kind of like just learning about strangers. Like this is unrelated to me. When I think oh, he was married to my mom at this time, it makes me feel so confused. But reading it like strangers, I'm like 'Oh, is he going to ask her out again?'"

"Yeah, it's so hard that you don't really remember your dad and now to have all this coming out. And of course, Janice has now been married for like thirty years to someone else."

"Ugh, too much to think about. Let me see what else she says."

Sol continues reading:

Your dad was sweet to me. He said he didn't know I was black at first, kind of like the guys you told us about on your dates. But I was used to going out with white guys back home. Other than that, race didn't really come up because we never talked about a future together.

Neither of us had much money, but sometimes in the morning he would bring me a flower that he had picked (I loved flowers even then), or we would just walk around downtown together after work. He showed me different neighborhoods, giving me the inside scoop on everything from growing up there. Of course, he must have avoided any areas where he thought we would run into someone he knew because I never met any of his friends. We were seeing each other only for a month or two. I was living in a little apartment near school, and once I felt like I could trust him, I would invite him to my place for dinner, and he would help me study and sometimes he stayed over. I was learning more about him, but like I said, it wasn't serious.

One day, we were drinking a bottle of wine at my place to celebrate him finishing the first phase of a project and this song came on the radio, "Love Will Keep Us Together." Patrick got this a look on his face and wouldn't make eye contact. I asked him what was wrong, and he said, "We danced to this song at our wedding." I asked him what he was talking about, and that's when he told me about your mom and sister. I still didn't understand, but when I finally figured out he had been separated only two months, I told him to leave and go back to his wife and baby.

I didn't want to talk to him or see him. I didn't know what to think—was he using me or what? I think I was more angry than anything about him not telling me the truth from the beginning. I tried to just throw myself back into my normal routine of school and work. But I was so exhausted all the time and feeling a little sick, it was hard to keep up. We were finishing up the fall semester. I finally went to the doctor after my mom and Jackie kept nagging me. I went to the student health clinic, and I didn't bring a friend or anything. I thought they would just tell me that I needed to get more sleep. The doctor did a physical, and the nurse drew some blood and took some urine. They said they would run a few tests to rule some things out. The next day, they called me with the news that I was pregnant.

Sol abruptly stops reading and puts down the letter. "Thea?" she says as she stares into the camera on her phone with wide eyes.

"Yeah. Wow," Thea says.

"I can't believe this. I mean, she kind of told me this when I saw her, but I was overwhelmed that day, and now here are all these details. I don't even know what to say. I can't believe I'm finding this out after all these years. My dad sounds like a mess too."

"Yeah, he really does," Thea agrees, not even trying to be nice about her dad.

"What if Janice had kept seeing him? What if that song had never come on the radio?! No Willow? No family? Or maybe he would still be alive?!" Sol starts to feel her throat tighten, a sure sign she's starting to panic.

"Sol, breathe," Thea says firmly, trying to calm her down. "You can't torture yourself like that with all those 'What ifs.' Is that the end of the letter?"

Sol closes her eyes and takes three deep breaths, holding for a few seconds after each inhale, just like she tells the students to do when she's trying to help them calm down. She opens her eyes and says, "No, there are two more pages. I guess Janice is really trying to get the truth out after all these years. Okay, here goes:

> After they told me, it's almost like my body embraced the situation and went all out. I could barely function because I was so tired and crampy. I was also in shock. I wasn't expecting this to happen, and I was flailing. I had no idea what to do. All I wanted to do was get my law degree and become a lawyer. I had to study for my final exams for the semester. But how did a baby fit into that?

> I called out of work sick a couple days but then forced myself to go because I knew I would need all the money I could get. In my mind, I saw pictures of my dream I had been working toward all these years getting a little off-balance. But I didn't have another picture. I didn't have a backup plan. I was determined to somehow finish. I called your dad to tell him and then decided I would approach the pregnancy the same way I approached school: preparation and perseverance.

> I dutifully went to my doctor's appointments. That day they told me I was pregnant, they had asked if I thought I would keep the baby. "Of course I will," I said. That was never a question for me. I talked to my parents about it, and they were surprised but

said they would help as much as they could. Like I told you before, every child in our family was treated as a blessing. People at school pretended they didn't notice anything—at least until winter was over and I stopped wearing bulky sweaters.

I already told you what happened next and how Jackie came down to help those two times and tried to convince me we could make it work. She always took her role as my big sister seriously. When she came, we spent the whole time talking about how to make it work. She offered to take care of you while I finished school. She didn't understand what was happening with Patrick. She thought he had abandoned me.

The more we talked, the more hopeless it felt. I believed the best thing I could do for you was to give you a chance at having a good life in a more stable situation. Jackie kept trying to convince me that we could do it, but I was focused on getting through the pregnancy without losing you, and then I knew I had to be willing to lose you for the rest of my life so that you could thrive.

After Jackie had talked to your dad that second time, and he said they wanted to raise you, I asked the hospital staff to never let me see you. I knew I would never be able to let you go if I did. I left Baltimore as soon as I could. Everywhere I looked was painful. I have never been back since then. To make some money, I did some training to become a paralegal. I thought I would go back to law school one day and finish. Then I met Calvin through one of my cousins, and we got married and had Shyla, and I guess other things became more important than my lawyer dreams. But I never stopped thinking about you as hard as I tried.

I'm so happy to know you after all of this. I'm sorry that this is what it took for you to know the truth. I hope you can forgive us for the way we handled everything. I want you to know that the most important thing to me was for you to have a chance. You are my missing piece.

Love,

Janice

Sol takes a deep breath and lets out a sigh. "Whoa. That's a lot."

"Are you glad she told you all that?" Thea asks.

"Yeah, I am. I have to know the truth. But it's a lot to take in. And I still have all this other stuff in the envelope to look at. Ugh, I don't know if I can finish it tonight." Sol lets out a huge sigh.

"Oh yeah, what's in there?" Thea urges, seeming not to hear Sol's last comment.

"Let me see…some of these are the letters she showed me already, but she said she went through some more old stuff. Oh my gosh! Here's a picture of her in Baltimore! Look at her. Can you see this?" Sol holds the picture up to the phone camera. "It looks like she's in Fells Point. I can see the Domino Sugar sign in the background. I'll send you a picture of it. Wow, I really do look like her, don't I? Look at that hair, though…so long and dark. It's gorgeous. Oh, here's her college graduation. And this one looks like her with her parents and brothers and sisters. I guess that means they're my grandparents and aunts and uncles. Shyla told me Janice's parents died a few years ago, though."

"Oh, that's too bad you didn't get to meet them."

"Yeah, it's going to be hard to get over that since they had thirty-six years to figure out how to tell me," Sol says as she stares intently at the photo. She then gently puts it on top of the pile she has already looked through and straightens the pile, then lets out a breath. "Okay, I think that's enough for me to go through for one day! Thanks for doing it with me."

Thea blows her a kiss. "Of course! You know I'm here for you! Good night, Sol, you're going to get through this!"

"Good night, Thea! You're the best!"

Jericho stands up and stretches when he hears Sol hang up. He then walks over and gives her the "puppy dog eyes."

"Okay, okay, let's go out back, and then I'll give you one treat," she tells him. He perks up at the word "treat" and runs to get his leash.

- 37 -

When Sol pulls up to the transplant center at nine o'clock on Thursday morning, she sees a blur of green. "Hi, everyone, I didn't know we were matching today!" she says, confused.

"Oh, we just thought we'd get in the spirit and surprise you. Green is the color for kidney disease awareness," her mom explains. Sol looks over at Thea and sees she's dressed to go to work after this, her long braids pulled up in a large bun, but she has also coordinated with the green theme with a gorgeous emerald blouse. Patty is wearing green "mom jeans," a green Loyola University sweatshirt—a different shade of green from the jeans, of course—and her favorite brown Birkenstocks. She even has a green woven fanny-pack.

"Leave it to you to make it an event!" Sol says laughing. "I wish I had known!"

Sol, Patty, Mickey, Thea, and Willow file into the transplant center. Patty and Sol have both done their basic blood tests and phone interviews, and this is their next step, a whole day of tests and interviews that will determine whether either will be approved as a donor for Janice.

The receptionist gives a surprised look when she sees

their group. "Good morning … everyone! Do all of you have appointments?"

Sol steps forward. "No, my name is Sol Garnett. It's just me and my mom, Patricia Thompson, that have appointments. This is just our support team."

"Oh, okay, here you are," the receptionist says, looking at her computer. "You can have a seat, and I'll call you in a few minutes. Did you want to go back together?"

"Yes, please," Sol and Patty say together.

They sit in the waiting area for just a few minutes, but Patty's hands don't stop playing with the bracelet she's wearing. She pulls it and then twists it until it cuts into her wrist. Mickey holds her hand on one side, but Patty's other hand doesn't stop moving. Sol looks at her out of the corner of her eye. Her whole life, Sol's mom hasn't liked anything medical. She tries natural remedies first for anything that she needs and has a whole cabinet full of different herbs and teas. Sol suspects that it's partly her mom's anxiety about doctors and not just her beliefs. Sol gives Patty's other arm a squeeze partly to reassure her and partly in hope that she'll stop her anxious twisting.

Without even realizing it, over the last couple of weeks Sol has started to imagine herself being a match for Janice and going through the surgery. She and Shyla have been texting, and Sol senses that underneath her chatty exterior, Shyla is feeling the weight of Janice's situation. Sol loves being able to help others, and maybe this is an extra special opportunity since she may be one of the only ones who could do it.

When the nurse calls Patty and Sol to go back with her,

the others say they'll be back later to pick them up, then they head out to their jobs.

The first doctor addresses Sol. "You're getting tested to match with Janice Broward at the Boston center, right? Now it says here that Janice is your mother."

"Um," answers Sol. Patty watches her intently. Sol hadn't thought about how to explain her family situation to strangers yet. After a second, she says, "Yes, she's my biological mother, and this is my adoptive mother." Patty hugs her around the shoulders.

The nurses sense Patty's anxiety and seem intent on reassuring her through everything, especially the tests like the CT scan. The parts that are education about the surgery are not as tense. When they do the video conferences with the various people at the Boston center who would be involved in making the surgery a success, Patty seems more comfortable because at heart she's a people person.

Different people at the center talk them through some practical matters Sol hadn't fully understood, such as the financial and insurance side of things. The staff also want to pin down who would be available to be their twenty-four-hour caregiver for a whole month after surgery. At this question, Sol and Patty both look at each other in surprise that they would need a caregiver for that long. When they're informed that a kidney donor wouldn't be able to lift anything for six to eight weeks, Patty starts asking question after question, thinking through the implications of what that would mean for running her store, receiving shipments, and putting up displays.

By the end of the day, Patty and Sol are both exhausted.

When they come back out to the waiting room, their support crew gives them hugs and Willow produces some "Superstar" stickers from her purse that she has left over from work.

"Thanks, everyone," Sol says. "I had no idea how intense that would be! I'm so glad you were here to support us!" She had been thinking that they could all go out to dinner together, but now she doesn't even mention it. She drives straight home with the car windows open, thankful to be back in the fresh air and done with meeting people for the day.

When she gets home, she takes Jericho for a long walk to loosen up her body after sitting for so long. She spends the walk thinking back through all the different tests and meetings of the day. *Would I really do this kidney donation? Who would take care of me after surgery?* The center staff said that if she matches, Sol can still change her mind up to the day of the surgery, so that's comforting to know she's not committed to anything if she doesn't want to be.

Jericho's tail wags constantly as they pass block after block of colorful rowhouses. He loves saying hi to the other dogs they see, but he especially likes meeting new people. Sol has always thought this would be a good way to meet a guy, but it hasn't happened yet. She has gotten to know quite a few of her neighbors while walking him, though. He's a great icebreaker.

Just as she's starting to relax and stop thinking about the transplant center, Sol gets a call from Shyla. She's immediately worried that something has happened with Janice. She's almost afraid to answer, but after three-and-a-half rings, she says, "Hello?" bracing herself for the worst.

"Sol! You'll never believe this—," Shyla says excitedly.

"Is everything okay?" Sol cuts in.

"Yes, sorry, everything is okay! Guess what! Mom got a match! It's one of my cousins! Remember how I told you the family is so big? Well, it paid off! I begged every single one of them to get screened, and even though some of the others have conditions that disqualify them, I think more than twenty people in our family at least got their blood type tested! So from that, there were a few potential people, but remember how I told you she was so hard to match because of her immune system? And then all the donors' situations...But Gordon, my one cousin, it seemed like he could maybe work out and then went in for the all-day testing, and he matched on everything and he said he'll do it!

"So they scheduled the surgery already! All this is happening so fast! But you know how Mom is getting worse and worse, the sooner, the better. Gordon's being macho about the whole thing like it's no big deal, but I think he's kind of scared. So I'm trying to be extra nice to him and helping him with all the logistics and talking to his insurance company and everything and trying to get the extra help for him, so he doesn't have to worry about any of that. His wife and I are teaming up to make it a good experience for him and she is amazing. I'm so happy someone in the family matched!

"But I wanted to see if you can come up. Will you come? It's going to be on Monday! Like get there 7:00 a.m. on Monday morning, and it takes several hours, but some of that time is just waiting. I would really love to have you there. Some others in the family will also be there, of course, but you're my only sibling so it would mean so much!" Shyla finally takes a breath.

"Oh my gosh, that's great!" Sol says, leaning down to pet Jericho. She had stopped walking when she answered the phone. "You'll never guess where I was this morning. My mom and I went to the transplant center to do our all-day testing!"

"What? Are you serious?" Shyla replies, a smile in her voice.

"I wasn't sure if I wanted to do it, so I didn't say anything earlier because I didn't want to get your hopes up. But yes, we both passed the initial screens and kept on going with the testing."

"That is amazing! Thank you so much, Sol! This means so much to me!"

"You're welcome! Okay, let me see if I can make it on Monday. I'll check and will let you know as soon as I can," Sol says. She thinks it's a good thing she has so many vacation days saved up. She straightens back up and steers Jericho toward home.

"I hope you can! You can stay at my house this time, okay?" Shyla says excitedly.

"Okay, I'll call you back!" Sol says, smiling. She can't believe this is happening right after she and her mom had just spent the day at the transplant center. She's so happy for Shyla and of course for Janice. She prays it will all go smoothly on Monday. She emails Zakirah that night about taking another day off.

- 38 -

The following night after work, Sol goes through the envelope that Janice sent her again. Now that she's planning to go up to Boston a second time, she wants to be ready with any follow-up questions she might have. There are a couple more pictures of Janice in Baltimore she didn't notice the first time she looked. There's another old family picture to which Janice has attached a sticky note that tells who each person is. There's a picture of Janice with Shyla as a little girl with a sticky note that says, "This is me at your age."

Sol turns to the letters in her father's handwriting. She wants to memorize everything. His writing is in all capital letters with a black ballpoint pen. Most of the stamps are a little crooked. As she goes through, she notices one address that's different from the others—West Cross Street. Did she miss this one before? She looks at the date on the postmark, and it's from November 22, 1982. It doesn't feel like there are any pictures inside. The paper is the same as all the others—paper from a white legal pad with perforations at the top. Maybe he wrote these letters from work on his lunch break. Did Mom even know he was sending them? Once she starts reading, she knows this is one she hasn't seen before:

Dear Janice,

I'm sorry, I never meant to hurt you. I hope you can believe me. I should have told you about my situation. I didn't think about how it would affect you. I guess I was running away. Everything in my life was going according to plan until we lost our baby. We never thought anything bad could happen to us. We thought we could change the world. It's like we got stuck after that. So we were arguing a lot, and one day I just left. But I didn't know how to go back, and the days just went by. When I met you, I thought maybe I wouldn't go back at all. I keep wishing for an easy answer, but it doesn't seem like there is one. I hope you can understand.

Patrick

Sol gets to the end and turns it over, but that's all there is. She reads it again. Then a third time. She thinks this is the closest she might ever get to knowing her story. She takes a deep breath, then looks back at the envelope. She turns it over in her hand and looks inside again to see if she missed anything. Nothing. Fifteen minutes later, she realizes she's just been staring out the window. She wonders what happened after that. How did her dad and mom figure out how to live together again after all that and with Sol coming into their lives as an infant? The more she finds out, the more questions she has.

- 39 -

"There are six emergency exits on this aircraft. Take a minute to locate the exit closest to you." Sol barely listens to the flight attendants' safety announcements since it's only been a couple of weeks since her last flight. She's flying up to Boston on Sunday morning. Shyla wants them to spend time with Janice before the surgery. This visit, Sol doesn't feel as nervous about being around them since she has met them already. She thinks that was the hardest part. But there is the surgery. And meeting the rest of the family. So she does feel a bit nervous. Sol is wearing her favorite yellow earrings that Willow gave her last year. She gives them a tug now to remind herself that she's not alone.

Shyla picks her up, and it's like they haven't stopped their last conversation. Shyla jumps right back in. "Okay, so we're going to meet Mom and Dad out for brunch at Home Sweet Home Café. They have THE BEST chocolate chip pancakes! You'll love it! Do you drink coffee? They make these amazing coffee drinks too—they're like works of art! Then maybe go to this pretty rose garden nearby that's in a park right by the water—Mom loves it there! June is such a good time for you to be here!

"She's looking forward to seeing you again, Sol! She said even though she hates her disease, she's so glad it brought you to her. And my cousin is being a champ about everything. Or at least acting like he is. His job is giving him three weeks short-term disability, so he will still get paid. I think that makes him feel more comfortable to know there will still be money coming in. We got *a bunch* of books and stuff for Mom to keep her occupied while she's in the hospital. Oh my gosh, how are you? You know how I tend to talk."

"All that sounds good," Sol replies, tugging on her earrings again. "I'm good, I'm glad I could come for this. I'm a little nervous about how everything will go with the surgery and meeting the rest of the family. Did you say they know about me?" Sol does wonder if things would have been different if Shyla and her friendly personality hadn't been involved in getting her connected with everyone.

"Well, some of them knew about you before, but now they all know. You know I had to tell everyone. And Mom did too! She showed your picture all around, and everyone thinks you look just like her. What did your dad look like? Do you have a picture of him? I'd love to see it. Not now while I'm driving, of course, but we'll have a LOT of time in the hospital tomorrow! And tonight! I can't wait for you to come to my house. I just love having guests. And you're my own sister! I bought the house about seven years ago when the neighborhood was still undiscovered, but now there are a couple of cute places that opened up around the corner, and there's a park I love to go run in."

Sol again takes in all the sights as they drive. "I'm looking forward to seeing it. Thank you for hosting me! So what relatives do you think will be there? Can you give me some sort of primer? I know there are a lot of people in the family!"

Shyla laughs. "There definitely are! Well, since it's a Monday morning, a lot of them will be at work, at least the younger generation. But you could definitely meet the Salt and Pepper twins, and the other twins—I just call them both "Uncle B"— might come too. For them, this is an exciting outing! Of course, my cousin Gordon's wife and son will be there, though I don't know how long they will stay because I think his son is only like three years old. I hope between all the adults, he'll be able to stay entertained. I think the transplant center even has a kids' play area.

"So that's them. My Great-Aunt Tabitha will be there—she's mom's mom's sister. She always shows up for everything because she wants to know every single thing that's going on with everyone. Oh my gosh, the family really wants to meet you. Of course, some of them knew about you all along but didn't think they'd ever have a chance to meet you. Aunt Jackie is definitely planning to come. She told me the other day she has been checking up on you all these years even though my mother didn't want to. So make sure you check your privacy settings on everything! Haha!"

Sol starts to feel a little more uneasy. "Okay, no pressure! Wow, that's a lot of people." At least it's not some sort of event that's actually centered around her.

Shyla glances quickly over at her. "Don't be nervous! I'm right here with you! Mom wants you there, and that's what's most important. Don't forget, you can always give me the look if you need me to start chatting away to take some of the pressure off. You know, they all have their own personalities, but as I told you, we were all trained that children are a blessing, so they are all happy to have you, even though you're kind of a latecomer to the family. You know there are lots of other 'stories' in our family. You can only imagine with a family this big. Every family has its share of drama. But we do roll deep. So Mom and Gordon should definitely feel the love. And especially with you coming up here again for this, it means so much. I know you had to take time off work again. I understand what that's like when people are depending on you every day. Anyway, here we are! And there's Dad's car, so they probably got us a table already. I hope you're hungry!"

Sol definitely finds it easier seeing Janice the second time around, and Calvin also makes it a little easier by being there.

"Thank you for coming, Sol," Janice says, smiling big as she greets her. "I can't believe I get to see you again so soon."

"I know, I can't believe they found a match so fast!" Sol begins, somewhat unwilling to address their relationship. She finds it easier to deflect the attention from herself at the moment. But maybe Janice feels the same way, so Sol tries to express care like she would to anyone about to go through a surgery. "It sounds like you have quite a fan club attending," she says.

"Yes, I'm so glad to have their support," Janice agrees.

The waitress arrives to take their orders, and Calvin says, "I think it's going to be four orders of chocolate chip pancakes! And maybe one small side of fruit so we don't feel too guilty!"

"And I heard so much about your coffee drinks," Sol adds. "I'd like to try the cardamom latte, please."

"Make that two!" Shyla shouts out, laughing.

Janice chuckles, then clears her throat, and they all get quiet. "So, I just want to say that going into surgery always brings up some questions. It's really a very safe and routine surgery, but there's always the chance that something can go wrong. Anyway, I wanted to talk with you about my will. I already talked to Shyla about this, so don't worry," Janice says to Sol.

"Oh...okay," Sol answers, caught off guard.

"I want to add you to my will, Sol. Is that okay with you? I know you have your own family, and I don't have any legal claims on you. I don't want you to feel like there are strings attached or anything. You never even have to speak to me again if you don't want to. But I do have some things I'd like to go down in my own blood family."

"Um, I don't know what to say," Sol replies. She looks at Shyla, and Shyla just nods.

"Okay, just hear me out, and then you can tell me. I don't know what's going through your head right now, but I can guess. Don't worry, I don't have millions to give you. But we do all right. As you know, one of my big loves is my garden, and I think about all the time and care I have put into it over the years. Every year, I collect the seeds from certain heirloom plants to grow the next year. Some of these plants have been passed on to me from my mother and grandmother. I would like you and Shyla to have the seeds and maybe keep them going. Actually, not just after I die, but I want to give you some to start next year. That way I can help you get them going."

"Oh, wow, after seeing your yard and garden, I know

that's a special gift. Thank you. But what if I mess them up?" Sol's eyes go wide.

Janice pats her hand. "I don't think you will. But that's why we can start soon, so I can coach you. And Calvin knows a lot too and can help."

Janice and Calvin spend the meal telling Sol and Shyla about the history of the different plants they've added to their gardens over the years and the care that goes into them. Sol wonders how much of this she and Shyla will remember, but she figures it's a nice, "safe" topic before Janice goes into this surgery. She's glad they don't have to talk about the possibility of her dying the whole time.

After brunch, they go to the park that Shyla had mentioned. When they get out of the car, Sol is amazed at the view. Somehow, she had forgotten how close to the ocean they were. She looks out in awe. She can't imagine seeing this every day when she's just driving through town.

As they walk around the brick path, Calvin and Janice act as tour guides, explaining the flowers, statues, and an area covered in painted rocks, a memorial to a little local girl who had died of cancer. A light breeze comes off the water and they all gape when they see a couple taking wedding pictures among the gorgeous pink roses. Calvin is the only one who's not too full of brunch to get an ice-cream cone, and they all sit and watch the ocean for a while. Shyla whispers that it looks like Janice is getting tired, so they head their separate ways. Shyla hugs her mom tight and tells her they'll be there tomorrow for the surgery. Sol just waves goodbye and starts walking to the car to avoid an awkward moment of deciding whether they should hug.

The drive to Shyla's house from the park is about thirty minutes. She lives closer to downtown since her office is there. When they pull up, Sol sees that the front yard is nothing like Janice's flower-filled paradise, but it matches Shyla's stylish personality. The green lawn is neat with a few striking flowering bushes. When Sol walks in, she sees beautiful modern and stylish rooms, again making her think Shyla should be in a magazine, but this time for her décor. After Sol drops her things in the guest room, Shyla says she wants to make the most of their time together.

"Okay, now I'll tell you everything about my life! It's easy since you're here. Let me start with all these pictures on the fridge. Well, you know Mom and Dad. Here are my cousins' kids—I call them my 'nieces and nephews' but they must be second cousins or once removed or something. They are sooo cute! Of course we had more twins! Oh my gosh, remember I told you about my ex-boyfriend? Well, I deleted all of his pics from my phone, but I haven't been able to part with these yet. We did have some really happy times. I don't know. Maybe he and I can be friends?"

Sol looks at all of the photos, especially the ones of Shyla's ex-boyfriend, which show them on a hike together looking sweaty and happy. "Well, I'm probably not the one to be giving relationship advice since I'm still single! But then again, I have dated a lot of guys!" she says, and they both laugh.

After she tells her the details of the photos, Shyla gets out two bottles of wine. "Okay, white or red?"

Sol chooses the red wine and checks her phone while Shyla turns around to open and pour them both glasses.

The next thing she knows, Sol hears Shyla singing, "Happy birthday"! She looks up, and Shyla is carrying over a cupcake with a lit candle in it. "I didn't forget it's your birthday in two days! We won't have a chance to celebrate tomorrow, so I thought I'd do a little celebration now."

"Aw, thank you! That's so sweet of you!" Sol smiles as she blows out the candle. They both raise their glasses to clink.

"I also got you a little something," Shyla says as she pulls out a tiny gift bag. When Sol opens it, she finds a beautiful silver necklace with a red stone in a simple round setting.

"This is what you call a 'little something'?" Sol responds. "It's gorgeous! I don't even know what this is. Thank you!"

"It's called a fire opal. I thought you might like it. It made me think of how your name means 'sun,'" Shyla says, looking pleased that Sol likes it.

"I love it! Will you help me put it on?"

Sol is touched by Shyla's thoughtfulness. She thought this trip would just be focused on Janice and the surgery, but Shyla made sure to make it a special time for her too. They chat for a while longer, and then Shyla says she has to do a little work since they'd be at the hospital the whole day tomorrow. Sol is tired after an eventful day and is thankful to go to bed early. She sends a few texts and falls into a deep sleep.

- 40 -

The next morning, Sol wakes up at 5:00 a.m., an hour earlier than she set her alarm. She hates it when that happens because she feels like she can really use the sleep. But she takes the opportunity to write in her journal.

Dear God,

I guess I just keep saying the same thing—I can't believe this is happening. Right now, I'm in the guest room at my sister Shyla's house. A couple of months ago, I didn't even know she existed and was related to me. Today is Janice's surgery for the kidney transplant from Shyla's cousin. I mean, my cousin too? Anyway, I'm so confused. I pray that all goes smoothly with the surgery! Janice was talking to me yesterday about putting me in her will. That kind of freaked me out! I mean, I'm glad to know the truth, but it's not like we have a relationship. She's still kind of like my friend's mom. So help me to sort that out. I'm nervous about meeting the rest of the family. I mean, some of them didn't even know about me! I guess it's a little easier because so much time has passed. It's not like I'm a child looking for a caretaker. So less pressure on them, I guess. I don't know how to feel about it. Will they welcome me or snub me? I think Shyla's affection for me will help with all of them, but I don't really know. And we'll be sitting in a hospital waiting room together all day? Again, I'm thankful that Shyla is talkative. Please help me today with my nerves! Help me to trust you. Today is not all about me. Bless Janice and Gordon today. Amen.

- 41 -

As Shyla and Sol drive to the hospital that morning, Sol texts Thea: *Here we go. On the way to the hospital and going to meet more of the family. Please pray for me and Janice and Gordon too! Thank you!*

Thea texts back a few minutes later: *I got you! Text me later and tell me everything!*

When they arrive, Sol is glad she got to pack her own clothes for the trip this time instead of having to find some last-minute clothes at a big-box store. She's dressed in her favorite red polka-dot button-down shirt, jeans, and ballet flats. She added the necklace that Shyla gave her and left her hair down, which she always feels gives her a bit of protection with its volume. She has her bag in the car ready to head to the airport that evening. Sol feels more confident and like herself. Still, she hangs back a little as she follows Shyla to the waiting area. She sees several people already there despite the early hour.

Shyla's "Hi, everyone!" confirms their identity as family. Sol now wishes they had made more of a game plan. At least she knows she can give Shyla "the look" if she needs help in a conversation. She doesn't have but a second to catch her breath before a short, elderly woman in a purple Adidas track suit and bright white Adidas tennis shoes rushes over to Sol. "You must be Janny's girl!" she says.

"Hi, Great-Aunt Tabitha!" Shyla intercepts the woman and gives her a hug.

"Hi, baby. I'm glad to see you, but first I need to talk to this one," she replies, nodding toward Sol. Her light brown eyes are bright and twinkling, and her pink-lipsticked lips are smiling.

Sol realizes there's no running now, so she sticks out her hand, smiles, and says, "Hi, I'm Sol."

Great-Aunt Tabitha ignores her hand and wraps her in a hug, saying, "I know who you are, and you're family. We don't shake hands with family. Now, come sit next to me and tell me everything."

As they walk to the empty seats, she points out the identity of the other family members, who are all watching them. "That's my nephew—Gordon's dad—and Gordon's wife and son. Those are two of Janice's other sisters. Next to them are Calvin's brothers, the Salt and Pepper twins— you can tell them apart by that patch of white on Salt's cheek. You can talk to all of them later. I'm the oldest so I have priority."

Sol gives them a wave and smile as Great-Aunt Tabitha propels them past. It looks like Gordon's dad and wife are both trying to tell each other that Gordon is going to be fine, although both of their faces show worry lines.

"Oh…kay," Sol says, semi-reluctantly agreeing to her questioning. Thankfully, Shyla takes the seat on the other side. "But can you give us an update on what's going on with

Janice and Gordon first?" Sol asks.

"Oh, they're just fine, getting prepped for surgery. Gordon will go first. The surgeon should come out in a bit and give us an update, so we might as well use the time to chat," Great-Aunt Tabitha replies, waving her hand like it's no big deal.

"That's why we met up with them yesterday, Sol," Shyla adds. "Mom may not even be able to see us today. But Dad will come out in a little bit."

"Like I said, don't worry about them. Now tell me everything," Great-Aunt Tabitha continues.

"Um, what do you want to know? Or what do you already know?" Sol replies, settling in for a grilling.

"Well, I knew about you from the beginning, so I know all about your daddy—I'm sorry he died, baby—and Janny asking him to take you. After that, we never thought we'd see you. We were all sworn to secrecy, and we never talked about you. But when Janny's kidneys failed, Jackie decided that Janny's life was more important than an old secret. Now Janny fought it. She didn't want to disturb your life. But once the cat was out of the bag, there was no getting that cat back in, if you know what I mean."

"Oh. Wow. It's just—" Sol struggles to process what she's thinking and feeling and can't quite put it into words.

"It's just what, baby?" Great-Aunt Tabitha says.

"It's just that I can't believe you knew about me, and I never knew about you," Sol finally says.

"Well, yes, I suppose that feels rather strange, but you know us now. So tell me everything. Are you married? Do you have children? Where are you living? What do you do for work? That will get us started."

The rest of the family ends their conversations and turns to listen in on what Sol will say.

"Aunt Tab, give her a break! We just got here. We have all day to chat!" Shyla exclaims.

"Thanks, Shyla. It's okay. I'm happy to get to know everyone better," Sol says. "I'm actually surprised you haven't told them everything about me!"

"Well, I thought I'd at least give you a chance before I fill in all the blanks!" Shyla says, laughing.

Sol pulls her water bottle out of her purse, takes a sip, and begins. "Well, you know my biological mother, of course, and the whole story that I just learned about. My mom got remarried when I was ten years old to my stepfather, Mickey. I have one older sister and one younger sister that have the same mom and dad. So that makes it kind of strange that I have a different mom than them even though I'm in the middle. I grew up in Baltimore and came back there after college down in South Carolina."

"Wait a second, you live in the city? Isn't that dangerous?" Great-Aunt Tabitha interjects.

"Yes, I do," Sol replies. "And yes, it does have its problems, but there's a lot that I love about it too. It's my home. I don't want to just run away from the hard things. I want to be a part of positive change."

"And that's why you're here too, right? Not running away from the hard things?" Aunt Tabitha quickly follows.

"I guess you could look at it that way. I mean, now I have a chance to be a part of this family that I never knew about. And at a time like this too. I mean, Shyla asked me to come, and Janice wanted to see me, so that means a lot to me. I guess I'm still thinking through everything."

At that moment, Calvin strides out from a door off the waiting room. "Hey, everyone! Gordon's surgery is starting now! Should be about two hours. Oh hi, Sol! Did you meet everyone? I see Aunt Tabitha is monopolizing you."

"Oh, Calvin, I'm just asking the questions that everyone here wants to know! You see they're all listening in!" Great-Aunt Tabitha replies, shushing him with her hand motion.

"Hi, Calvin! It's okay. Is Janice doing okay? Was she nervous?" Sol answers.

"She's doing just fine. She said to say hello to everyone out here and thank you for coming. Gordon also says hi to everyone. He seemed a little nervous but is definitely being strong. He really wants to do this for his aunt—and the whole family really—so he is also feeling good," Calvin announces to everyone.

"He really did want to do this! He's been talking about it nonstop since he found out!" Gordon's wife adds.

"Daddy's getting cut open with a knife!" Gordon's three-year-old son chimes in. "And they're going to take out one kidney bean but leave one in there. But they're going to sew him back up like when I ripped my shirt and he'll be as good as new!"

They all laugh at the mention of the "kidney bean" and the three-year-old's understanding of what's happening. It breaks the tension, and Calvin's authoritative presence bringing an update seems to comfort them too.

Now that the focus is momentarily taken off of Sol, she uses the opportunity to look around at the other family members. No one has given her any strange looks yet, so she feels okay. But she wonders what her role here is. Should she try harder to circulate and meet everyone? She feels like she's following Shyla's lead—and then of course Great-Aunt Tabitha has been talking with her the whole time—so she thinks she's okay. They seem nice so far, but Sol still feels unsure. She's thankful the focus today is on Janice and Gordon and not just on her. It seems like as good a way as any to meet them.

"Calvin, I heard you're planning a party in a couple weeks for when Janny and Gordon are feeling better. Are we doing a barbeque? Tell me everything because you know I will bring one of my special fruit tarts—but the flavors have to go with everything else," Great-Aunt Tabitha says.

Shyla leans over to Sol and explains, "Aunt Tab used to be a pastry chef at this famous hotel here—the Parker House. Since she retired, our family gets to reap all the benefits! We come up with all kinds of reasons to have parties just so she'll make her legendary fruit tarts."

"Not just legendary—award-winning!" Calvin chimes in. "Yes, please, Aunt Tabitha, we would love to have one! I was thinking about a barbecue, but I haven't decided yet. With all of you here, it's a great time to plan and keep our minds from worrying."

"Gordon loves barbecues, so that's perfect," his wife says. "Especially barbecued chicken, baked beans, and coleslaw."

"Great!" Calvin replies. "You know Janice loves a barbecue, and we can make those shish kebabs she always asks for. I wonder if this surgery will change her appetite at all. I've heard the effects once you have it can be almost immediate! I mean, we have been managing her disease so long, it will be nice to see her feeling better. Maybe we'll even go on a cruise or something!"

"I know you've traveling up here a lot lately, Sol, but if you can make it back for the barbecue, please come! I can pay for your ticket!" Shyla exclaims. "Then you could meet everyone! And I mean, everyone! At our last family reunion on Mom's side, there were what—eighty people? And you know one of my cousins is a DJ, so he always gets everyone up dancing. Our family tears up the Electric Slide!"

After they finish discussing details of the post-surgery party, the conversation quiets down a little. Sol looks over and it seems like Great-Aunt Tabitha has dozed off. It really was an early morning! Shyla and Sol head to the café next door to get coffee and snacks.

"Are you doing okay?" Shyla asks as they walk over.

"Yes, everyone seems nice so far," Sol says. "Thanks for introducing me. Great-Aunt Tabitha is kind of hilarious."

"Oh, yeah, she is one of our interesting characters. The family is full of them! I don't want to scare you away by telling you everything up front! Oh my goodness, you'll find out about all of them soon enough. The group at the hospital right now is a pretty tame introduction, especially now that Aunt Tab is napping! She always wanted a family of her own, but she never got married or had any children. But she has been the best aunt to everyone. And you can see she's very 'involved' (aka nosy) in everyone's lives!

"She's pretty harmless, though. She tries to be careful with her gossip! She says she still may get married yet! With her baking and her awesome personality, she attracts all the men! But she is sharp as a tack and will not put up with any foolishness, so no man has been able to make the cut yet. She always said it's better to stay single than to marry the wrong man and be committed to him for life."

Thankfully, the line at the coffee shop is short, and they are able to get two full trays of drinks and a bag of snacks to take back to the family. Shyla insists on paying for everything.

Once they have their orders in hand, Sol continues the conversation. "Oh wow, maybe I will be like her, then! She seems amazing and has the right attitude, I think. My marriage prospects haven't been making the cut either! I think I told you about the guy Franklin. You'll never believe what happened with him the other day! I'll have to update you, but he's out. I feel like this is the problem with online dating—you're dating from the start. It's not like you know each other casually first or have friends in common."

"Oh no, I'm sorry! Hopefully that means there's a better guy out there for you! But I get what you're saying. Once my relationship with my coworker ended…Oh, his name is Mark, by the way…I decided I was going to take a break from dating for at least a year. Oh, I will have to tell you that long, complicated tale too about him. I don't know how I'm going to meet anyone once my break is over, though. I know tons of people meet online, but then there's the flip side of it like you're saying that no one ever talks about.

"Let's get back over there before Aunt Tab's tea gets cold. But I want to see your profile once we get settled again. I think we're going to have plenty of time to talk."

They carefully carry the trays of hot drinks back to the family and manage to make it without spilling anything. Sol can't wait to drink her coffee. It seems like a lifetime ago that they first arrived.

- 42 -

When they get back to the waiting area, nothing much has changed, except that now Calvin is the one dozing off. The sun coming in the big window is making the area warm and cozy, perfect for napping. Even Gordon's son is curled up against his mom. Everyone else is either on their phone or reading a magazine.

"Here you go, Aunt Tab," Shyla says as she sets the tea down.

"Thank you, baby."

"I remembered to put a splash of milk in there for you too," Shyla adds.

"Just how I like it! Now, Sol, you had a break. Are you ready for more questions?" Great-Aunt Tabitha says.

"Actually, Sol was going to show me her dating profile," Shyla says.

"Oh, well you can show me too, then, Sol! I've been thinking of getting one of those myself, so you can show me how it's done!" Great-Aunt Tabitha exclaims.

Sol laughs. "Well, I don't know if I'm the best person to ask since I haven't had a lot of luck myself, but I'm happy to show you how it works." She hands her phone over and both Shyla and Great-Aunt Tabitha peer over it to read.

After a few seconds, Great-Aunt Tabitha blurts out, "Your profile says you're white. Baby, you are not white. What is going on?"

"Aunt Tab! She just found out about Mom!" Shyla exclaims.

"You thought you were white your whole life?" Great-Aunt Tabitha asks.

Sol feels out of her depth. She doesn't know the answers to a lot of questions right now. She stares at her newly discovered great-aunt in a stunned state and finally nods slowly.

"Oh, baby, I'm sorry, I guess I forgot. That is certainly an adjustment," Great-Aunt Tabitha says and pats her arm.

"You are still Sol," Shyla says as she puts her arm around her and squeezes. "Just with a little extra soul!" she adds and laughs.

Sol can barely force herself to smile.

"I'm sorry, Sol," Shyla says. "Great-Aunt Tabitha's right. This must be a huge adjustment. I mean, nothing changes but everything changes. For better or worse, this country still cares if you have one drop of black blood. I guess if I had never gotten in touch with you, you could have just been white your whole life unless you got a DNA test or something."

Sol feels like she needs to say something at this point, but she doesn't want to say the wrong thing. She decides to go for as much honesty as possible. "Thanks, you all. It is an adjustment, as you say. But I don't want you to think I'm upset because I found out that my birth mother is black. Everything is just a lot to process, and then with Janice and Gordon doing this transplant. It's been so much happening so fast."

"I'm just glad I have you in my life! Now, let's look at these guys that are trying to holler at you!" Shyla says as she looks back at Sol's dating app. "Oh, this guy is cute. Looks like you had a little conversation going there. Oh wait, was he the one living with his parents?"

"Yes! Can you believe it? That's Raymond. He's still been messaging me but I'm like…uhh…"

Just then, a strong voice calls out from across the room, "Okay, we made it. What's the latest?"

They look up to see two women and a man in their sixties walk into the waiting area, but Sol isn't sure who they are and can't even read the tone of voice or determine which person was talking. She slides her phone back into her purse. One of the women takes the lead. She's tall with close-cropped white hair, no makeup, dark blue shirt and slacks, dark lace-up shoes, and a confident air. Calvin stands up to greet them and tells them what's going on. Shyla smiles and waves but waits for Calvin to finish. She leans over to Sol and says, "Those are Mom's sisters and brother. The one in front is Aunt Jackie. Don't worry, I'll introduce you."

The siblings make their way over once they are done being briefed by Calvin. Shyla stands up, and Sol follows her lead. Before they can say anything, Aunt Jackie says, "This must be Janice's long-lost daughter. Wow, you look just like her." When Sol hears her voice, she can now tell that she's the one she heard when they walked in. The voice is also not quite as warm as the others. Aunt Jackie is now looking her up and down, which makes Sol a bit uncomfortable, but she tries to force some calm into her voice.

"Hello, I'm Sol Garnett," she says, and extends her hand

for a handshake. Aunt Jackie shakes her hand and makes space for the others to do the same.

"So, Sol Garnett, we finally meet you. I always kept tabs on you and didn't understand all the secrecy. The way families are these days, it's almost like no big deal," Aunt Jackie says. Sol senses there's more to the way Aunt Jackie feels about her since there's an edge to her voice.

Shyla stands next to Sol and squeezes her hand. Sol addresses Aunt Jackie. "Janice told me you're the one who helped when she was pregnant with me. Thank you for doing that. Without you, I might have never been here."

"Well, your father was definitely not there," Aunt Jackie replies, with an eye roll.

Sol is taken aback, but she tries to see the situation from Janice's sister's perspective. She tries not to show any emotion in her response. "I'm just learning about everything now," she says. "I'd love to know anything you want to tell me." She has learned from working with the students in her program that people just want to be heard and acknowledged. She doesn't want this new aunt to feel this way about her, but she tries not to react with her own attitude.

"I know he died when you were young, and I'm sorry. But the man I knew about was nothing but a player. He played my sister—didn't even tell her he was married—got her pregnant, and left! My sister, beautiful young woman in law school, working and trying to make a life for herself. He just saw someone who could make him feel better about his messed-up marriage and used her. Leaving her pregnant and alone. I mean, I'm glad he was able to talk your mom into taking you after you were born because he definitely didn't do anything during the pregnancy. But yeah, he sweet-talked his way back into your mom's life just like that. I guess it all worked out for everyone, though. If he had lived, that is."

Tears well up in Sol's eyes. No one has ever talked about her dad like this, except the one hurtful comment from Franklin. She doesn't really have many memories of him herself because she was only five when he died, but she has pictures, and her mom told her stories. She doesn't know what to say. She looks down at the floor. The carpet is those square tiles that you can change out when they get spills, but there is a stain on one that she guesses they hadn't had a chance to replace yet. It looks kind of like a kidney, now that she thinks about it. She does her best to focus back on the reason she is here today, to support Shyla and Janice and Gordon as they do this transplant.

"Hey Sol, let's go find the restroom. I think it's down this hall somewhere," Shyla says as she guides her away from Aunt Jackie. Sol keeps her eyes on the floor, but as they leave, Shyla gives her aunt a worried look and shakes her head.

When they get to the restroom, Shyla checks to make sure they're alone and then says, "I'm sorry, Sol. She shouldn't have talked bad about your dad like that. I think she's been carrying that around for a lot of years. She's worried about Mom too. She's always been protective of her like that."

Sol keeps her eyes downcast. She knows once she says a word, she's going to start sobbing.

"Hey," Shyla says as she puts her arm around her. "Aunt Jackie may not be warm and fuzzy. But she gets stuff done.

Don't forget she's the one that brought us together, and I will forever be grateful for that. I hope you feel the same. I know everything is overwhelming right now, but hopefully now that she got that off her chest, she can calm down a little. She really wanted to meet you and probably even surprised herself by saying all that. I talked to her last night. But we don't have to go back there right now. I think we have another hour before the surgery is done. Do you want to go for a walk or something?"

"Thanks, Shyla," Sol says as she lifts her head to look in the mirror. "I am glad to have met you. Yes, let's get some fresh air. Isn't there a park nearby?"

"Yeah, the way Mom feels about flowers, she probably requested a room with a view of the park too!"

As they make their way to the front entrance of the hospital, Shyla greets a few more family members who are just arriving. "Wow, your family does roll deep!" Sol says, forcing cheer into her voice.

"Yeah, some of them just said they can come over on their lunch break. This is definitely a big deal for the family too. We've never had a family-to-family transplant before! They'll be talking about this for years to come!"

As they walk around outside, Shyla chatters about everything they see, from the best thing to order at an Italian place they pass to a couple sitting at a bus stop. After a few minutes of this, Sol interrupts to ask Shyla, "So how are *you* doing? Are you worried?"

"Of course I'm a little worried, but you know, I actually feel really excited. We have been waiting for this for so long, and it should make such a difference for her! Especially with Gordon being pretty young. I just hope everything goes smoothly, and her body doesn't reject it. She's been talking about all the things she's looking forward to doing, especially getting off dialysis! But just having more energy for the kids and stuff, traveling. And her garden, of course!"

Just then, Shyla gets a text from Calvin saying that Gordon's surgery is done, and all went well. She says, "Let's head back. This is exciting! Why didn't I think to get balloons or something? I wonder what Gordon would like. Shoot, is there a store around here? Or maybe we should just go to the hospital gift shop?"

"Yeah, let's check out the gift shop!"

They rush through the gift shop and grab several things each, including a card that sings "Let's Get It Started" for Gordon and a solar-powered dancing flower for Janice. When they get back upstairs, the family is all on the edge of their seats as though something might happen any second. After a few minutes of waiting, everyone starts to relax again, and after several more minutes, they start reading the magazines they've put down. Finally, someone comes out and says Gordon's wife can see him. A few minutes later, she texts Gordon's dad a photo and says he's doing great. The entire group starts screaming "Woohoo!" and "Hallelujah!"

Calvin tells Sol and Shyla that the surgeon said Janice's surgery will be another three to four hours. The family members who had been there since early in the morning start to disperse. A few of them go to find lunch, but some say they have to leave and trust that Calvin will let them know how things go. Jackie and her siblings are still there but sitting on the other side of the room with their backs to Sol and engrossed in what they're doing. Gordon's mom arrives, and Gordon's son goes home with his grandfather. The Salt and Pepper twins come back to the waiting area carrying three large pizza boxes for everyone who's still there. After they eat, the family works their way through the magazines on the tables in the room, and then some of them go to the gift shop to buy fresh ones. Sol prays intermittently in her head for the surgery when she thinks about it. The rest of the time, she tries to distract herself by chatting with Shyla or reading magazines. Sol and Shyla both look for new games to download on their phones. The solar-powered flower they got for Janice occupies them for a few minutes as they look for an optimum location to place it to get the most sun.

After hours pass, a different surgeon finally comes out and tells them that Janice's surgery is done and that so far everything looks good! Sol didn't realize her whole body had been tensed until this moment when she lets out a huge sigh of relief. Calvin and Shyla hug each other, and both start crying. "I can't believe it!" Shyla sobs. "Finally!"

Sol smiles around the room at the family, who are all standing now and rejoicing animatedly. She feels a little like an outsider in the scene but reassures herself that's normal since she just met most of them. She's glad she gets to share this happy moment.

Calvin and Shyla spend a couple of minutes talking about the logistics of the rest of the night. They still won't be able to see Janice for a few hours, so they agree that Shyla should take Sol to the airport now so she doesn't get stuck in rush hour traffic and then can come back after that.

Sol takes a few minutes to go around the room and say goodbye to everyone, telling them she hopes to come back soon. As they drive to the airport, Sol again feels like she can't believe this all just happened. *Thank you, Lord.* Shyla drops her off at Departures with a hug. "Thank you so much for coming. I'll send you updates! Bye, Sis!"

- 43 -

Dear God,

Happy birthday to me! Thank you for another year, and wow, it has been action-packed! I want to remember to be thankful, but there is so much to think about. And I'm just so tired! All the traveling and drama has taken it out of me. But thank you so much that the surgery was successful. It's the first birthday that I know the woman who actually gave birth to me. Help me to have energy today and to enjoy the day, even despite the confusion and shock I still feel. I keep going over and over everything in my mind. Janice, Shyla, Jackie, Great-Aunt Tabitha, Gordon and his family, Calvin. And here, my mom that raised me and Dove and Willow and Mickey, my work, my house, Jericho, my church, my life. I feel kind of happy but kind of confused. I don't know how to untangle everything. I'm so happy that Janice got her transplant, and I will hopefully have more time to get to know her and that whole family. And maybe Aunt Jackie will warm up over time. Maybe. That whole exchange at the hospital just raised more questions.

- 44 -

"Hey, Faye! I missed you all! Can you catch me up on every-thing?" Sol says as she enters her office ready to tackle work.

"Hey, Sunshine! Happy birthday! Of course I can! Swing back over here once you get settled in."

Willow joins Sol at her desk and gives her a hug and deposits an eco-friendly reusable container with a smiley face Post-it note in front of her. "Sunny lemon bars for you, birthday girl!"

"Aw, thanks, sis!"

"Meet me for lunch and tell me everything? My treat, of course."

"Aw, I wish! I really need to catch up on what I missed. But you'll be at Mom's house tonight, right? I'll fill you in all together. I can't believe it's my birthday already. Time is flying."

When she checks her email, Sol does have one from Dove with a gift certificate for Koco's Pub, which has the best crab cakes in Baltimore, hands down. That is a treat she'll definitely be looking forward to using! Sol is glad Dove sent her something, even though she didn't say much more than "Happy Birthday!"

She spends the day completely focused on her work and blocks out all other thoughts. They have to wrap up the program for the year and create the annual report, which will show how successful Read-Imagine's partnerships were in Baltimore this year and hopefully get them more funding, which will allow them to work with more schools. By the end of the day, she's feeling better for getting things done and having sort of a normal day and goes home to take Jericho for a long walk. She craves the familiar things like work and walking her dog amidst the upheaval in her emotions caused by finding out all of these new things about her identity.

After their walk, she heads to her mom's house, and when she walks in, the smell of Old Bay seasoning reminds her that they are having a crab feast tonight. She looks down at her yellow, ruffly shirt and knows it will not survive the mess from picking the meat out of the crabs.

Willow is already there, and Sol gives quick hugs all around. "Happy birthday! How was your trip? How is Janice doing?" they all question her at once.

"I'll fill you in once we're all settled. But first order of business, do you have an old T-shirt or something I can borrow? I totally forgot we were doing crabs tonight!"

"Not just crabs, but my famous potato salad too!" Mickey chimes in. "Let me get you a shirt."

"Oooo, I love your potato salad with all the hard-boiled eggs and celery!" Sol gushes. "Thanks!" She quickly changes into the faded orange Orioles T-shirt he gives her.

Once they are all elbow-deep in crab shells and corn on the cob, Patty asks, "So how did the surgery go?"

"Shyla just texted and says they are both doing well so far!," Sol says. "The technology is pretty advanced since they have been doing kidney transplants for a while now. Shyla and I met up with Janice and Calvin for brunch on Sunday so we could see them before the stress of the surgery day. Oh yeah, I almost forgot, it seems so long ago. She said she wanted to put me in her will and give me some stuff now."

"Oh, really?" says Willow. "Like what kind of stuff? Did you bring something back? Was Shyla okay with it?"

"Oh, Shyla and I are both getting them—seeds for some heirloom plants that have been passed down in the family, and I guess maybe a little money too, I'm not sure. But you know, I think Shyla is so happy to have a sister that she would give up her whole inheritance! She has been so welcoming. I can't wait for you to meet her! Oh yeah, I will have to tell you what happened with Aunt Jackie too. She was not so welcoming."

"What?! Are you serious?" Patty's head snaps up, and she's staring intently at Sol. "Janice's sister—the one who came to live with her?"

"Yes, I'll tell you all about it in a minute. Let me finish telling you about the surgery. So they go in early in the morning, but a lot of the time is just prep time and lots of waiting. There were already several family members in the waiting room when we got there at 7:00 a.m.! Oh my goodness, you all would love Great-Aunt Tabitha—that's Janice's mother's sister! She used to be a pastry chef at this fancy hotel there and has apparently had streams of admirers for years but never got married. So she's involved in everyone's lives in the family. They were talking about this fruit tart she makes.

"Oh yeah, they are going to have a barbecue to cele-brate the surgery in a couple weeks. I want to go because it would give me an opportunity to meet more of the family. I don't want to miss my chance since some of them are quite elderly. Unfortunately, Janice's parents died just a few years ago. Anyway, Great-Aunt Tabitha wanted to know all about me from the moment I arrived. So I chatted with her for a long time. Calvin would give us updates, and the surgery went well! He says Janice started feeling better right away! Can you believe that? Anyway, she does still have a while for recovery. Gordon is doing great too! He will be showing his scar to everyone. That is an amazing thing he did. I mean, he's only thirty years old and has a young son. His son was there and is so adorable!

"So everything was going so well, and I was feeling not too awkward until Aunt Jackie arrived. Yes, Mom, she is the one who came to help Janice when she was pregnant with me. I think she's still mad about the whole situation, and I just reminded her of it."

Patty looks stricken. "What do you mean? What did she say?"

"Well, first she looked me up and down and didn't say anything. Then she was talking about how Dad was a player. Mom, is that true? I mean, I thought I knew about him, but I just found out last month you were separated, and you're not even my biological mom, so I guess I don't know as much as I thought."

Sol knows that talking about her trip and getting to know Janice and the Broward family might hurt Patty and the rest of them, but she figures that she has the right to feel anything and everything after they kept this from her for so long.

Everyone turns their eyes to Patty. Mickey puts his arm around her, even though it's covered in crab seasoning, seeming to want to give her support. Patty tries to start talking a couple of times but stops each time. Her eyes go up to the left, like she's trying to remember something. As they stare at her, Sol has a faint memory of a show she had watched about if your eyes went one direction, you were telling the truth, but if they went the other way, you were lying. But which way was which? And why was she thinking about her mother lying to her?

"Given the situation, I can see why Jackie would say that," Patty slowly begins. Sol thinks, *Is that a non-answer?*

Patty continues, "I mean, your dad was dating her sister when he was technically married to me. Janice broke things off with him when she found out. That probably would have been enough to cause Jackie not to like him. And then Janice found out she was pregnant. You know all that already." They nod and continue to stare at her. *Could there possibly be more?* Sol thinks.

"Mom, really, is there anything else you haven't told us?" Sol whispers. "We deserve to know the truth."

Patty takes a deep breath. "Girls, we love you. Your father and I both loved you. All of you, all the time. But we didn't always get along with each other, and yes, we did separate for a while. But once we were back together, we were together until the day he died."

"And when did you get back together?" Willow asks angrily. "It sounds like I almost didn't get born."

Patty keeps her eyes on the crab shell she's been toying

with. "Not right away. He stayed at his friend's house for the whole time Janice was pregnant with Sol. He wanted to be there for Janice and do the right thing, but Janice's sister never let your dad see her.

"I think her sister actually offered to move in with Janice and help raise her. But Janice decided she wanted me and Patrick to take you, Sol. She's really an amazing woman, even though I never knew her personally, and of course, I resented your dad being with her. And our marriage did work out. But it wasn't perfect, of course. When he came back, we instantly had a new baby. Like I told you, we named you Sol because you brought light back into our family. And I think that time apart was really a wakeup call for your dad.

"He missed Dove so much too. I remember finding out later that he used to drive by that playground we always went to because he wanted to see her. But I never talked about it because I never wanted Dove to remember not having him around. She loved you so much, Sol, and played with you all day. Your dad and I went to counseling for a while and I joined a mom's group that helped me too.

"I had to figure out how to run the shop and take care of you all. Looking back, I remember being so sad after the miscarriage when your father and I were separated, but when he came back with Sol, we were a family again and I was just trying to pour into this family and also build my business.

"Was he a player? I don't think he was. I mean, I never expected him to date someone when we were separated and trying to work things out, but we were both lost, and that's how he handled it. I don't know what Jackie is thinking now, but maybe you can ask her one day. I hate that she's not being welcoming with you, but wasn't it her idea to get in touch with you in the first place?"

Sol throws her crab-covered paper towel on the tables and says glumly, "Yeah, but just to find a kidney! I guess she wasn't really interested in me as a person."

"Well, you never know what's going on in people's heads. Maybe she still wishes she could have raised you. I mean, look at you! You're amazing!" Patty says.

"Agree!" Willow shouts. "But seriously, Mom, is there anything else we need to know? Are you really my mom? Do we need to do DNA tests or what?"

Willow is trying to lighten the mood, as usual. The tension releases a little bit, but they are still feeling uneasy.

"Yes, Willow, you are Patrick's and my biological daughter. There is one more thing, actually," Patty says.

They look at her with surprise.

"Well, I guess you're old enough to know about everything now. Mickey, are you okay if I tell them?" Patty asks and Mickey nods. "You almost had a little brother too. Mickey and I were pregnant, but I lost him at fifteen weeks," Patty says as she starts to tear up. Mickey hugs her and tears up too. "After that, I just couldn't try anymore. Too much loss."

"Oh, you guys, I'm sorry," says Willow. She and Sol get up and come around the table to hug Patty and Mickey. "Our little brother. Did you name him?"

"Yes, his name was Brooks Michael," Mickey takes over. "He would have been twenty-five years old now. We were really sad, but we know how blessed we are already. You girls know I love you like you're my own DNA. That's why we went through the process for me to formally adopt you, so you would never question that."

"We love you too!" the sisters say as they group hug again.

"One question, Mom. How did we not notice you were pregnant?!" Willow asks.

"Remember how I went through that peasant blouse phase—those gorgeous handmade blouses from Guatemala?" Patty says. They all laugh.

"We remember! It seems like you never quite got out of it either. Once a crunchy granola mom, always a crunchy granola mom," Willow says. "And speaking of crunchy granola, I brought key lime pie!"

"Yeah, let's not forget we're here to celebrate the sunshine in our lives, our true daughter and sister by blood and love!" her mom says. "We do have a few little things for you." She starts setting gifts on Sol's lap, trying to avoid the crab mess in the process.

"I just received these beautiful stained glass ornaments you can hang in your window for the shop, and I thought you would like this one. And Mickey got you this Orioles shirt. You can never have too many of those!"

"Aw, thanks, you guys!"

Willow jumps in, "And this one is from me. I got us tickets to that play you wanted to see at Center Stage so we can go together!"

"You did?! I'm so excited! Thanks, everyone!" Sol says. "One more thing, speaking of Dove, I finally talked to her and caught her up on everything, but she didn't believe me. She thinks the whole thing is a scam."

"Oh no!" Patty says. "I'll call her tomorrow. This is my responsibility, after all."

"Okay, thanks, Mom." Sol hopes that's one less thing she has to worry about. She heads to the kitchen sink to do a thorough scrub of her hands before she picks up her yellow blouse and heads home.

- 45 -

Dear God,

Wow, family. Even though I'm finding out my family is far from what I thought it was, thank you for all of them! Even Aunt Jackie who gave me attitude. Thank you for the extra family and also my awesome friends that are like family to me.

Will I ever have a family of my own? Help me with this dating thing! I feel like I'm running out of time to have children too. God, I know I have to trust you, but it's hard. Is having my own family in your plan for me? I'm glad I'm finding all this out before I do have my own children, though. Continue to shape me into the woman you want me to be, whether or not that includes a family of my own. But if it does, I want to be ready!

- 46 -

A couple of nights later, Sol gets a call from her mom.

"Hey, Sunshine, I just wanted to check on you. I know you've been going through a lot, and we didn't get to talk one-on-one at your party. How are you doing?"

"Thanks, Mom. I'm doing okay. Thanks again for the ornament! I love it! I hung it in my window, and it's making all these pretty patterns when the light hits it." Sol tries to force cheer into her voice, but she feels very tired.

"You're welcome! I thought you might like that. I also wanted to see if you have any other questions for me. I get the feeling you don't really trust me after all this," her mom says tentatively.

Sol sighs. She wasn't ready for a heavy conversation tonight but doesn't want to miss the opportunity to learn more.

"Yeah, Mom, you're right, the player comment about Dad was a surprise. And just finding more things out about him. You always gave us such a positive image of him, and we never got a chance to know him as a real person because he died when we were so young. So I'm trying to figure out how all this new information fits into my understanding of who he was. And I guess how I feel about him too. I mean, it was great when he was just this perfect, fairy-tale dad. But now—" Sol breaks off.

"Yeah, now he's a real person who messed up," Patty says. "I would love for him to be a perfect dad too. I guess that's why I only told you the positive things. And there were so many positive things! He was a great dad. But all of this..." Now Patty is the one who breaks off.

Sol clears her throat, stalling. "I don't even know what questions to ask. Are there more things you want to tell me? I do really want to know the truth. I mean, I'm thirty-six—oh wait, I'm thirty-seven now—and all of this is still affecting me."

"Hmm, you're right," Patty says, pausing to take a sip of what Sol guesses is one of her favorite herbal teas. "Let me think. Okay, let me tell you some stories. Some of these things you might know already, and some of them might bring up questions or give you a better picture of him. You know we both grew up here, but we didn't go to the same schools or anything. He grew up in South Baltimore, and I grew up in Mom and Dad's house that you know. I didn't know him when he was younger, but our lives overlapped. He was also six years older than me, which is a big difference when you're younger. He played baseball since he was tiny and loved to go fishing. Those things he brought into his adulthood and you may even remember. He played T-ball with you when you were little. He used to say that by the time you were grown up, women would be allowed to play in the major leagues and you and your sisters would be playing for the Orioles!

"He was drafted to serve in Vietnam, but he had a high

lottery number, and they actually never did call the men with that number to serve. He may not have had to go either way since he was in college. I think he always felt conflicted about that because he had friends he grew up with who went and never came back. Or they came back, and they weren't the same person who left. That whole generation of men…You know your two uncles served. Your dad was like so many college students then who were protesting against the war.

"By the time we met, he had graduated and gotten a job with the city government. I think you know the story of how we met—we were both looking around at a little health food stand down at the farmers' market, and he asked me about carob chips. He was a good cook too! I was finishing up my degree then, and when I graduated, we got married. We went to Acapulco for our honeymoon, and that's what originally planted the seed for my store. We didn't have money to buy much at that time, but we loved to walk around the markets and see all the beautiful handmade clothing, art, and jewelry."

"Oh yeah, Mom, I knew some of this but definitely not everything," Sol interjects. "What happened after that?"

"Well, we were just a young married couple. We had a little apartment, and we were both working. I was working as a receptionist then. Some of our friends were around and our families, of course, so we spent time with all of them. We had some great times together as just a couple but wanted to start a family when the time was right. After about four years, we got pregnant with Dove. Her name symbolized our commitment to peace, and we also wanted to honor our friends that didn't come back from the war. Having a baby changed things, but we had so much help around, we didn't struggle. I stayed home from work after that so I could be with her, and then we got pregnant again. Did I ever tell you this?"

"Yes, but you didn't tell me much. Go on." Sol doesn't want to stop the flow of information.

"Dove was just barely walking then, and we were chasing her all around. The new pregnancy was a surprise, but we were excited. Everything with my body felt pretty similar to when I was pregnant with Dove, so I expected it to be the same. We were so happy, and we would talk about all our plans for what we wanted to do and what we wanted for our kids.

"Then just about a month after we found out, one day I felt sharp pains in my belly and then I noticed blood. I was hoping it wasn't what I thought it was. But the bleeding got heavier and went on for days, and I knew we had lost the baby. We had already told a bunch of our family members because we were so excited. We were talking to my belly all the time and had told Dove that she was going to be a big sister—not that she understood. After that, I couldn't do anything. I laid in bed for days. I was so sad. Patrick had to take off work. He didn't know what to do. He was so sad too but felt like he had to be strong. We didn't tell anyone at first. We were just not answering any calls and not seeing anyone.

"Patrick told people I was sick. I mean, I was sick—at heart. Finally he told my mom because he had to go back to work. She came and took Dove for a couple of days, but that made it worse, me being there all alone. So she started coming over during the day. But we couldn't go on like that forever.

"Your dad was doing the best he could, but I think he didn't know what to do with his feelings. I think for him it was more anger than sadness. We started arguing. You know, he just wanted me to feel better but didn't know how to make that happen. I didn't know either. I was so lost in my grief I couldn't even see past myself. So one day he left and didn't come back. He called to say he was going to stay with his friend for a while." Patty pauses for a minute, and Sol can hear her taking a few more sips of her tea.

"Mom, I'm so sorry about your baby. So that makes two miscarriages. Some of my friends have gone through that, and I know it's so hard. But I can't believe Dad left you like that!"

"I know," Patty says sadly. "I don't think he meant to stay away. But days turned to weeks, and then weeks turned to months. Honestly, the days went by without me noticing. Thank God Dove was too young to remember those days. I missed him, but I don't think either of us knew how to relate to each other after that. Like we were living this dream life, and then we just weren't. Looking back, I wish I had gotten help—seen a counselor or found a support group or something. But it's always clearer when you look back, right? And that kind of thing was just not talked about then. So you know what happened next, I think."

"Yeah, I happened! I still can't really believe all this."

"Well, believe it. You happened, and I'm so glad you did. When your dad called to tell me that Janice had just had his baby and she wanted us to take you, honestly, I was so shocked that he had started a relationship, I just hung up. I didn't know what to say. You know, we were still married, and there he was telling me that.

"The more I thought about it, the angrier I got. But you, Sol. I couldn't stop thinking about you. It was like I was awake for the first time in months. I had lost one baby, but here you were. This was before I even told your dad to please bring you home. He kept calling almost every hour because he said Janice needed to know quickly—I'm not sure why—and I finally told him yes.

"I think Janice got someone she knew from law school to do the paperwork. I don't think I ever thought twice about what she must be feeling. Someone told me once, 'Grief is greedy,' and that is so true."

Sol jumps in and heatedly says, "Wait a second, are you now telling me that you only took me to make yourself feel better? Like a replacement baby?! The reason Janice gave me up was because she had preeclampsia during her pregnancy and was in the ICU and deep in debt from the hospital bills!"

Patty's voice is calm when she says, "No, I'm just trying to be honest with you. I didn't know that about Janice's debt. Just from the second he told me about you, I knew I wanted you to come live with us. I was still grieving our baby that we lost, but you were here, and we could focus on you and your future.

"Anyway, your dad was still staying at his friend's house, like I told you the other night. When I called him to tell him my decision, he said he was going to go to the hospital to pick you up that same day and would be coming home that night.

"So after that, we started trying to work on things to make our marriage better. I was slowly coming back to life. It was hard for me to get past your dad having been in a relationship, but I did want our marriage to work out. Who knows what would have happened if Janice hadn't ended their relationship or if she hadn't decided she wanted us to take you. You may have had a completely different life. But I'm glad you didn't. I'm so glad you're with us. But I know you want to know your biological mom, and I will support you fully in that.

"You and Dove were best friends and growing so fast. Then we got pregnant with Willow. Since all your names have special meanings to us, you may think we named her that because of the weeping willow and our grief, but really, we were thinking about flexibility and grace—the ability to bend to the circumstance.

"Patrick loved being a dad and played with you all for hours. I will have to see if I can find some pictures I tucked away. I think it's time. After he died, I tried to just push a lot aside so I could focus on raising you three." Sol hears the clink of Patty setting the cup down on the saucer.

"I would love that, Mom. Thanks for telling me all this." Sol figures she'll keep her mom talking as long as possible and get the answers to all her stored-up questions. "Can you tell me more about how he died? All I ever knew was that it was a car accident. I only have faint memories of that time."

Patty sighs deeply and is silent for a moment. "Of course I'll tell you. But sweetie, it was awful. December 15, 1988. Our apartment was over near Patterson Park. Your dad was driving to work in the morning. He usually left around 7:45. That morning, he took Fayette Street to go across to his office. They had just finished building I-83 that ended there, and there was a light right there where the highway ended into downtown. Your dad was going through the intersection and someone either ran the red light or hit a patch of ice when they tried to stop and ran right into him. He never liked to wear his seat belt. He always said he felt like it was choking him. So he got thrown from the car."

"Oh my gosh!" Sol covers her mouth in shock. She had always just accepted that "he had died in a car accident" but had never asked for more details.

"One of his coworkers was driving the same route and saw the accident, and he recognized the car. Do you remember that brown station wagon? It had the "Save the Whales" bumper sticker, and he knew it was Patrick. He tried to stop, but the police made him keep driving. When he got to work, he found my number and called me. I started calling all the hospitals right around there, and I found him at Mercy Hospital."

Patty takes another sip and a deep breath. "By the time I got there, he was already gone. I never had a chance to say goodbye. He died of head injuries, they said. I stayed by his bed for hours. His parents came and my parents came, and I don't know who else. It's a blur. I just was in shock. Finally they came and said they had to take the body. I mean, 'the body'! Like he was just a piece of meat, not a person. I still can't get over that."

"Oh my gosh, Mom, that's terrible. That is so sad. So what happened to the other driver?"

"He had some injuries too—I think some broken ribs and a concussion—but he survived. The thing was, they were never able to conclusively say he was responsible for running the red light because it was really icy that morning. We did get some money from his insurance company and of course your dad's life insurance, which allowed us to buy this house, but Sunny, I didn't want to live without your dad for all the money in the world. When we got back together, our family was stronger than ever, and we had you and Willow and Dove. I didn't know how we were going to go on without him. This time, though, I knew I couldn't fall apart. I had done that before, but now there were three of you. I was determined.

"Thankfully, that's where our big Sipinski family comes into play. When your husband leaves temporarily, that's one thing. But when your husband dies, people step up to take care of you. So your aunts and uncles and grandparents and cousins all pitched in to help. I'm sure you remember them all being around all the time. It was a lifesaver. I tried to just save all my grief for at night when you were sleeping, and I think it mostly worked. Of course, you all missed him too and didn't fully understand, except Dove. She was devastated. Even to this day, I can still see how that affected her."

"Yeah, I loved having all of them around. I do remember that. I'm so glad they were there to help us." Sol's mind starts flipping through memories from her childhood.

"Me too. So that's more of the story. Is that enough for one day, or do you have more questions?" her mom asks.

Even though Sol had been planning to keep her talking indefinitely, she now feels completely exhausted from this conversation. "That's a lot to think about. Thanks for telling me, Mom. I think that's enough for one day."

"You're welcome. When you're ready with more questions, I'll be here. I love you, Sunshine."

"Love you too, Mom."

- 47 -

It's a new season. Sol is eager to move on from her experiences with Franklin. And she decided not to go out with Raymond again either. She's trying to learn from her experience with Franklin to listen to her gut. She has a lot going on, but dating is also a good distraction when things are so heavy. Her dream is to find someone she can share life with—the good and the bad. Someone who is a lot of fun but can also be serious. She has the greatest friends and sisters, and she loves hanging out with them, but there's something different about being someone's "one person." There's also something about being a woman and being seen as attractive to a man in that way.

When she gets home from church on Sunday, she decides to try a new dating app and start fresh. All new descriptions, photos, and of course, her newly discovered ethnicity. Hopefully she won't run into Franklin again on this app. Or any other guy she's gone out with before, for that matter. She chooses a photo of her and Jericho for her main profile picture. She wants to scare off anyone who doesn't love dogs! A picture of her lounging and reading a book, a subtle nod to her work with the literacy program.

Hopefully there is a guy out there who likes to read too! And one of her and her group of multicultural friends at an Orioles game. That one includes a lot of things she loves. Okay, maybe just one more of her at the beach!

For her description, she writes a draft and texts it over to Thea's husband, Quentin, for feedback. She's found it's good to get a man's opinion on this part to make sure what she's trying to say is coming across. Her height hasn't changed, of course. She thinks it's a little strange they ask that but guesses it's important to some people. For ethnicity, she checks out the choices. She kind of wishes there was an "It's complicated" choice, but she finally selects "multiethnic." The whole idea of dating based on ethnicity rubs her the wrong way anyway, but this is how things are right now, and she wants to be truthful. For her potential matches, she chooses "Ethnicity: No preference."

She texts over a screenshot of the whole thing to both Thea and Quentin, and after a few minutes, they both give her a thumbs-up. *Let me know what the matches are like over there!* Thea adds.

Sol takes a deep breath and makes her profile live. She looks through her immediate matches and a few seem interesting. "Here we go again, Jericho," she says to her dog. She wonders if she should just have Jericho assess the guys for her or if it's kind of like how people don't introduce every person they're dating to their kids until they are more serious. But maybe he can sniff out the good ones. She feels like she really might need to tweak her approach.

Just as Sol sets her phone down, it rings. When she answers, it's Shyla and she's sobbing. "Mom's body is rejecting Gordon's kidney!"

"What?! I thought she was doing great!"

"She was doing great but not anymore. I guess something was off this morning with her numbers, and so they were just running some more tests to be sure. They did an ultrasound and a biopsy, and I don't know what else. I just got here about an hour ago. I mean, Mom didn't really notice anything different, but now they're trying to treat the rejection with meds, and I think there are some other options if that doesn't work, but I'm just hoping they can get it under control! Ugh, you know I told you her immune system was high risk!"

"Shyla, I'm so sorry! What will happen if they can't make it work?"

"I don't know. They're going to keep trying more things."

"Is there anything I can do?"

"I don't know. I can barely think straight. I wanted to talk to someone about it, so thanks for getting back to me. Just pray for us. I'm actually going in to talk to the doctor now, so I'll call you later."

Sol closes her eyes and says a quick prayer that the doctors can fix whatever's going on with Janice's new kidney, then spends the rest of the day lounging with Jericho, still trying to recover from her eventful week. She even goes to bed early, hoping to get a couple of extra hours of sleep.

- 48 -

What is it you're supposed to do when you can't sleep? Is it get up and do something else or continue to lay there? Sol has so many thoughts running through her head, thinking about Janice in the hospital, Shyla's sobs, dating apps, her own identity, and everything that has happened in the past couple of months. She tries the deep breathing technique she learned from Willow. Sometimes it works, but she finds she's impatient. It's definitely not working tonight. She decides to get up and make some tea. Jericho follows her to the kitchen, and she gives him a treat. "You're a good friend, Coco."

While she waits for the water to boil, she again starts thinking about how no one really understands everything she's going through. They're trying to be supportive, and that's awesome, but they can only go so far. Who can she talk to about all this? Then she remembers that Thea had texted her the links for some support groups. Which one would be most helpful right now? Is it remotely possible that one of them has a member that has a newly discovered biological relative in the hospital? She decides to check out the one for the people finding some unexpected stuff from

DNA tests. Someone must have at least found out they were a different ethnicity than expected. That's definitely on her mind from setting up her new dating profile.

She starts looking around on one of the sites. All of the people's stories are about finding out they have a different father. Or finding out they were adopted altogether. She almost forgot how unusual her story is to have a different mother but to be with her biological father. Except she knows some babies are raised by another family member while the mother takes on the role of a sister or aunt. It's just so complicated.

The one thing that she sees over and over again is that it's a traumatic event to find this out when you're older. Your whole life people have been withholding the truth from you or lying to you outright. And that's what you've built a life on. When she reads that, she immediately identifies with it—trauma. The urgency of Janice's situation has consumed a lot of her thoughts, and she knows this will take a while to untangle anyway. She thinks about how things may have been different if she had found out—Mom had just told her, for instance—without all of this other stuff going on. What she would have done or thought or how she would have processed everything. She thinks about calling Thea but it's way too late. She keeps clicking around on the site and sees there's a private group she can join. Before she can change her mind, she fills out the application. After this small action toward taking care of herself, she decides to try to go back to bed and see if she can sleep.

- 49 -

An hour later, Sol is still lying in bed staring into the darkness. She decides to try to get some of the stuff out of her head by writing in her journal again.

Dear God,

What if Janice's kidney transplant fails??!! Can you help her? Am I supposed to help her? If I'm a match, I think I would do it. You would make me brave and able to do it. Encourage Shyla's heart. You are the healer. I feel so helpless, but I know you said to bring our cares to you. And you showed us all the time you were here on earth that you want to heal people and you care about our physical bodies. Please help!

I also need help on what to do with all these thoughts about my identity. Help me sort them out and get the understanding and answers I need. I was raised as a white person, but now I find out I'm only a half-white person. And in this country, that makes me black, or at least biracial (a term I hate). But I look mostly like a white person, so people treat me like a white person. So I don't have the same experience as other black people. Seriously, who am I? I know I am your child, but it matters who my biological family is too, right? Of course it matters. But do I do something different? I have a whole new family through Janice. But do they want me? How could they give me up in the first place? Aunt Jackie wanted to keep me, at least. It seems really convenient that Janice got married and was able to pay off all that debt and was able to have and keep Shyla. Did she ever think about me? She says yes. I mean, she seems nice, but what kind of mom gives up her baby? Would Aunt Jackie taking me have been better than Dad taking me? Why couldn't he just stay with Mom? Maybe he's really the one to blame in all of this. But then I wouldn't be here at all. I guess it would be different if Dad hadn't died so at least I could have had one biological parent raising me. But who could have known that he would die?

I know I have to trust you, God. You knew everything and you know everything. But what do you want me to do now? There's no going back. I guess most families these days are unusual anyway. No one even uses the terms "broken family" or "blended family" anymore. We are all just making it work. I guess what's good for me is that I have more people to connect with, not less. Of course my white family is all based on a lie, but then again, my sisters were lied to also. I mean, Dove doesn't even believe it. I wonder if Mom talked to her yet. I'm glad she's at least admitting it's her responsibility. I didn't ask to be adopted into this family or to have it be a secret. What about Mickey? I wonder if he knew. He has always been a great stepdad/father to us, but is this something he even knew about? I'm sure both sets of our grandparents had to know that Mom was never pregnant with me. They were at least complicit in the cover-up. I don't remember them ever treating me differently. Or did they not know the whole story? Every time I talk to Mom and get some answers, somehow I wind up with more questions.

- 50 -

It's 9:00 a.m. and this is her third trip to the coffee machine already. Sol is struggling to stay awake after her sleepless night. The coffee isn't helping. She doesn't have any school visits on the schedule today, so at least the kids won't catch her falling asleep in class. She tries to stay on her feet and move around as much as possible to stay alert. She makes a loop by Willow's desk for the fifth time, and Willow asks if she wants to grab lunch.

"Oh, wow, it's still morning, isn't it? How will I make it through this day?" Sol asks. "Yes, let's do it! I have to stay awake!"

They go to a café down the street with patio seating. After Willow decides on a new dish she has been wanting to try and attempts to talk Sol into getting the other one she wants to try, Willow turns to Sol with a concerned look. "I'm worried about you, Sunshine of my Life. Tell me what's going on."

"What do you mean?" Sol replies, surprised. She wasn't ready for a heart-to-heart talk.

"You're walking around like a zombie, and you are running yourself ragged with all this travel and extra work projects. It's like you're trying to avoid having a conversation."

Sol looks at her blankly. "Oh."

"So? What's really going on? Are you avoiding me and/or our whole family?" Willow's look is part hurt and part empathetic.

Tears well up in Sol's eyes, but she wills them back down. She takes a deep breath and decides to try to be as truthful as possible. "Oh, Willow, I'm sorry. Don't take it personally. I guess I am kind of avoiding you all right now. I just have a lot of questions. And every new question leads to another question. I'm so glad you love me and have been supportive. This is just such a weird time, and I don't really know how to handle it. I just started looking at some of the support groups for different things like people who found out they were adopted when they were adults or people who got unexpected DNA results. They all say it's a trauma. So I guess I'm going through trauma, but it's so unusual it's not like there are a lot of people that can relate. And I can't help feeling like I don't belong anywhere. I know you love me, but it's really hard. And then to have Janice going through this health crisis right now too, I'm so caught up in that. And not only that, I find out my mother is black, which doesn't really change anything, but it does add a new aspect to my identity, and how do I deal with that?"

Willow has been listening with a concerned look on her face but now seems to shake Sol's concerns off with a move of her hand. "Oh, Sol, I know it's a lot. But we love you! You're our family! That's all that matters!"

"That's not all that matters!" Sol snaps at her.

Willow recoils at Sol's tone.

"Oh, I'm sorry, Will, I just can't sleep with all this on my mind, and it's made me so edgy. I know you love me, and I love you too. We are sisters and nothing can change that. But it's a lot more complicated."

Just then their food arrives, and they eat in silence for several minutes. "I appreciate you checking on me. I know you want to help me," Sol finally says.

"I do! But I don't know how. Should I just focus on the fact that nothing has changed in our relationship, or should I try to talk about all the changes you're going through? Or should I just distract you by talking about something else? This jackfruit 'pulled pork' sandwich is amazing, by the way. Do you want to try it? Too bad you got the quiche instead of that Thai sweet potato bowl. You know I wanted both of them!"

"Yeah, I guess I just had to go for the comfort food today. I'm not feeling like I need to shake anything else up right now." Sol takes a bite of Willow's sandwich. "That's pretty good though!"

"How can you help me? I don't know exactly. I'm just trying to figure everything out myself. Of course I don't want you to treat me any differently or walk on eggshells like I'm about to break any second. Did you all know anything about me having a different mom or did you ever suspect it? These are some of the questions that are going through my head. Like who in the family knew and kept this from me all these years."

Willow finishes chewing and says, "No, Sol, I wasn't even born when all that happened. How could I have known? I mean, it's not like anyone told me and asked me to keep it secret. When you were looking through pictures at Mom's house the other day, it did seem weird that there weren't any of Mom pregnant with you, but it's not so weird to not have a complete photo chronology of your life. There were pictures of her holding you when you were just an infant. I mean, we do look a little different, but it's not like I look really similar to Dove either. You know, looking back, there are some things that may have been strange, but I definitely didn't think anything of them at the time."

"Well, that's good. I can't stand thinking that you and Dove were lying to me too. What things are standing out to you now?" Sol is looking for any and all information that will help her piece things together.

"Remember when Dove started to get all into our family's genealogy because of that class project she had? This was when the websites were just starting, so it's not like it is now. But didn't she try to go downtown and do a records search at the courthouse or something? And Mom was saying she couldn't take her, and they got into an argument about it. I wonder if Mom was afraid she was going to find something out. I don't know why Mom didn't just tell you. I mean, you're a grown woman. And now for it to come out like this just makes it harder!" Willow takes a huge bite of her sandwich and offers Sol a sweet potato French fry.

"Oh yeah, I had forgotten about that. Did you know Mom told me they give you a fake birth certificate when you get adopted? Wait, I wonder if we got a new birth certificate with Mickey as our father. Now that would be really weird." Sol almost laughs thinking that she and Willow could relate as adoptees with fake birth certificates.

"That would be so weird! Another thing I remember was Grandpa Sipinski sometimes saying things that didn't make sense. And I don't think he ever forgave Dad for leaving Mom. He never really shared happy memories like the rest of the family. You know how sometimes he would start talking on and on about what a father and a husband is supposed to do. I thought maybe it was because we were starting to get into serious relationships and he didn't want us to marry the wrong guy, but now I can see how he could have been talking about Dad."

"Ugh, you're right. But wait, do you think that Mickey knew?" Sol helps herself to three more fries from Willow's plate.

"Oh my gosh, I'm sure he knew! But maybe not. Sol, you have to talk to Mom and ask her all your questions."

Sol sighs. "I know. Every answer I get leads to more questions."

- 51 -

Sol's tinfoil dress is staying together with some duct tape and a prayer. Thea's annual World UFO Day celebration is always fun, and this year it's also a good break from everything that has been on Sol's mind all week. She had never heard of the occasion until Thea and Quentin started having these parties. They started it as a joke one year since the meteorologists were predicting torrential downpours for the Fourth of July and they had already ordered a ton of food, but it was such a hit that they made it an annual tradition, and it has gotten more elaborate each year.

Sol arrives in her homemade dress and Bubble Wrap accessories looking fierce and joins the twenty-five or so people who are already there in Thea's space-themed backyard. Sol knows most of them from being friends with Thea for so long. Some are Thea's or Quentin's family, but most are friends from different stages of their lives that she has met or hung out with along the way.

As usual, Sol does a quick scan for any single men who Quentin may have invited. He does try to look out for her! Her scan is a habit from her many years of singleness, but she doesn't really expect to meet anyone since they haven't mentioned anyone. She would love to meet someone through a friend rather than a dating app, though, so she is always a little hopeful. Unfortunately, she doesn't see anyone new in the crowd. However, her scan does detect Thea dressed in an amazing Grace Jones-inspired look! Thea's braids have been taken out, and her hair is done up in an amazing sci-fi style with temporary light blue hair color added. Sol rushes over to get a picture before both of their outfits fall apart. She has learned from previous years to make sure to bring backup clothes since that could very well happen!

As she fills up her plate with Rocket Ships (alternating fruit on a stick with a strawberry point at the end), Saturn's Rings (onion rings), and Alien Chompers (burgers with olive eyeballs and cheese fangs), Sol's joined by one of Thea's old college roommates. "Hey, Sol! How are you? I don't think I've seen you since last year's party!"

"Hey! You're right, I can always count on seeing you here. I love your outfit, by the way!" Thea's former roommate is dressed in a shiny lime green dress with green swimming pool floaties attached to her ankles, ears, and hanging down her back.

"Thank you, yours too! What have you been up to this summer? Traveling?"

"Oh, just a little. I went on a quick trip to Boston, just a little family thing. What about you?"

Thea's friend gives her a play-by-play of her cruise on the Mississippi River, complete with her suitcase getting accidentally dropped in the water. Sol says "uh-huh," "really?" and laughs in all the appropriate places, but in the background, her mind is wondering if she should have said more or less about her own trip. She wasn't really ready for that question, but she knows it's just typical small talk for this gathering.

Thea calls them over to take pictures by the "spaceship" her husband has rigged up, and they all proceed to update their social media. It is fun to see everyone else's pictures from all over the world who are having their own UFO parties.

The DJ, Quentin's cousin, decides to amp up the music to "everyone on the dance floor" level, and they all dance until they're sweaty, exhausted, and most of their costumes have lost at least one piece. Thea awards the "Best Alien" crown to one of her coworkers, who it looks like has a lot of cosplay experience. His costume has lights, moving parts, and even squirts slime when you get within a certain distance.

After most of the guests leave, Sol stays to help clean up.

"Thanks for helping. It makes it so much easier," Thea says when they finally plop down side by side in two patio chairs. "So how are you doing? Catch me up on everything." She reaches down to start peeling off her knee-high boots.

"No problem. It was good to get my mind off everything for a little bit," Sol replies. "Oh yeah, I finally got a chance to look at some of those websites you sent me. I have so many thoughts running through my head! But I don't have the energy to talk about it right now."

"I bet you do! There's a lot to digest. It will probably take a while. What's the latest with Janice?" Thea takes a sip of her green bubble tea.

"I actually heard from Shyla yesterday. She says they tried everything, but the transplant did end up failing. So Janice is back on dialysis, back on the waiting list. They let her keep her spot on the list, but it's still unlikely that she would get a match off there.

"Shyla and Jackie started talking to the few family members that were still possibilities. Gordon volunteering had made some of them more willing to try. They're also setting up a website and doing more social media stuff. I told her I would share it to my network, and we're all brainstorming anyone else that might have a wider network. Plus I'm still waiting to hear on my results from the transplant center."

"Oh, so another waiting game combined with Shyla's kidney campaign. But you may still match. Do you think you would do it?" Thea raises her eyebrows at her.

"I don't know, but more and more I think I would." Sol leans back in the chair.

"Big decisions! I hope you hear from the center soon. Maybe give them a call if you don't so at least you can feel like you're doing something proactive. Oh yeah, sorry I didn't have any guys here today for you to meet! You haven't told me anything about the new dating app. No leads?"

"Ugh. No leads at all! In a way, it's good not having to deal with guys I'm not interested in, but in a way, it would be nice if someone was interested in me!" Sol rolls her eyes.

"Sorry, Sun! Maybe that new app is just wack." She slurps the last of her bubble tea. "But I think I read somewhere too that black women get the least play on dating apps! You changed your ethnicity, right?"

"What?! They do? Yeah, I changed it to 'mixed,' I think."

"Yeah, maybe it's the myth of the angry black woman or whatever, I don't know. I think some guys just have an idea of what the different ethnicities mean. That's probably what happened with Franklin. Although he could also just be a plain old racist. Or maybe that's just saying the same thing."

"Ugh. Well, I don't really need any extra 'excitement' now anyway! What's going on with you?" Sol's ready to change the subject.

"Just getting ready for this party has been taking up all my extra time! The kids were so happy to go to 'Grammy Camp' at my mom's house, and it was nice to have a break, but I miss them so much when they're gone! We try not to call and video chat with them much because we don't want them to miss us and misbehave for my mom. We're thinking 'out of sight, out of mind' is best."

"Well, it was a great party, as always! Seventh year of doing it?" Sol shoots her a big smile. She doesn't want to bring down the mood.

"It's actually been eight years of planning, but remember that one year it was flooding, and we had to cancel?!" Thea laughs.

"How could I forget? I know your friends are all 'ride or die' but that was even too much for us!"

"I don't blame you! We ended up just having a movie marathon inside with like five or ten alien movies! I think most of the people fell asleep on my floor in their alien costumes!"

"Legendary." Sol bestows her bubble wrap crown on Thea's blue hair.

- 52 -

The next few days are blessedly uneventful.

On Wednesday, Sol gets a text from her mom as she comes in from walking Jericho: *Hey, Sol, can you talk?* Sol sees she also missed a call when they were out walking, but she doesn't recognize the number. Sol wonders what her mom wants to talk about. They had been texting over the past few days, and Sol told her about the transplant failure and sent her pictures from Thea's party so she could see how the foil dress turned out.

Her mom answers on the first ring. "Hey, Mom, what's going on?" Sol says.

"Hi, hon, did you get a call from the transplant center today?"

Sol looks at her phone again. "No, I don't think so. I just had a missed call though." She starts mixing together Jericho's food in his bowl.

"Oh, that was probably them."

"Oh, okay," Sol says, distracted.

"You'll never believe this," Patty continues. "They approved me as a donor for Janice."

Sol jerks so hard that Jericho's bowl falls off the

counter, and his food goes everywhere. "What?! I thought you were just doing this to support me! I never thought you'd be a match!"

"I know. I was. I mean, I was doing it to support you. I didn't think I'd be a match either. Do you want to go call them back?"

Sol looks down at Jericho happily eating his kibble off the floor and takes a second to think, then says, "Mom, I told you that Janice's body rejected Gordon's kidney. So it's kind of a big deal. I've been thinking about donating if I match."

"Oh really? Well, you don't have to decide now. This will just give you more information." Sol catches a glimpse of herself in the reflection on the glass and notices the worried look on her face. She remembers how the people at the center said she could change her mind up until the day of the surgery. So that takes care of not wanting to donate. But what if she doesn't match at all? At least Patty did. That makes her feel a little better knowing there's at least one match out there.

"You're right. You're totally right. Okay, let me call them back. I'll let you know." After she hangs up, Sol takes her time picking up the phone again to dial.

"Hi, this is Sol Garnett returning your call," she forces herself to say confidently when a voice answers.

"Hi Sol, we have your results from the testing to match Janice Broward."

"Okay…"

"Unfortunately, her immune system makes her really difficult to match. I'm sorry, but your test results show that you're not a good candidate to donate to her."

"Really? Are you sure? I'm her daughter." Sol sits down hard on the edge of her chair. Jericho looks up from his food but stays where he is.

"I know, I'm sorry. We are sure. Do you want to put your name on the list for the exchange in case we have an eligible donor? It's a long shot, but there's no harm in trying."

"Um, yeah, sure, thanks. I have to go," Sol says as she hangs up abruptly.

Patty calls a minute later. "What did they say?"

"I'm not a good match."

Sol immediately starts crying. She didn't realize she had so much pent-up emotion, but now it all comes out. Jericho comes over and puts his head on her leg.

"I know, hon, I know," Patty says. "It's okay."

"I don't even know why I'm crying."

"It's okay, just let it out. Is Jericho there with you?"

"Uh-huh," Sol squeaks out.

"He's a good boy. Why don't I come over? I'll bring you some dinner."

"Okay," Sol says, then lays down on the couch and closes her eyes and cries. She didn't realize how much she had started counting on being a match and being able to donate to Janice. The more she had gotten used to the idea, the more it seemed like the perfect story—her finding out about Janice and then being able to help her.

- 53 -

"Sol, honey, wake up."

"Oh hey, Mom, I must have fallen asleep," she croaks, feeling groggy all over.

Her mom sets the food down in the kitchen and then comes and sits next to Sol on the couch and wraps her arms around her. "You know, I never thought things would happen like this. I thought we were doing the best thing for you. And I guess maybe we were a little selfish too. Okay, I know we were. And now that Janice's kidney disease has progressed, this is a huge thing to be going through all at once. I'm sorry, Sunshine."

Sol doesn't reply. She just sits there in her mother's arms and lets herself be comforted.

After a few minutes, Patty says, "Have you talked to Shyla? Is Janice doing okay?"

"Yeah, she's doing okay, but Shyla is really discouraged. She was so relieved to have finally found a donor and thought that was going to at least give her mom like ten good years. But now it's like starting all over. I told her I would try to come back up again and visit soon. Good thing it's an easy trip and there are lots of flights every day from

Baltimore to Boston. You know, I feel bad for her too being an only child and going through all this alone. She is close with her cousins, but I mean, you can't imagine how excited she was to find out she had a sister. So I do want to be able to be there for her."

Patty keeps holding her and strokes her long hair gently. "I know you do, Sol. And I'm so glad that you all are getting along so well! We've put you in a tough situation, but you are handling it with such grace and maturity. I'm really proud of you. And I'm glad you're still talking to me! I know how angry you were when you first found out. I know we have a ways to go to rebuilding trust and figuring out how our lives are going to be from here."

"Yeah, I was really mad at you. And I can't help wondering how things could have been different. I mean, what if Janice had died before I had a chance to meet her?"

Patty's hand stops moving. "You're right, so we really owe it all to Jackie for the truth coming out. I know she wasn't very welcoming with you, and I can only imagine what she thinks of me. Well, come on and sit at the table, and we'll eat while we talk."

Patty starts pulling food out of the bag she brought. "Mickey made that South American chicken and rice we all love. Let me make you a plate."

Jericho follows them over and lays down at Sol's feet in cleanup position just in case anything happens to fall on the floor.

"Thanks, Mom."

They eat, and Sol tells her about joining a new dating app. Even though her mom listens and supports her and has herself always had several black friends, Sol feels like there's only so much she can understand about this specific situation. In reality, there aren't many people who could really understand living your life as white and then finding out in your thirties that you have a different mom and she's black. Not to mention trying to date in the midst of it. So she guesses she should just be thankful that they do have a good relationship and she can talk to her about it a little. She tells her about what happened with Franklin, and her mom was livid. She knows that her mom wants the best for her in terms of a husband and life in general, so that is good, but sometimes it can feel like pressure. Or like it's her fault that she's still single. She hasn't gotten any matches yet, so she's not sure if it's just this new app or the ethnicity thing. Or maybe it is her fault. But she decides she has too much on her mind to worry about it right now.

Patty starts packing up to leave. "So, would you be willing to donate to Janice?" Sol says. "I know you didn't expect to match, and it's a lot to ask, but she really needs to find someone. You won't believe how upset Shyla was when I talked to her. I told her I would try to help her as much as I could. I guess I thought I would match and be able to donate. The center didn't seem to think a paired exchange was very likely, but I told them to put me on the list. I have to do something."

Her mom stops packing the food and looks at her. "Sol, it is a lot to ask. I want to think about it a little and talk to Mickey. I mean, you know how I feel about doctors, so I don't know. And plus all that time off work and Mickey has to take care of me that whole time. It's a big decision.

I'll let you know."

"Okay," Sol says, not wanting to force the issue. "Thanks for coming over." When her mom closes the door, Sol collapses back on the couch and closes her eyes.

- 54 -

Thank you, Aunt Jackie, for helping me know the truth. A couple of nights later, Sol decides to visit the site about people who found out they were adopted when they were older, "late-discovery adoptees." Most of them had been raised by two adoptive parents. Some of them have a positive adoption story but still want to know more about their biological parents, even if only for health information. Some of them had hard times with their adoptive parents and never felt like they fit in their family, so they are relieved to know they're not related by blood. Some of them have had positive reunions with members of their biological family, some are still searching, and some were again rejected by members of their biological families. Some of them have missed their chance because none of their blood relatives are still alive.

This gives Sol so much to think about. She's a little different because she knew her biological dad for her whole life. Well, the first five years of her life. And now she knows her biological mom. She has some answers but still feels betrayed because no one told her the real story for all those years.

The sites say she may start to remember things that were

clues. This is just what Willow had been saying at lunch the other day. People always talk about how she and her sisters look different, but that's true in a lot of families. Then there's all the confusion over her ethnicity and her name. But she really has to attribute a lot of it to her name leading people down that path. She loves her name, but it does make it more complicated. Her looks—it's hard for her to be objective, but she thinks she just has olive skin and tans easily. One of her Italian friends has hair that's kinkier than hers. This is why talking about "race" is such an illusion. She hates the word anyway, but now she has to come face-to-face with it in a personal way.

In terms of the adoption, she knows several people who were adopted or have adopted children of their own, especially at her church. She always thought it was this altruistic thing like "Oh, they are so selfless to adopt that baby..." until she started learning more about it and hearing stories from the adoptee rights movement. She and her sisters were also formally adopted by Mickey, so they have a bit of experience with it. Now it's so weird to think she was adopted twice—once by her mom when she was an infant and once by Mickey at age ten-ish. There's a fairy-tale aspect to the idea of adoption, and she even starts thinking about stories like Cinderella or Little Orphan Annie. And then there's the idea of adoption in Christianity. She always has known that she was adopted into God's family. Even Jesus himself was adopted and raised by a man who was not his biological father. So it's nothing new.

She thinks she's not *so* mad about the adoption but more that no one told her the truth. What do they think of her that they couldn't tell her? That she couldn't handle it? The more she thinks, the angrier she gets. But this is going nowhere. She needs answers.

- 55 -

Willow, Sol, their two dogs, and about fifteen containers of various food and drinks all squeeze into Willow's MINI Cooper as they head across the Bay Bridge to the Eastern Shore the next day for Mickey's annual family reunion. Part of the tradition is that the sisters always drive together even though the car gets a little cramped, especially now that their crew includes the dogs. Usually Dove would be with them since she typically comes home for a visit in the summer, but Sol doesn't mind that work kept her in California for now. That's a whole other unresolved issue.

As she has been doing since childhood, Willow closes her eyes and sings the song "Old McDonald Had a Farm" as they drive across the bridge to distract herself from being scared of heights. Sol has been tasked with driving for just this reason but sneaks a glance toward the Bay to see how many boats are out. The dogs stick their heads out on either side of the car, which makes Sol a little nervous even though she knows the other cars aren't that close.

It's a typical "hazy, hot, and humid" day in a Maryland summer, and they are sweating but don't want to turn on the air conditioning and miss the smell of the summer air and outdoor sounds.

When they arrive at the park, they unload the car and quickly throw off their bathing suit cover-ups and run into the water to cool down and wash off the sweat. They are among the first to arrive, so they aren't slowed down by greeting relatives on the way. Thankfully, Mickey's family has always been very welcoming to them and doesn't treat them any differently than the other family members. They were all so happy for him to meet and marry Patty and automatically have three children. His parents just wanted more and more grandkids, so that sped up the process!

Because the girls were young when Patty and Mickey got married, they've been a part of the family for several decades now. For the past ten years or so, his parents have taken to asking Sol and her sisters when they're going to get more great-grandchildren. Dove seemed the likeliest to fulfill their dreams when she got married, but she and her husband hadn't told anyone about their decision not to have children, and then Dove decided marriage didn't really fit into her plans at all. Sol is still just praying for a husband who will be a good companion and treat her right and be a good father to Jericho and her (hopefully existing someday) children, and Willow is happy just dating and traveling for now.

The picnic area starts to quickly fill up with family, and the sisters make their rounds greeting everyone. They spend the afternoon eating, wading in the water, and listening to family stories. Someone has decided that this year they would have games with prizes, and so they team up for a three-legged race where every single team falls over when their legs are tied together. The ring toss has the targets marked with old family baby pictures, and some of the Thompsons become so competitive that Mickey's great-uncle, who is approaching one hundred years old, has to intervene.

Sol and her mom decide to sit out the Hula-Hoop competition, and after fending off all the relatives that give them a hard time about it, position their chairs up next to each other to cheer. "Hi, Sunshine, good to see you! Did you get some of the pineapple stuffing?"

"Hi, Mom! Yes, it was delicious! Mickey's family definitely has some great recipes they pass down through the generations. Did you ever try to get a copy?"

"Yes, I did, years ago, but they said it was top secret! Can you believe that?" Patty looks incredulous.

"Oh no! I guess that's just another reason for us to keep coming to the reunions!" Sol has already moved on to dessert and challenges her mom to a watermelon seed-spitting competition.

They both laugh and watch the participants in the game. After a few minutes, her mom speaks. "I'm actually glad I got a minute to talk with you because I was going to call you this weekend."

Sol puts her plate down on the grass beside her where ants promptly swarm it, then turns to her mom. "Is everything okay? Oh, did you talk to Dove?"

"Yes, everything is okay. I did talk to Dove, and it was a hard conversation. I think it's going to take her some time to get used to it, and like you, to forgive me for keeping the truth from you all." Patty closes her eyes for a second, then open them again.

"Yeah, that makes sense. Is that what you wanted to tell me?" Sol is glad her mom at least took care of that and wonders how things will be with Dove the next time they talk. And also wonders when they will talk again.

"No, I wanted to tell you that the transplant center actually called me again this week about coming in to get retested against Janice's latest results. I talked with Mickey about the whole thing, and I decided I can't do it."

Janice says this matter-of-factly, and Sol stares at her, her jaw dropping open a little bit. She doesn't know what to say, but finally sputters out, "What? Why?"

"I'm sorry, hon, I know how important this has become to you, but I just can't." Patty tries to put some tenderness in her voice, but Sol can tell her mom hopes she'll drop the topic.

Sol starts to feel her face get hot and not just from the summer sun. "Yeah, I know, you said that. But why not? At least tell me the reason. Don't you think you've kept enough from me over the years?"

Patty grimaces. "Sol, I know that's your biological mother, but I barely know her. I never met her in person, and this is a lot to ask. Surgery and then weeks of recovery and then living life with only one kidney. Who's going to run my business while I'm recovering? What happens if my other kidney goes out? Plus you know how scared I am of even going to the doctor."

"What?!" Sol's voice starts to get louder, and she gets more upset. Willow glances over at her to see what's going on. "Without her, there is no ME! Is that what you want? Was

I just an inconvenience that you got forced into because you thought that's what you had to do to get Dad back? And now, you don't even care if she lives or dies! You 'don't know her'! How easy for you to say that! What about me? That's where I come from, and I've only just met her! And there are no other potential donors! I seriously expected more from you, Mom. Or should I say, 'Adoptive mother, Patricia'?!"

"Honey, hold on..." Patty says and tries to put her arm around Sol. Sol shrugs it off.

"Don't even try it. It's not going to be that easy to smooth this over. We are talking about a woman's life here. And not just any woman, my biological mother, who I just met because you lied to me all these years!" By this time, Sol is practically screaming and she's starting to shake. Willow edges closer and closer to monitor the situation but doesn't intervene.

"I know you're upset," Patty tries again. "But I can't see a way to make this work."

"What? That is the most selfish thing I've ever heard. People do this surgery all the time and live the rest of their lives with one kidney. It sounds like it's just a convenient excuse. At least you didn't try to blame it on poor Mickey. Has all of this—my whole life—been all about you? Did you take me in just to make yourself feel better after you lost your baby and to try to save your marriage? Did you even want me at all? Maybe you were just jealous of Janice anyway since she had Dad. Is that what this is all about? You still haven't forgiven her for stealing your husband?"

Sol finally stops to take a breath. Patty looks at her as though she's been slapped. In the distance, Mickey looks over to see what's going on, and Willow motions him to stay over there and to try to keep the rest of the other people on that side too.

"Sol, I always wanted you. You have to believe me," Patty says.

"Why? Why should I believe you? You lied to me for the past thirty-seven years. You can make up any story you want at this point. Did you think I was just going to be okay with this whole thing? That's what it seemed like at first, right? 'Oh, Sol is getting to know her half sister, isn't that cute?' Well, maybe it took me a little longer to process the situation. God knows I'm still processing. But this just shows me I never really was a part of this family. I mean, who would you give a kidney up for? What if it were me? No, not me, probably not. Maybe Dove or Willow since they're your blood children?"

"I know, I was wrong to lie to you. But that doesn't mean I don't love you. This is what I was afraid of." Patty lets out a huge sigh and covers her face with her hand.

"Oh, so you wish you could go back to when you were still lying to me so you don't have to face the situation? Geez, you really have your priorities straight."

"That's not what I said. I didn't want you to hate me. I didn't want you to feel like I loved you differently than Dove and Willow. I didn't want you feel caught in between these two families."

"Well, guess what, Mom, that's the reality. You not wanting it to happen wasn't going to stop it. And you just made it worse. And now—what is this, a sick joke that you went to the center with me? 'Oh, this will be a cute memory. Let's dress up in green shirts and make a party out of it.' Forgetting that my biological mom was sick and getting sicker and that's why we were going in the first place!"

"No, Sol, that's not what I was thinking at all. I was trying to be supportive, that's all. I never thought I would match, and it put me in a difficult situation."

"Yeah, but guess whose situation is a lot more difficult than yours…Janice's. Okay, well, I'm done talking about this. I hope you reconsider," Sol says and gets up and walks toward the car. This is one of the times she regrets the carpool situation. She's so worked up, but there's no way to really escape. She veers off and starts walking down a nearby path in the opposite direction from the rest of the group. Her phone starts ringing, and it's Willow wondering what happened to her.

"I saw you and Mom arguing. Are you okay?"

"No, this whole adoption story is just complicated. More and more stuff keeps coming up. I know it's not a good time for this. I don't want to ruin the party for everyone." Sol quickens her step to put more distance between her and the party. She doesn't want to ruin it, although she still hasn't found out if Mickey has been lying to her too.

"Well, things are winding down a little bit. What do you think about staying for like thirty more minutes, and then we'll head out? Let's plan to stop at the custard stand on the way back too! Maybe that will cheer you up a little, and you can tell me everything."

"Okay, I can do that. Yeah, that custard always helps. I'm going to just walk for a little bit, and then I'll be back." Sol follows the path deeper and deeper into the woods while mosquitoes swarm around her. It seems fitting to her in her current mood.

- 56 -

Dear God,

1. I can't believe that Mom got approved to donate a kidney to Janice.

2. I can't believe she says she won't donate.

3. What are you doing?

4. Mom and I are fighting but I'm not going to back down. I need answers. Did you seriously have to make my life so complicated? Okay, so your life on earth was complicated too. I know you understand.

5. Show me a way forward.

6. Thanks for always being there.

- 57 -

Jericho sniffs at the peaches and blueberries Sol has picked out but decides the free-range chickens are more interesting. The two of them are at a farm stand in a rural area of Baltimore County. Sol has been avoiding her mom for the past two weeks. Patty has texted and called and even tried to get Willow to intervene, but Sol isn't ready. She's been putting all of her attention into her work, and with any free time, is taking Jericho for long walks and drives. Today she took the afternoon off. As they're getting back in the car, she gets a text from Shyla: *Hey, are you free this weekend for a visitor? My work conference got canceled, but I want to get out of here. The Yankees are in town. Haha.*

Sol replies: "Ew, the Yankees are the worst! Haha. Yes, come down! I'll get my guest room ready! Just send me your flight details, and I'll pick you up! I'm at the farm stand right now, so I'll get some extra!"

Sol immediately gets in touch with Thea and Willow to make plans. She's so excited for them all to meet. She doesn't know what she's going to do about her mom, but for now, she's still not talking to her. But maybe meeting Shyla would make Patty reconsider about not donating? After all, she *is* a mom. The women come up with a loose plan that includes an Orioles game, church, and live music at a winery nearby with ample time to relax and do nothing. Sol isn't sure how much time Shyla will want to spend one-on-one versus in a group, so she just tells the others to be on standby until she can get more info. Shyla is a talker, so Sol suspects that she'll be happy to have a group for all of those activities.

When Sol picks Shyla up from the airport later that night, Sol finds out she's right. Shyla says she can't wait to meet everyone. It's pretty late, so they head back to Sol's place and plan to get all of the activities going the next day. Shyla is so excited to meet Jericho, and he is in love with all the attention she gives him. She asks if she can walk him, and they go out for a walk around the neighborhood with Shyla alternating between baby talking to Jericho and filling Sol in on the latest with Janice and the rest of her life.

Sol decides to steer them toward the Johns Hopkins campus because she knows it will be lively on a Friday night. It's Shyla's first visit to Baltimore, and Sol wants it to be a good one.

Shyla looks fascinated by everything they pass, but her attention always returns to Jericho. "I wish I could have a dog, but my work schedule is sometimes so unpredictable, I don't know if that would be a good life for a dog! I don't want to be selfish about it! But 'Oh, Jericho, you're such a good baby, aren't you? You bring so much happiness to your mama, don't you?'"

Sol laughs. "He does! Dogs are really the best. But I think that's a wise decision. You don't want a dog that's going to just be alone all the time or that you have to pay all this money for doggie day care for. But you'll get one someday! In the meantime, Coco is super happy to have you visit him!"

"He's the best! I have a few friends with dogs in Boston, and I try to get them to let me dogsit, but only one person has ever taken me up on it! I have even done the matchmaker thing to find out what breeds are good for me and what type of dog I would like. I'm learning so much! So far, I'm thinking a greyhound! Did you know they're actually super chill dogs? You would never believe it because they run so fast, but you can adopt a retired greyhound, and they just sleep all day! Plus, their hair is short and they're pretty affectionate. I definitely want an affectionate dog but not one that's super slobbery! I have a hard enough time keeping things clean!"

"Hey, that's an idea, did you ever think about dogsitting professionally—on the side, of course? Then you could just have a dog or two when it's convenient for you. Or maybe you could volunteer at the shelter?"

"Good ideas! I will have to look into it! I was thinking about offering volunteer law hours to the shelter, but honestly, I just want to snuggle the dogs! I spend enough time doing law!" Jericho pulls them toward a group of college students who are standing in a group eating French fries.

"Well, I'm sure they would love to have you. How is the law, by the way?" Sol tugs Jericho's harness the other direction so he'll leave the fries alone.

"I'm actually getting a little antsy at my firm. This happens every four to five years. I may just need to switch it up and change my specialty. I guess I just get a little bored once I've mastered one area. I think deep in her heart, Mom wants me to be a Supreme Court Justice! But I'm thinking about doing environmental law maybe, I'm not sure. And listen to this, remember how I told you that my ex-boyfriend, Mark, works at the same firm with me? Well, last week we were both working late, and he asked me if I wanted to go get something to eat, so I did. It was nothing fancy—we just went to this little place for fish and chips and beer, but it was definitely nice to hang out with him again."

"Oh really?" Sol gives her an inquiring look and wiggles her eyebrows. "So what are you thinking?"

"Well, he's dating someone new, so I'm not really thinking anything. I mean, we tried to make it work for three years, so it's not like anything is different now that would cause it to work if we tried again. But maybe we'll be friends. I mean, that is a super weird thing for me to say about an ex because I don't even believe in that! But it was so good to talk to him, and we have all those years of history. Didn't I say I was taking a break from dating anyway?!"

They slowly make their way through groups of college students while Jericho sniffs everything, and then they wind their way back around to Sol's place.

Sol makes sure that Shyla is all set with everything she needs for the night and sets the coffee to start brewing at just the right time the next morning. Jericho seems a little torn between whose bed he wants to sleep beside, but he finally settles on his usual spot next to Sol.

- 58 -

On Saturday, Sol, Willow, and Thea have planned to go to a winery "up in the county" that's having a live band. Sol explains to Shyla that Baltimore City and Baltimore County are two separate things, and the city isn't a part of the county. Sol's used to this since she grew up here, but she can see how it may seem a little strange too. After a carb-heavy breakfast and lots of coffee at her favorite quirky place to take visitors, Papermoon Diner, Sol and Shyla pack up a picnic basket full of water, fruit from the produce stand, and snacks. Willow said she was going to make lunch for all of them, but Sol thinks she'll bring extra just in case one of Willow's culinary experiments doesn't exactly work out. Plus, she thinks more food is always merrier!

When they all arrive at the winery, Sol excitedly introduces Shyla to Willow and Thea. They chatter away and are happy to get to know each other. They stake out a spot under a tree. The day's starting to get really hot, so they try to find a space in the shade, but the competition is fierce. The grapevines all around make such a pretty scene, and the grapes are starting to ripen. They head into the tasting room to find which wines they like. Shyla exclaims over everything. "I feel like I'm in a movie! Or Napa or something! I can't believe this is right near you but seems like a totally different world! I would be shocked if we have any wineries near me with the weather up there, but I will have to look. That would be amazing!" she says.

Once they pick out their wines to start with, they get settled on their blankets, and Willow and Thea start asking Shyla questions. "How is your mom doing? Tell us everything. What's it like to meet Sol after all this time? Is she what you expected?"

Shyla laughs. "First of all, cheers! To my new sisters!" she says. "You know I'm including you all whether we share blood or not. I went from being an only child to having four new sisters! Too bad Dove isn't here. Now tell me what sizes you wear because I'm coming to borrow your clothes!"

"Oh yeah, Shyla is a bit of a style mogul!" Sol adds. She looks over at Thea, who is wearing a body-hugging leopard-print dress today that she had explained was inspired by Eartha Kitt. Sol knows Thea understands about being a style mogul.

"Hey, we all have our passions!" Shyla says laughingly. "Mom is doing okay. She says to tell you all hi and to please come visit soon. I kind of think she's lying to me, though, and trying to put on a brave face so I don't worry. I talked to Dad about it and he feels the same way. I mean, we do talk to her doctors too, and I've done my own research. There's a huge community of people who are either on the kidney waiting list or have had a transplant already, so there are a lot of stories out there. But at the end of the day, she's just really hard to match. That's why we were so excited when

Gordon–that's my cousin—matched and was willing to do the transplant. You know, all these crazy thoughts are going through my head like, 'Can I pay someone for their kidney?' I'm seriously thinking about the market for body parts! I understand now how desperate people do desperate things. I just want her to live as long as possible!"

"Oh wow, yeah, I can see how that puts you in a really hard spot!" says Willow with a concerned look on her face.

Sol's mind is racing, thinking about Patty, but she tries to keep a neutral face. She thinks she had better keep a close eye on how much wine she drinks so she doesn't say anything she'll regret. She didn't tell anyone the real reason for their argument. She's angry at her mom, but she doesn't want to create extra drama. She's still hoping Patty will change her mind.

Just then, the band starts playing, and the women look around to check out the rest of the crowd. "Hey, we're all single, right? I'm going to try to find some guys for us!" Willow says.

They all laugh, and Sol feels thankful for her younger sister who always finds a way to cheer her up. The food that Willow brought all turned out delicious too! Sol is so happy that they are all getting along. She did feel a little nervous about them meeting. Sol doesn't want to feel caught between the two families, and she's glad that Thea and Willow can now partially share in this new aspect of her life.

The band is mostly playing oldies and when "Shout" comes on, everyone jumps up to dance with the small group that has formed on the grass. They are all crouched down on the "softer" part when someone accidentally bumps into

Sol. She loses her balance and falls over onto the grass and looks up to see Mickey.

"What are you doing here?" she blurts out.

"Well, hello to you too!" he replies, laughing.

"Sorry, I just didn't expect to see you." Sol tries to recover quickly. "Did you know we were going to be here?"

"Oh, I don't know. Your mom just said an oldies band was playing and that was enough for me! Maybe one of your sisters told her." Mickey shrugs.

"Oh. Where are you sitting?" Sol asks neutrally.

"We're right over there. See your mom? She said she needed a little more time to warm up before dancing. Or did she say, 'more wine before dancing'?" Mickey laughs at his own joke.

Sol is annoyed but tries not to show it. She doesn't blame Mickey, but now that she thinks of it, maybe he deserves it too. She looks around for Willow, but the others have disappeared. She wonders if she could have set this whole thing up. She knows it's not unusual to see people you know out and about around Baltimore. It's one of the things she loves about it. Even now, she looks over and sees a teacher from one of the schools she works at. But if her sister deliberately put them together, she is definitely going to be angry.

She's not ready to see her mom, and especially not with Shyla there. But it looks like she doesn't have much of a choice. She can't tell them that her mom's a match for her bio mom's kidney transplant—at least not yet. She's going to have to make the most of it. She says a quick prayer, "Help me, Lord."

She finally locates her sisters and Thea getting another

bottle of wine at the tasting bar and joins them. She whispers to Willow, "Did you know Mom is here?"

"What?!" Willow replies. Sol looks at her closely to see if she's faking it, but it doesn't seem like she is.

"Did you tell her we were going to be here?"

"No, I didn't. But you know what? I think the event was listed in an email that Mom forwarded to me. So maybe that's how it happened."

"Uh-huh. Well, you know I haven't talked to her since our fight."

"Yeah, and what was that fight about anyway? I mean, you're going to have to talk to her sometime. And don't you want her to meet Shyla?"

Sol takes a deep breath. She does want her mom and Shyla to meet, but she just wishes she had been able to do it on her own terms. But maybe this is what needs to happen—for her mom to see that Janice has a daughter who cares about her (a daughter besides Sol!) and that her decision to not donate is affecting other people.

She turns to Shyla and tries to act nonchalant. She hasn't told Shyla she and her mom had a fight, and she doesn't want to get into the reasons. "Hey, Shyla, guess who I just bumped into…literally! My stepdad, Mickey. He and my mom are here. I guess they heard that there was a band today too!"

"Oh my gosh! Are you serious? I've been wanting to meet them! Where are they?" Sol knows there's no turning back now.

The three of them head over to where Patty and Mickey have their fold-up chairs and what looks like an entire smorgasbord of food on a portable table with an actual cloth tablecloth, Shyla talking excitedly the entire way.

"Hi, girls!" Patty calls out as they approach.

"Hi, Mom, I didn't expect to see you here," Sol begins, and then tries to brighten up her voice. "This is Shyla, Janice and Calvin's daughter."

Shyla shakes hands with Patty and Mickey with a huge smile on her face. "I'm so excited that we ran into you! I was hoping I'd get to meet you all this weekend, but I didn't know it would be here! I just met Willow and Thea and am getting all the dirt on Sol! You must have more stories that you can share! Oh, what wine did you all end up getting? We got the Chardonnay and Riesling just because it's a little warm—okay, blazing hot!—out, but I really want to try them all. We'll see how far we get! Willow made some delicious chickpea sandwiches, so they are totally spoiling me! It looks like you have a good spread over here too. But how can we sit still when they're playing these great oldies?! These are the best songs to dance to!"

Shyla finally takes a breath and Patty jumps in. "Shyla, it's so nice to meet you! We've been hearing so much about you. We're trying a bottle of rosé—here, take a little cup to try it. Do you all have dessert? Mickey made his heavenly mud brownies. Here, take some of those too!"

"Oh wow, thanks! Should we bring our blankets over? I mean, we did get a tiny spot in the shade, but it looks like the sun is moving, and we will be blasted with heat soon." Shyla is catching on to the Maryland weather.

Sol gives her mother a meaningful look, hoping to communicate that she didn't want to join with them, but her mother goes for the middle road. "We'd love to have you join us, but it's okay if you want to just have some girl time too."

"Aw, you're so sweet! Well, Willow thinks she can find guys for all of us here somehow, so we'll see how that goes!" Shyla says.

"I do see a couple of cute guys around, so I hope it works out!" Patty says, laughing. "We'll see you on the dance floor!"

The women return to their blanket and proceed to eat and drink all the goodies. "Sol, what was that about? You seemed a little icy with your mom," Shyla says.

"Yeah, sorry, I just wasn't prepared to run into them. We had an argument," Sol replies.

"Oh really? About what? You didn't tell me."

"Let's just enjoy our day. I'll tell you later."

"Okay, but I'm glad I got to meet them anyway. I was hoping we could squeeze that in this weekend, but I didn't want to make a big deal out of it. I don't know if you feel like you're in an awkward position or what."

"I appreciate it. I mean, the whole past couple months have been kind of awkward and hard. But I'm glad you got to meet them too."

The sisters spend the rest of the afternoon tasting wine and dancing. They do find some guys to dance with, but they're old enough to be their dads. It turns out they came with the band and live in Pennsylvania. They all agree that it was still fun, and even though they have been eating all day, they stop at a creamery on the way home for some fresh ice cream. They agree on their plans for the next day, and Sol and Shyla go back to Sol's place, and after taking Jericho for a quick walk, they both crash on the couch.

"Wine always makes me so sleepy," Sol says.

"Me too! Why is that?" Shyla says as her eyes close.

They both wake up two hours later, let Jericho out in the shared backyard, and change into pajamas. "Okay, I know you're a lawyer, but does that make you not want to watch *Law and Order*? The original one, that is," Sol asks.

"No, I love *Law and Order*!"

Sol makes sure to set the alarm for the morning, and they proceed to doze on and off in front of a *Law and Order* marathon. Sol eventually wakes up and makes her way to bed. She leaves Shyla to decide whether she can drag herself to the guest room or just wants to stay on the couch.

- 59 -

The next morning, Sol wakes up to find that Shyla did make it to the guest room sometime in the night. She quickly gets the coffee brewing, sets out a few breakfast snacks, leaves Shyla a note, and takes Jericho for a walk. The morning feels humid but not overly hot—yet. She thinks about what to wear to church. Despite the outside heat, she always has to take an extra sweater or two to combat the air conditioning in the church building. One of the pastors once told her they keep it low to keep people awake! She decides to wear her red capris with her red sandals, a short-sleeved black and white polka-dotted blouse, and a white cardigan.

When she gets back, Shyla is at the table drinking coffee. "Thanks for hooking me up, Sis! You know I need my coffee to start the morning off right!" Jericho goes straight over to her and starts nuzzling her arm. "Hey, cutie pie!" she says to him. Sol hands her a treat to give him. She figures, what's a little more spoiling?

"I love my coffee too! Can I make you an egg sandwich or omelet? Or something else?"

"Egg sandwich, please, and make it a runny yolk with extra cheese, please!!"

"Coming right up!"

After they finish getting ready, they head off to church. Shyla said she usually only goes to church on Easter and Christmas Eve, but she said she'd love to see what Sol's church is like since Sol is so involved there.

On the way over, Shyla says, "So what's going on with you and your mom, really? I know you didn't really want to talk about it yesterday."

Sol takes a deep breath. "I guess it's good I got my coffee if we're going to start the morning off talking about this. It's really complicated, but finding out your mom was my biological mom brought up so many things. Number one is that she lied to me for so many years. And I guess asked the rest of the family to lie too. I mean, your mom lied to you too—by omission. How did you feel when you found out?"

Shyla is staring out the window, taking in everything they drive past just the way Sol did when she went to Massachusetts. She turns her head to look at Sol. "Hmm, you're right, they definitely kept things from us. I mean, my situation is so different from yours. When I found out, I was so focused on finding a kidney donor for my mom that all I thought was that you were a potential donor! And of course, I always wanted a sister. But it's so different for me because I always had my two biological parents with me. I never questioned any of that."

"I never questioned it either. And now I feel even worse that I didn't suspect it more. I mean, even just looking at us, you can see how different we look. But I always just brushed it aside because everyone else did. Plenty of siblings look very different. A lot of times, one will take after the mom and the other will take after the dad, and they will look totally different. I mean, all I had to go off of for my dad was some old pictures, but I believed the story the whole time." Sol reaches over to turn the radio down.

"Did they treat you differently?" Shyla asks.

Sol takes a second to think. "No, not that I can remember."

"Did your mom say why they didn't tell you?"

"She said she was afraid of messing up our relationship. And the longer she waited, the harder is became."

"Huh."

"Yeah."

"I'm sorry this has been so hard. I mean, I kind of just barreled right into it, not really thinking about how devastating it would be for you. I was only thinking about saving my mom—our mom."

"Of course, you did what you had to do."

They pull up to the church, and Sol quickly asks Shyla how she wants to be introduced. "You can just keep it simple and say my name. Don't worry about telling everyone the whole long story!"

They greet several people on the way in, and Sol sees at least one single guy checking out Shyla. She doesn't blame him—her sister looks amazing. Too bad the single guys at church are few and far between—and typically a lot younger than she is! Sol's open to dating younger guys, but, of course, they have to be open to dating an older woman. And now, a woman of color. That conversation with Franklin pops back up in her head. *Do guys really think like that?* she wonders. She hopes not at her church, which she had deliberately selected because it was multicultural and diverse in ages and income levels too.

Sol's so excited that a couple of her favorite songs, "Great Is Thy Faithfulness" and "Way Maker," are in the worship set. She loves how her church mixes the traditional hymns and new songs together. Shyla sings along with them too. Sol says a prayer of thanks for her new sister. When the main pastor gets up to preach, he says, "Today, we're going to talk about a subject that's really hard for most of us— forgiveness. Maybe that's why we pastors don't preach on it that much, because it's hard for us too. But we should. Because unforgiveness is what keeps those hurts hurting us long after they happen."

Sol and Shyla both kind of gasp when they hear the topic and then look at each other with wide eyes. Sol scribbles on her program, "Can you believe this?!!"

Sol listens in a daze as her pastor explains how forgiveness isn't saying that what the person did is okay. She replays her conversations with her mother in her head. *Did she say she was sorry?* Sol asks herself. She has no intention of "letting her mother off the hook" after lying to her for so many years. She internally groans and rolls her eyes but tries to keep a neutral face on the outside. She hears someone blowing their nose in the back of the room and wonders if they're crying. The pastor asks them to close their eyes and think about someone they need to forgive. *Seriously?* Sol thinks. "That wasn't hard to think of someone, was it?" he asks after they open their eyes. Sol wonders where he's going with this and if he can read her mind.

"Now imagine that you're God, and the person you thought of was you," her pastor continues. "When He was thinking about someone He could choose to forgive, there were millions of people that had done bad things to Him— we call it *sin*. He thought about you and what you had done, and He also thought about what you were still doing and had no intention of stopping. He thought about how you weren't thinking about Him at all or apologizing or changing your ways. And then He made a decision. He said yes, I will forgive her, yes, I will forgive him. I will give everything I have to make things right between us. And then He sent Jesus to die so that could happen—to take the punishment so you didn't have to take it. Now I want you to think about that person again that you had in your mind. The Bible says, 'Forgive others because God forgave you.' You may not want to do it, but there it is."

The rest of the service passes in a blur, and on the way back home, Shyla asks Sol, "So what did you think about the sermon?"

"I can't believe that was the topic. God always does stuff like this to me."

"Are you going to forgive her?"

"No, I still don't want to. I mean, I don't know."

"Okay. Well, you have a lot to think about."

"Yeah, I keep meaning to start looking for a therapist to help me sort through everything, but there has been so much going on. What about you?"

"He wasn't lying when he said it wasn't hard to think of someone that you need to forgive. I was thinking about my ex. I know I still have to fill you in more, but there was one thing he did that really hurt our relationship. One Sunday, a bunch of people from our office went to the Patriots game together—someone had a connection to get us tickets. Meanwhile, I was in West Bridgewater hosting my cousin's baby shower. Oh my gosh, it was amazing too! And the baby is super cute. She is like three now! You'll probably meet her soon. Anyway, he ends up getting drunk at the game because of course they were tailgating beforehand, and he ended up making out with another woman—a white woman, no less, but that's another story. The worst thing was that it's another woman in our circle of friends, so I still see her. Once he sobered up, he told me about it, and he felt horrible and asked me to forgive him. I said I did, but I don't think I ever really trusted him again after that, and I kind of held back in the relationship. So maybe I never really did forgive him. Maybe that was what finally did us in."

"Ugh! I can't believe he did that! I'm sorry!"

"Yeah, it really hurt me. But now I'm thinking about the whole forgiveness thing again. Maybe I'm just hurting myself now. Ugh, it's so complicated! Anyway, thanks for taking me to church with you! I think that was just what I needed. And I was reminded that God is in control of Mom's kidney, not me. So that lets me breathe a little easier."

"Good, I'm glad! Thanks for coming with me! I promise, the rest of the day won't be so heavy!"

"Phew, I hope not!"

- 60 -

After Sol tries unsuccessfully to lend Shyla an Orioles shirt and has changed her own outfit into Orioles orange, they meet up with Thea and Willow at a bar across the street from the stadium.

Thea is naturally dressed in the style of Lisa "Left Eye" Lopes from the group TLC and even has eye black under her left eye. "I can't believe you let her come here wearing that Red Sox shirt!" she cries out playfully.

Sol laughs, then says, "All right, ladies, do you want a drink out here, or should we just go in? I think Willow's *boyfriend*—oops, I mean 'friend' is selling beers inside today."

"Haha, can't we have both?!" Thea says.

"Boyfriend and friend?" Sol teases.

"Ha. Ha. Drink out here and in there! Let's definitely get a hotdog out here too. Then I'll be ready for my FAVORITE stadium food!" Thea says.

They hang out and people-watch all of the fans coming through. It's not as wild as when the Yankees or Red Sox are in town. The Orioles are playing the Washington Nationals today, and Shyla gets plenty of teasing for her Red Sox shirt, but thankfully the crowd seem to take it in fun. Orioles fans are known for being pretty welcoming to opposing teams' fans, and since the Nationals are not a big rival, everyone seems pretty relaxed.

They get into the stadium just in time for the anthem, their purses filled with peanuts and pistachios to shell. As they make their way to their seats out in the center field "bleachers," they run into one of the stadium beer vendors, and Willow immediately starts to blush. Even though the guy is covered in sweat, his brown eyes seem to be laughing, and he still looks super attractive. Or maybe the sweat makes him more attractive, especially since his muscles are flexing carrying the bin of beer and ice, and his shirt might be just one size too small. The women can all see that there's something going on between these two.

"Hey ladies, who needs a beer?" he says.

"Me!" they all say at once.

Sol thinks that even at $10 per beer, the stadium beers are worth it just for the experience.

"Come see us in section ninety-four!" Willow calls out.

"Uh-huh," they all tease her.

"Spill the beans, Willow!" Sol cries out. "He is sooo cute!"

"It's no big deal," Willow protests.

"Yeah, right!" Thea says. "You can see the sparks flying through the air!"

"Okay, so we went out a couple times. I met him one day when I was walking Granola and he was playing ultimate frisbee in the park. I mean, Granola just happened to take off running to try to catch the frisbee and well…we may have gotten a little tangled," Willow explains.

"Oh, rEEEally? Tangled?!" Sol prods.

"Well…" Willow says.

"Spill it!" Thea cries.

"I'm meeting his mom tomorrow," Willow says with a giant smile on her red face.

"WHAT!?" they all say at once.

"They're having a cookout, and he invited me."

"Whoa, meeting the parents already! This is serious! Girl, I don't blame you at all!" Thea says.

Once they get settled in their seats, they start getting into the game, and Shyla says she has to admit that Oriole Park is kind of nice. Sol takes her for a tour around, and they get some pictures with the giant bobbleheads in the kids' area.

"I won't forget this," Shyla says.

"I'm so glad you could come!" Sol replies and gives her a hug.

The game is not super exciting since both of the starting pitchers have great records and keep the number of hits low. The women use the opportunity to continue chatting.

At the end of the fourth inning, Thea takes Shyla to get her favorite stadium food, the waffle fries with crab dip on top, while Willow and Sol scout out the new food places that have opened this year.

"Wow, you all really love your crabs here, huh?" Shyla says.

"Try one," Thea answers.

Shyla takes a fry covered with dip, and within seconds, she says, "We have to get back in line. I need my own! Those things are delicious!"

Meanwhile, Willow takes the opportunity to talk with Sol. "Okay," Willow says, "tell me what's really going on with you and Mom."

"I'm still mad at her, but I tried to play nice so Shyla didn't feel completely awkward. Plus, I was hoping meeting Shyla would change her mind a little. I was going to plan to stop by even if we hadn't run into them."

"Change her mind about what? What are you talking about?" Willow's brow is scrunched up in confusion.

"Will, I really need to tell someone, but I need you to promise to keep it to yourself." Sol doesn't know if it's a good idea to tell her, but she feels like it's too much to keep to herself. And maybe Willow can run some interference if she needs her.

"I will. You know you can trust me."

Sol swallows but doesn't say anything.

"Sol?" Willow says after a whole minute passes.

"Mom got approved to be a kidney donor for Janice," Sol finally whispers.

"What?!"

"But she doesn't want to donate," Sol adds.

"What? Why not?"

"I don't know. She says she's afraid of hospitals or whatever and is worried about who will run the shop. I don't know, whatever she said seemed like a really flimsy excuse to me. And I'm like, hello? You kept this secret from me all these years, and now you don't care if she lives or dies?!"

"Oh, Sol, now I understand better. I knew you were mad at her about the lying—and you have every right to be. But this? I'm really surprised."

"I know, I guess that's partly it. She has always taught us to be kind and serve other people, and you know she and Dad were like all about peace and love and volunteering, but now, in a real situation, she refuses. And it's not like it's a stranger! Well, I mean, kind of a stranger to her, I don't know." Sol stops talking long enough to get an order of nachos.

After they're done at the counter, Willow says, "Do you think she could still be jealous or something after all these years?"

"I mean, I guess. But would you let someone die over that?" Sol loads a nacho up with jalapeños and cheese and crams it in her mouth.

Just then, they hear, "Okay, now I see why you come here! This crab dip!" They turn around to see Thea and Shyla both carrying trays of food.

"You know it!" they reply.

Willow leans over to Sol. "We'll talk more later," she whispers.

They stay to the very end to see the Orioles win in the bottom of the ninth inning and to give Willow more time to flirt with her beer vendor guy. When she's not flirting with him, she looks around for guys for Sol and Shyla, as well as other potential guys for herself. Between the win and Willow's boy craziness, they have a great afternoon.

- 61 -

After Sol takes Shyla to the airport that night, she spends some time thinking about the weekend and pulls out her journal.

Dear God,

Thank you for a good weekend with Shyla. I didn't miss what you were saying about forgiveness, but I'm just so angry at Mom. I know you want me to forgive her, and I know you put me in that family for a reason. But I just can't do it on my own. I'm going to need you to help me to even want to forgive her. And Lord, I pray for Janice. If Mom won't donate, please send another living donor! I pray that she gets a new kidney and is able to live for many more years and that I can get to know her more. I know nothing's too hard for you, so please help. Thank you. Amen.

- 62 -

That Tuesday, Sol's mom texts her. *Can we talk? Please.*

Sol thinks through everything that has happened, especially the sermon about forgiveness.

Okay.

They agree to meet that evening at the arboretum again. Sol calls Thea on her way home, and they pray for the discussion.

"I need God to really help me because I am not feeling her at all right now," Sol says.

"Well, it's good that you're meeting with her. It's a step. Just see what she says," Thea replies.

After Sol takes care of Jericho and eats a quick dinner herself, she bumps his nose with her own and says, "Here goes."

Two months have passed since they first met here, and Patty told her the story of her birth. The trees are now all full of leaves and the flowers are in full bloom. There are people scattered here and there walking or playing on the expansive grounds. She sees her mom walking toward her wearing a flowy, patterned sundress and her favorite Birkenstocks. When they meet, Sol gives her mom a stiff hug, and they sit on the same bench as before. *In loving memory of Iris.* Sol thinks it seems fitting. *Here we are again,* she thinks.

Her mom toys with her wedding band, twisting it around and around on her finger. Sol watches the kids playing in the meadow, trying to guess their ages and what books they like to read. She's not going to be the one to talk first.

Finally, Patty turns to her. "Thanks for agreeing to talk with me, Sol. I know you're angry and you have every right to be upset that I kept the truth from you all these years."

Sol sits silently, staring straight ahead, her face set into a hard expression. She feels like they've already had this conversation.

Patty's own face gets a pleading look. "I wanted to ask you to forgive me. I know I don't deserve it. I know I was wrong, but I can't go back and do it right. I should have told you when you were a lot younger. I hope you didn't feel like I treated you differently at all. I always loved you just like the other girls. I thought I was doing the best thing, and then I was just scared."

Sol doesn't respond.

Patty tentatively takes Sol's hand and holds it. "Will you forgive me? Please, my precious daughter?"

They sit in silence, with Sol's mind racing. *Will I forgive her? I've been asking myself the same question,* she thinks.

Sol pulls her hand away but turns to look at her mom. "Mom, I honestly don't want to forgive you. I can't believe you did that to me—thirty-seven years. But I feel like God really is asking me to forgive you, and so I want to try. We even had a sermon on forgiveness at church on Sunday. So, I forgive you."

Patty starts crying and hugs Sol. "Thank you."

They sit for a while watching the evening shadows get longer. After some time, Patty says, "There's something else."

Sol looks at her and shakes her head. "Mom, no, I don't think I can handle anything else right now."

Patty smiles like she has a secret and says, "I think you'll be happy."

"Oh, okay. I guess you can tell me then." Sol braces herself for the worst.

"I changed my mind about donating a kidney to Janice. I'm going to do it."

"What?!" Sol stares intently at her mom.

"It's the same as how you feel about forgiving me. I don't *want* to do it, but I feel like maybe it's what I'm supposed to do. I was surprised by how upset you were when I said I decided not to. So I've been thinking about it a lot. I talked to Mickey some more, and we figured out a plan to make it work. I mean, I want to do it for you. To make up a little bit for keeping you from her all these years. So you can have longer to know her."

"Oh wow, Mom. I'm in shock. Thank you so much! I can't wait to tell Shyla!" Sol smiles involuntarily, and she feels tears on her face.

"It was so good to meet her this past weekend. I'm glad she could come down."

"Me too! So can I tell her?"

"Now?"

"What better time?"

Sol pulls out her phone and video calls Shyla. Shyla answers right away with a surprised look on her face.

"Everything okay?" she says. "I just got home from work and was trying to change real quick to head back out to my swing dancing class, but then I ran into this old friend in the parking lot so I'm really running behind, and I can't find the shoes I wanted to wear—"

"Shyla? Hi, yes, everything's okay. But Mom and I have some good news and wanted to tell you right away."

"Oh! Got it! Hi, Mrs. Thompson!"

"Hi, Shyla! Sol, do you want me to tell her?" Sol nods and Patty proceeds, "I got approved as a kidney donor for your mom, and I want to donate."

"What?!" Shyla says and breaks into tears. "Oh my gosh, I can't believe this—are you serious?" Shyla continues crying and laughing at the same time.

"Yes, I'm serious. I want to give you all as many years as possible together."

"Sol told me you got tested with her, but I thought it was just moral support. I never thought you'd be a match or that you would really consider doing it! Or I guess I never even asked if you were. But this is amazing! I can't wait to tell Mom! She is not going to believe it at all! Then we can figure out when we can schedule the surgery. The sooner, the better. When can you come up? Don't worry, you'll be in and out. Sol knows the routine from the last surgery. Then you'll just take it easy for a couple weeks. I'll book you into the best hotel here, right by the hospital to make it as convenient as possible. Sol, you'll come, right? I'll get you adjoining rooms—"

"Yes, thank you, Shyla," Patty says. "That sounds good. We'll figure out all the details. You're right, Sol agreed not to say anything about my results until I had some time to think about it. But now that I've decided, she wanted to tell you right away!"

"Oh my gosh, I still can't believe it. Oh my goodness, I still have to get going to my class. I'll call you tomorrow, okay, Sol? Give your mom a big hug for me!"

They hang up, and Sol leans over and gives her mom a hug. "Thanks, Mom."

- 63 -

Dear God,

Wow, you work fast! I can't believe Mom changed her mind about donating. Now I just need you to let Janice's body accept Mom's kidney and work with it! Please!

So was that tied up with my decision to forgive Mom? The timing seemed too perfect to be a coincidence. I still need you to help me forgive her every day and move forward.

I also need help with still figuring out this whole identity thing. Maybe it's easier because I've built a whole life already, or maybe it's harder because this whole life I've built wasn't based on knowing the whole truth. Where do I go from here? I definitely need to find a therapist who deals with identity issues or maybe adoption issues. The support groups seemed helpful too, so maybe I'll start there. Guide me to the right thing. Amen.

- 64 -

Sol logs on again to the website for people who found out they had a different parent than they thought. She's not feeling as fragile now as she was when she first looked into it. She's had a little time to get used to the new information about herself. She realizes that her story could have been a lot worse. She just has more family now, but since she is older, it doesn't have to be the main thing that defines her. It's not like she needs a parent to provide food and shelter at this point, and she doesn't have to live with her siblings.

She knows from working with her students that the stories can be heartbreaking. She works to help them continue to develop and create more hope and tools for building their own stories. She also just knows the value in showing up for them every day and being an adult who cares about them. She thinks there can probably never be too many of those.

On the other hand, some of the "nontraditional" families she's gotten to know have been the most beautiful—people choosing to love and serve one another, working together to fill a gap with a strong foundation. The older she gets, the more she knows that things aren't so clearly delineated, and A plus B can equal all sorts of things.

She hasn't followed up on her application to join the private discussion group. She scrolls through her email and finds a link to get into the group. As she browses the topics that people have posted about, one word comes to mind: shame. It isn't everyone's story, but Sol notices that a lot of the secrets and lies and cover-ups came from pregnancies that weren't supposed to happen based on the circumstances. Everything from children born from rape and incest, which Sol could understand not wanting to talk about, to teenage moms, affairs, sperm donors. Sometimes it was more about keeping it a secret from the spouse than keeping it a secret from the child. But in all of these stories, the child was hurt. How can you address pain if you keep it covered up? What information do we have a right to know as humans?

Certainly, most people want to know the truth about their identity, even if it's negative. Most of the secrets posted about in the group came out due to DNA testing. Everyone reacted in different ways. Sol wonders if she should post. She doesn't know if she's ready to "go public" with the news, even though she knows it's not really public since it's a private group. She hasn't even told anyone beyond her own family and Thea. And Franklin, of course. She does a private eye roll about that. It feels good to know she's not alone, though. She continues to read the stories and thinks how things have changed so much. With the rising popularity of DNA testing, what could before be hidden forever is now bound to come out. But with social media and all the online groups, it also means you don't have to go through it alone.

As she's browsing through, she does a double take when she sees someone post about counseling. She reads that there are now counselors who specialize in working with people like the ones in the group (aka NPEs—not parent expected), usually because they are one themselves. This seems like a message from God or something since she keeps putting her own counselor search on the back burner. She clicks on the link and immediately sends emails to five of the counselors before she can change her mind.

She guesses she should also look into the whole kidney donation thing more too if Mom is going to donate. When Gordon was donating, she didn't have to do anything, she just showed up to be supportive. She tries to remember everything she and Patty learned when they went to the transplant center for their testing and counseling.

There are lots of great resources online to learn more about the process, but she keeps getting caught up in people's stories. She tears up several times as she reads about people dying waiting for a kidney or a best friend who donated to save their friend's life. There is even a pop star who got a transplant from her best friend.

She finds out that some other countries have you opt out instead of opting in to being an organ donor, and that has helped with the number of available organs. She doesn't want to think about the organ black market, like Shyla mentioned, but she's starting to understand how people can get to the point where they see that as their only option. But it looks like the US has a way to go to make organ donation an attractive option, from paying for recovery time to simply increasing public education. Sol thinks she registered to be an organ donor years ago, but she checks her driver's license to see if it's on there. It is. But of course that's only if she dies and her organs are still usable and useful.

She emails her boss, Zakirah, while it's on her mind to request a meeting. She wants to get time off to be there for the surgery, and she thinks it's time to fill Zakirah in on everything. They have a good working relationship, but Sol doesn't consider them to be close. Thankfully it's summer, so the program is a little slower since they're aligned with the school year. They take the time to do a lot of foundational and operations work, as well as working on marketing and programs for the upcoming year. Sol's pilot program to get the volunteers more involved with policy change at the city, state, and federal level has been approved for the upcoming school year, and she's hoping to get some results so they can continue to get funding for it in the coming years.

Sol figures she can at least be checking in and put in a few hours of work while she travels and helps take care of her two moms. Wow, her two moms. She hopes Mickey and her sisters will also be able to take some time off. Her mom will want to come back here to recover, right? So Sol will be torn between being in Massachusetts and here? She knows that both of them have big circles of people to support them, so she's not a sole caregiver or anything, but she feels pressure since she's the tie between the two families. *Well, Dad was, wasn't he?* she thinks bitterly. She shakes her head and tries to shake the thought off. *Lord, help me to remember the blessing here,* she quickly prays. She's so glad to have met Shyla and Janice and the rest of the family and know more about who she is. But she thinks she's still in shock a little bit. It's been a whirlwind. She sits there and hops from thought to thought, from website to website.

- 65 -

"Be a good boy for Aunt Faye," Sol tells Jericho as she drops him off at her friend's apartment. After three weeks of planning and coordinating, Sol, Patty, and Willow are flying to Boston. Mickey will drive up later since he couldn't get away early.

It's amazing how they can just schedule the transplant like an elective surgery. For the people who are on the waiting list and get a kidney from a deceased donor, they have to have a suitcase packed, stay in town, and be ready to go any day, whenever a kidney becomes available. And that could take years.

"Mom, what books did you bring to read?" Sol asks. "That's one thing I love about traveling. I'm on this airplane and even though they have Wi-Fi, I pretend they don't so I can take a break from work emails and messages."

Patty pulls a book out of her bag and holds it up. "I brought this book about online marketing and how to build a successful online store. Mickey and I are planning for the whole store to convert to online in the next couple years. I can't believe you all are coming with me today. But I'm so glad. It's like a family trip, even though it's not exactly a pleasure cruise. Too bad Dove isn't here. What should we do for sightseeing today? This will probably be my only chance. And you girls have never been there, so we have to do some touristy stuff!"

"Definitely!" says Willow, who leans in from the row behind theirs. "I was looking online at all the must-see things there. We have a lot to pack in! If we do the Freedom Trail walking tour thing, we can see a bunch of stuff on the way. Are you up for that, Mom?"

"Let's try it! I haven't been there in what, forty years? I do remember going to this great stall in the market there. They had jewelry from all over the world and stories about the people that had made it." As she's talking, Patty holds up two pretty handmade necklaces she's wearing right now, as if to demonstrate. "They really inspired me when I was planning my own store. Of course, that could've been at the market in Philadelphia too—I can't remember. So many years have gone by!"

"You're not that old!" Sol and Willow both say and laugh.

None of them get very far in their books because the flight is so short, and they get caught up in their sightseeing plans.

After they land, they make their way to the hotel and take a few minutes to freshen up. Willow tells Sol she's convinced all of the guys here will look like Matt Damon or Ben Affleck, so she needs a few extra minutes to do her makeup—just in case. They decide to take an Uber over to the Old South Meeting House so they can quickly start their tour and from there walk toward Quincy Market where Patty may possibly have gone to a jewelry stall forty years ago.

At each historical marker, Patty imitates a tour guide as she reads from the descriptions on her phone. Sol is glad that her mom seems happy and they have these activities to keep them occupied rather than thinking about the surgery all day and night. When they get to Faneuil Hall and Quincy Market, they discover that a lot has changed since Patty was last here. It's more like a mall than the little stands that Sol was expecting. She decides that it's the perfect time to buy some gifts to bring back to Faye to thank her for watching Jericho since it's a tourists' paradise. She tries to find the cheesiest things imaginable and ends up buying socks that look like lobsters, a keychain that says Boston slang phrases, and a tin of Boston Harbour Tea. Patty finds some beautiful, handmade scarves from Cambodia and decides to buy herself one to commemorate the occasion. Willow buys two essential oils she can't find at home.

After their shopping, they are all ready to eat and head to the North End where Willow has picked out an Italian restaurant for them. As they're finishing up their pasta, Mickey texts Patty to say he made it to the hotel, so they order him some lasagna to go. He says he can come pick them up, but Sol insists he meet them at the famous cannoli place instead of the restaurant. As they walk the two blocks over, they see a crowd of people on the sidewalk and wonder what's going on. As they get closer, they realize that Mike's Pastry really is famous and there's a line out the door. Twenty minutes later, it's finally their turn to order, and they decide to splurge on a dozen cannolis just to make it worth it. As they push their way out of the shop, they spot Mickey's car down the street, and Willow quickly stops for an

Italian ice from a street vendor on the way.

On the short ride back to the hotel, Sol gets a text from Dove: *Hey, are you with Mom?* She shows it to Willow. Willow shrugs. Sol hasn't talked to Dove in weeks, and she remembers that Patty had said Dove was upset when she had told her the truth about everything.

Yes, we're headed back to the hotel from sightseeing. Sol texts back what she hopes is a neutral answer.

I still can't believe you got her involved in this. Dove's reply tells Sol there's nothing neutral she can say. But Sol decides that now is not the time to deal with Dove's anger.

We'll have to talk later. Love you, Sol texts back, and puts her phone away.

- 66 -

The coffee they make in their hotel rooms is enough to get them out the door the next morning but won't keep them going for too long. They are supposed to be at the transplant center at 7:00 a.m. Sol keeps thinking about the café that she and Shyla had gone to the last time they were here and hopes she can make a trip over there ASAP. Sol, Willow, Patty, and Mickey run-walk the one downtown block from the hotel to the center, passing morning garbage trucks and commuters. The rest of the huge hospital campus looms around them. Once they enter, they find themselves directed to the same area as for Janice's first surgery.

Shyla and Calvin are already there, and somehow they've stopped by Dunkin' and have loads of doughnuts and coffee. Sol thinks that's a good start to the day! Shyla introduces Patty, Mickey, and Willow to her dad. "This time it's your turn to fill up the waiting room!" Shyla says. "Thanks again, everyone, for supporting Patty in donating. It means so much to us! And I'm glad I get to see you again too!"

Patty has to say hello quickly and go back to prep for the surgery, but for the rest of the crew, it's time to hurry up and wait. Calvin says the rest of the family will be coming later. They seem to have adjusted their plans this time based on the first surgery. Sol doesn't mind because it gives her a chance to visit with them without feeling like there are too many relationships to manage. And she appreciates the time to get some sugar and caffeine flowing through her body.

As they dig into their doughnuts and coffee, there's no sound except chewing. Shyla gets through two doughnuts and one cup of coffee, then gives Mickey and Willow a brief overview of what to expect for the day. Patty's surgery will be first and will take a couple of hours.

They take their time eating, taking trips to the restroom, and checking out the rest of the floor. After a while, Shyla says to Mickey, "I didn't get to really talk to you all at the winery. I want to know all about the girls when they were young. I'm sure you have lots of stories!"

"Oh, do I ever! Where to begin?" Mickey jokes. "Should I tell them the one with the shark?"

Sol and Willow groan.

"Okay, okay, not that one," Mickey says. "Well, she's not here to defend herself, so I'll start by telling a story about Dove. She was the one that gave me the hardest time when I started dating Patty. But I guess it makes sense because she was the oldest. You know the way I won her over? Playing office! I have my own business, so I would give her office supplies, give her old checkbooks for expired accounts, and let her write checks, and before you knew it, she had created a whole fictional business, and I just acted as her assistant! Now seeing her in the corporate world, it makes perfect sense!"

Sol thinks Shyla probably got Mickey talking on

purpose so he wouldn't be sitting there thinking about Patty's surgery. There will be enough hours in the day to worry. That's a story she had never heard. Leave it to Shyla! Sol wonders what other stories he might tell.

Mickey continues, "Now it's Sol's turn for a story. Sol has always loved dogs, so when she was little, she would sometimes take care of dogs in the neighborhood. It was the day of Willow's birthday—Willow, was that your tenth birthday?—and Patty had made her this huge chocolate cake and decorated it with Backstreet Boys—remember that band? Anyway, Sol had brought the dog over to our house for a few hours. The next thing you know, Patty walks through the kitchen, comes back out, and says, 'Mickey, did you put the cake somewhere?' We couldn't find the cake she had made anywhere! Then we see the dog. Wiggles. His white coat was covered in so much chocolate, he looked like a Dalmatian! He ate that entire cake!"

"Oh my gosh, I forgot about that!" Sol adds. "And then I had to stay out in the yard the rest of the afternoon to see if Wiggles would get sick! But it didn't seem to bother him one bit!"

"I'm still mad at that dog for eating my Backstreet Boys cake!" Willow says, mock pouting. They all laugh.

"Now isn't it time for Calvin to tell us a story about Shyla?" Sol asks.

Calvin looks startled when Sol says his name. "Dad, are you okay?" Shyla asks.

"Oh, yeah. Sorry, I was just thinking," he answers, rousing himself from his thoughts. "A story about Shyla, huh? I think we have a Backstreet Boys story too."

"No way!" Shyla retorts. "New Kids on the Block forever!"

"Oh yeah, sorry to mix up the boy bands," Calvin says, teasing Shyla.

All of a sudden, they hear a voice: "I hope you saved a couple of doughnuts for me!" Great-Aunt Tabitha comes around the corner laughing, followed by Aunt Jackie.

Sol and Willow stiffen a little seeing Aunt Jackie. Shyla takes it upon herself to introduce everyone since she's now familiar with all of them ,and Sol is thankful for her chattiness.

"It's like déjà vu all over again, isn't it?" Great-Aunt Tabitha says to Sol and Willow. "I can't believe we're back here in this same waiting room. But we're so blessed to have your mom donating. It's a feat to find just one living donor, much less two."

Sol just smiles at her and squeezes her hand. Aunt Jackie surprises them by smiling and being friendly and warm.

"What's going on with her?" Sol whispers to Shyla as they look over to see Aunt Jackie laughing with Calvin.

"I don't know, but I bet Aunt Tab had something to do with it," Shyla whispers back. "Or maybe she has miraculously mellowed in the last couple of months."

Shyla, Sol, and Willow go back to flipping through their magazines while keeping one eye on Aunt Jackie. Mickey must have forgotten about what Sol said about the first surgery visit because he acts as friendly as ever.

After a few minutes of chatting with Calvin, Great-Aunt Tabitha takes the seat next to Sol and says loudly, "So did you find a man on that dating site yet?"

"Don't worry about Sol," Shyla fires back. "What about you, Aunt Tab? You said you were going to set up a profile too."

"Believe me, I have enough men without adding anybody from that matchmaking site. All I have to do is whip up one of my famous desserts, and they line up for my number. Now, as to who I will actually give the time of day, that is another story. I'm still looking for one that is worth giving up all the others for! But I stay entertained!"

"So does that mean you have to keep baking for them to keep them interested?" Sol asks.

"No, baby, that's just to get their attention. But I do surprise them with a treat every now and then to let them know I see when they're taking good care of me. I believe they call that 'positive reinforcement,'" she says and laughs. "So what happened with you? Have you had any dates with new people?"

"Honestly, the last time I checked, no one was interested. But it's been a while! I've been so busy with everything else."

"Too busy for a love life? Well, I guess it does take some effort at the beginning."

"Definitely effort to sift through them and get through the first date, if they make it that far!"

"Right, and then you can just put them on a maintenance plan!" Great-Aunt Tabitha says. "Well, listen, we have time to kill today, so hand your phone on over to me, and I'll sift through some of them for you! Don't worry, I have good taste!"

Shyla leans over and whispers, "Actually, she really does."

"Sure, why not? That will give me an excuse not to be on my work email all day." Sol laughs and opens up the dating app and hands it to her great-aunt. "Just swipe left for the guys who should get left and right for the ones that might be Mr. Right!"

Shyla leans over Great-Aunt Tabitha's phone to see the dating app and give her input. Sol looks across the room, and it seems like Calvin, Mickey, and Jackie are having a serious conversation. She leans back in her chair and closes her eyes. It looks like Willow has already dozed off.

When Sol wakes up, Great-Aunt Tabitha hands Sol's phone back to her. "Okay," she says, "I found a few contenders on there! Now it's up to you to follow up! Let me know how it goes!"

Sol laughs and thanks her and assures her she'll keep her posted. She starts looking to see who Great-Aunt Tabitha has selected for her.

A few minutes later, the surgeon comes out to tell them that Patty's surgery is done, and she did awesomely. Sol, Willow, and Mickey all hug each other. *Thank you, Lord!* Sol says a silent prayer. The Broward side of the family smiles and claps. The surgeon says Janice's surgery will be next, and that will take several more hours.

"Phew," says Mickey. "I'm glad that's over. I'm going to go get some fresh air. Can I bring anyone anything?"

They all decline his offer, but as he's walking away, Calvin jumps up and jogs after him. Sol sees Calvin put a hand on Mickey's shoulder and hears him say, "Hey, let's talk for a minute while you walk."

"Don't worry, I'll text Dove," Willow says.

"Thanks, Will."

They all turn their attention to their phones for a few minutes. Suddenly, Sol hears a sharp intake of breath from

Shyla and looks up to see a man walking into the waiting room with a happy face balloon. "Who is that?" Sol says to Shyla. But Shyla has already stood up and is walking over to him.

"Oh, you don't know who that is?" Great-Aunt Tabitha says. "That's her boyfriend, Mark."

"What do you mean boyfriend? I thought they broke up," Sol asks, surprised.

"Well, take it from me, I don't think they're going to stay broken up much longer. Did she tell you the story? Something about her being black and him being white and working at the same law firm, etc., etc. Flimsy excuse, if you ask me. He's a nice young man. He better hurry up and propose, though, because Shyla is a catch! She won't stay single long!"

The next moment, Shyla walks over with the rugged-looking stranger in tow and introduces him. "Sol, this is my friend from work, Mark. Mark, this is my long-lost sister, Sol! Her mom is the one donating to our mom. Okay, that sounded a little confusing, but I think you know the backstory. And here's her younger sister, Willow, and her dad, Mickey, is here too. Can you believe they all came up for this? Sol, I was so surprised that Mark showed up. I told him about mom's surgery, but I didn't know he was coming. He said he wanted to be here too. Plus, he has known her for what, like three years? Anyway, we'll be back; we're going to just see if we can drop this balloon off in her room."

"Nice to meet you, Mark. I've heard so much about you," Sol says. When he turns around, Sol raises her eyebrows at Shyla, silently telling her, *We have a lot to talk about!*

The rest of them sit in silence, each caught up in reading a magazine, being on their phones, or "resting their eyes." All of a sudden, Willow calls out, "Does anyone have a six-letter word for 'crescent-shaped legume'?" and they all start laughing.

"Why are you laughing? I'm so close to finishing this crossword!"

"KIDNEY!" they yell out together.

"Oh yeah!" says Willow laughing and playfully hitting her forehead with her palm.

Calvin comes back and says he and Mickey found a TV in a lounge down the hall if anyone is interested. "*The Price Is Right* is still on after all these years!"

Mickey comes back after a while with fresh newspapers and magazines. Turns out he went back to the hotel and took a short nap. They all spend the next few hours in and out of the room, walking around, looking out the window, checking out the gift shop, going for food, and updating each other on what they find. Shyla tells them that the rest of their family decided to come tomorrow instead, so hopefully they can actually see Janice, but they are thinking about her and want Shyla to send hourly updates. The Salt and Pepper twins are in charge of disseminating information to the rest of the family.

Finally, a different surgeon comes out to say that Janice's surgery is done, and everything went well.

They all hug one another. Calvin and Mickey both look relieved. Aunt Jackie asks if everyone wants to come over to her house for dinner later, and Sol and Shyla look at each other as if to say, *What's going on with Aunt Jackie?*

They make a pile of gifts and cards for Calvin and Mickey to deliver to Janice and Patty when they are allowed to see them. The men are planning to hang out as long as they need to in order to see their wives. The rest of them disperse with plans to reconvene at Aunt Jackie's house later.

"Phew, I'm exhausted from the stress of this! Plus I'm hungry!" Willow says.

"Let's get pizza and go back to the hotel for naps!" Sol says. "Shyla, do you want to join us?"

"Aw, thanks, Sol, but I'll see you later at Aunt Jackie's. Mark and I are going to grab lunch. I know she said you don't have to bring anything, but I'll tell you Aunt Jackie does have a weakness for fancy cheese if you want to make an extra-good impression."

Sol gives her a wide-eyed look while Mark isn't looking and gives her a quick hug. "Thanks for the insider information! See you there!"

- 67 -

Sol and Willow take Mickey's car that evening to go to Aunt Jackie's house. Mickey is still at the hospital. Sol hopes she can navigate these "rotaries" that seem to be on every road in Massachusetts. Willow holds two chunks of specialty cheese as their gifts for Aunt Jackie. It turns out there was a Whole Foods right next to the transplant center, so they were able to find some good ones pretty easily. Not that Sol knew much about the cheese world beyond the basics, but the cheese expert at the store helped them with recommendations.

Sol has spent the afternoon thinking about the family dynamics of the two families and herself as a bridge in the middle. Well, maybe she's not the only bridge anymore now that Janice has one of Patty's kidneys. It was really Aunt Jackie who made all of that happen, though she probably didn't predict it would work out quite that way. Sol finds herself wondering more and more what Aunt Jackie, Janice, and her mom are all thinking. She wonders whether she will ever know the answers or whether they even know the answers.

She has heard back from three of the counselors she contacted and is glad she has some appointments coming up. This is the twistiest life story. Either way, she's thankful she had a loving family to grow up in. It was the secrets that have recently been revealed that have shaken her. Maybe she should thank Aunt Jackie tonight for being the one who started the reveals in motion.

After a few wrong turns, they pull up to the house almost on time and find Great-Aunt Tabitha in the front yard playing with an adorable little chihuahua. "Oh, Ferdinand and I thought we'd wait out front for you so we could be the welcome committee!" she says as they disembark.

They each hug her and pet the dog, then head to the front door. "Thanks, Great-Aunt Tabitha! It's good to see you! Is this your dog?"

"No, he's Jacqueline's dog but I pretend he's mine whenever I want, and Jackie doesn't mind if I borrow him from time to time. It's a win-win!"

Sol laughs. "Aw, I understand! Dogs are great, but they're a lot of work! My dog is staying with my friend Faye while I'm gone, and I bought her three thank-you gifts already! He loves it, though. He thinks I don't know how much they spoil him when I'm away! Just like with kids, it's good for them to have an extended family!"

As they make their way inside, Sol sees that Jackie is in the kitchen and Shyla is out back managing the grill. She greets Aunt Jackie and gives her the fresh sheep milk pecorino Toscano cheese she brought. "What can I do to help?" she asks.

"Hello, Sol. Thanks so much for the cheese. How did you know this was one of my favorites? We're all set in here, but you can go out back and see if Shyla needs anything," Aunt Jackie replies with a smile.

Sol heads out back and sees that Willow is trying out a game of croquet. "I told her to try it so she would stop hovering over me and asking if I needed anything!" Shyla says and laughs.

"Well, then I guess I won't ask you if you need anything," Sol says.

"Actually, I didn't want to put Willow to work, but you are a different story! Can you put these veggie shish kebabs together for me? They're inspired by Willow, but I'm excited to try them too! I found the recipe when I was looking online, and they seemed easy enough. You know cooking is not really my thing, but I'm pretty good on the grill! Plus Aunt Jackie is a great cook, so we don't have to worry. She will let me know if my stuff is not good! Anyway, I got the chicken cooked already. Yikes, hopefully it's done in the middle. Ooo, and try out this sangria I made. I may not be a great cook, but I can definitely mix some stuff together and make it taste good! Did you all get a nap today? It was such an early morning again. I was so tired but also wired—"

"Stop right there, Ms. 'I Broke Up with My Boyfriend'! What was Mark doing at the hospital, and did you think you would get away with not spilling every single detail? And what happened at lunch? You wanted a sister—this is what sisters do!"

"I know, I know, I was going to tell you!"

"Uh-huh." Willow comes up to stand beside Sol; they both stare at Shyla with wide eyes.

"Well, I guess I'm trying to still figure it out myself. But he knows Mom, and he wanted to support her."

"Well, he wasn't at the first surgery," Sol says.

"I didn't tell him when the first surgery was. I didn't know he would show up today either, but we were talking about it the other day. And he knew how worried I was when Mom's body rejected Gordon's kidney. Who could have known that Patty would come through?!"

"Well, that was nice of him. So what's the latest on what you're thinking about him? And wasn't he dating someone new?"

"He is a nice guy. But it didn't work out for us. I thought he was dating someone new too, but I guess not anymore."

"And is it worth trying again?" Willow asks.

"Maybe." Shyla starts humming and returns to tending the food on the grill.

"The humming says it all, Shyla!" Sol laughs. "So did you figure out what's going on with Aunt Jackie?"

"I think she's going to bring something up at dinner. But that's just a guess. She hasn't said anything to me. I've been here since 5:00 p.m. and keep dropping hints, and I've been snooping around too. I asked Great-Aunt Tabitha, and she just smiled and said life is a highway. Who knew she listened to pop music?! I think she definitely knows what's up but is not going to say. Oh, she brought some homemade coconut cake too! Save room for that!"

Just then, Aunt Jackie pops her head out the door and says, "We'll be ready in ten minutes! How's my grill master?"

Shyla gives her a thumbs-up.

Fifteen minutes later, they've all piled up their plates and gathered around the table. Aunt Jackie clinks her glass and asks for their attention. "Keep eating, keep eating. I just have a few things I want to say. You're probably wondering why I wanted you to come over. I know I gave you a hard time when I first met you, Sol. And I said some things about your father that hurt you. So I wanted to apologize. I'm sorry.

"I don't want to make excuses, but it's been hard for me too because I just want the best for my sister. Her kidney disease has been affecting her ever since she was in her forties. I don't know how much you know about her story, and I don't think she would volunteer it on her own, but there are some things I wanted to share. And I want you to hear it from me. I was there. You're sisters, so you know what it's like when something is going on with one of your sisters. When Janice got pregnant by your father, we were all devastated. First of all, we didn't even know she was seeing him. Then she found out he was married. And white. And then she got so sick during the pregnancy, we didn't know if she might die giving birth."

Even though Aunt Jackie had told them to keep eating, they have all put their food down and are listening intently.

"But she was so committed to having you, despite the circumstances. We wanted to protect her, but there was no protecting her when her heart was already tied to you. So I went down when I could to try to help take care of her while she was pregnant. I visited her in the hospital and saw your sonograms. She would not see your father at all. She wasn't in love with him by any means, but she was in a bad place. She was so angry that he had not told her about being married, and at that point, she felt used by him. She had all the hormone ups and downs of pregnancy and that didn't help. Already, her law career was derailed, and she was feeling lost. I tried to be an anchor for her. She was completely torn about what to do once she had you. I told her we could raise you together, that I would help her. Our parents wanted to help her too, but none of us had much money. Even when she got preeclampsia and had to go on bed rest, she still refused to give me your dad's number and was determined to keep you.

"It was only after she gave birth to you, and we saw the first bill from the hospital for almost $50,000 that her mind started to change. I told her I would help her, and we would figure it out. She said, 'No, Jackie, you have your own life to live.' I had just gotten a new job as a bailiff at the courthouse here and was seeing a guy I thought I might marry. She said, 'There's no way I can keep this baby. I won't even have money to buy diapers! I don't even know how I'll take care of myself.'

"And that was that. She never changed her mind. She wouldn't give in to me trying to persuade her. She knew this decision would change her life forever. When she asked me to call your father to ask if he would take you, I went off on her. I thought he was a player. I thought there was no way that he could be a responsible father. Although I still have some negative feelings toward him, he and Patty did right by you, Sol. I'm sorry you lost him."

Willow puts her arm around Sol's shoulders and gives her a squeeze. Sol leans her head against Willow's.

"I kept an eye on you ever since you were born. I was always thinking I could go get you if needed. You are still my sister's baby. I have friends in Baltimore that were my eyes. Once your father died, I didn't know how your mom would be able to handle the three of you, and again, thought

I could rescue you if needed. Janice said she always knew she made the right decision, and she was confident they would take good care of you. She is a lot more trusting than me, but I'm glad it worked out. I didn't want to be right. She missed you so much, but she tried not to dwell on it. She thought it would make it harder. Once she married Calvin and had Shyla, she tried to stay focused on them. I would send her updates if I found anything out. Of course, the rise of the internet and social media made it easier. She was really proud of you, but she still didn't want to rock the boat even as you got older. Of course, the older you got, the harder she thought it would be for the truth to come out.

"And now we've come full circle. The truth is all out. It's time for forgiveness and new life. Look at how you've turned out. You're a beautiful, wonderful, generous woman. I'm proud to be your aunt. And Willow, I'm happy to have you as my niece too! And hopefully I'll get to meet Dove one day too. Cheers to our new extended family!" They all raise their glasses for a toast, and when Sol looks around, she sees that everyone is trying to hold back their tears or just letting them flow down their faces.

Sol takes a minute to collect herself, then says, "Thanks, Aunt Jackie! I think I understand more now what you said when we first met. I really do owe so much to you, from before I was born to now getting a chance to meet Shyla and Janice and all of you. So let me propose a toast to you, my long-lost aunt, the one who makes things happen! Cheers!"

The rest of the evening passes with funny stories from both sides of Sol's family. Aunt Jackie pulls out some photos of Shyla when she was little, and they all ooh and aah over her and pictures of Janice when she was younger. When it's time to say goodbye, Aunt Jackie hands Sol an envelope.

"I found this a few months ago when I was thinking about Janice's story. It's a picture of Janice when she was pregnant with you. I think you should have it," she says.

Sol throws her arms around Aunt Jackie. "Thank you so much! You don't know how much this means to me!"

"You're welcome, Sol. And I want to let you know that I'm here for you, and I'm sorry for the way this all happened."

Sol feels something cold on her bare toes that are sticking out of her sandals. She looks down to see Ferdinand licking her foot. She stoops down, picks him up, and gives him a hug. "Thanks, Ferdinand." She shakes her head and laughs.

- 68 -

Dear God,

Wow, I can't believe this day. This is a major one. So much has happened in the past few months. There I was, just going about my life, never knowing there were all these secrets hidden beneath the surface and drama about to take place. Would I have written this story for myself? No, I think I would have made things a little easier. But without all the drama, I guess I wouldn't be here. And then I could easily have gotten aborted or given to another family. Every little thing had to line up for this to happen.

And then Mom matching Janice for a kidney?!!! That was really, really unexpected. I mean, I didn't even know if I would get tested, much less donate! And here we are. You are a really surprising God. Lord, I pray that this transplant is successful. I pray that Janice's body doesn't reject it. Give her many more years to live.

I pray for our relationship. Help me to get to know her in whatever capacity you want me to know her now. Help me to forgive them all. I don't want to stay trapped in my anger and hurt. I don't want to pass on a legacy of secrets and bitterness. Help me to heal, now that the wounds are exposed.

Thank you so much for Thea and my sisters. My *three* sisters! I don't know what's happening with Dove, but help us to get to a good place. And then Aunt Jackie added a whole other dimension to the day with her apology and revelations. I'm so glad I don't have to have a tense relationship with her. It seems like she's coming to terms with everything too. She just has that big sister protective thing for Janice. I can't believe she gave me this picture of Janice when she was pregnant with me. It feels like such a missing piece and helps me to picture their lives back in the day. She was so young!

And what about Dad? He has stayed pretty fixed in my mind until now. I don't really have many memories of him, but at least we have photos. But this whole thing has added another dimension to the story of him. What do you do with the story of someone who has died? Can that change over time with new information? Can you tell the truth without feeling like you're disrespecting them? I guess I thought he wasn't really affecting me, but maybe he still is. Is that why my relationships with guys haven't worked out? Am I waiting for them to abandon me?

Phew, I'm so glad I'll be starting my counseling soon! Thank you, Holy Spirit, that you are our counselor too! Amen.

- 69 -

This is as disheveled as Sol has seen Calvin yet, and probably ever will. She can tell he tried to straighten himself up, while Mickey didn't even bother. They both have stubble on their faces, and Sol slips Mickey a piece of mint gum. The husbands have spent the night at the hospital, both unwilling to leave their wives, and Shyla, Sol, and Willow have come to relieve them. Willow wanted to stop by the gift shop on the way in, and Shyla and Sol had continued upstairs. After greeting their dads, Sol goes to Patty's room, and Shyla goes to Janice's room. "Time for a shower!" Mickey calls as he leaves.

"Mom! How are you feeling?" Sol says as she sees her mom sitting up in bed waiting for her. Her mom looks okay but nowhere near her normal level of energy.

"Hi, sweetie. I feel good, a little tired. But I want you to do something for me. Will you ask the nurse to bring a wheelchair for me?"

"Sure, Mom. Do you want to go for a little walk? This room is getting a little stuffy, I guess." Sol quickly pops into the hallway for a nurse, determined to do whatever she can to help her mom.

When she comes back, her mom says, "Yes, I want to

go on a very short walk to Janice's room. There's something that I want to say to her."

"Oh, okay. Let me tell Shyla we're coming over." Sol sends her a quick text, not knowing what to expect from this talk her mom wants to have with her other mom.

"How do I look?" Patty asks, straining her neck to see her reflection in the glass.

"Like you just had surgery and spent the night in the hospital! But still gorgeous, of course!" Sol tells her.

"Ha ha, thanks, Sol," her mom says as she fluffs her hair and quickly puts on ChapStick.

The nurse helps her mom into the wheelchair, and as Sol pushes her into the hallway, she sees Willow just starting to come off the elevator. She gives her a one-minute signal with her finger before her mom can see her and quickly turns to wheel her mom in the opposite direction.

When they reach Janice's room, Sol knocks lightly on the door, and it looks like Shyla has been helping Janice with some beauty touchups of her own.

"Wheel me right next to her bed, please," Patty requests. Once she's at Janice's right arm, Patty reaches out her hand for a handshake and says, "Nice to finally meet you, Janice."

Janice returns the handshake and says, "You too. Who would have guessed we would meet like this? And after all these years."

"Not me. It's been a long time." They look at each other thoughtfully.

Shyla and Sol take seats by the window and try to give their mothers some space. At the same time, they don't start a conversation of their own and strain their ears to hear every word the women are saying over the noise from the air conditioning and hallway.

"It has been a really long time. I can't believe you gave me a kidney. Thank you. I know thanks will never be enough but thank you from the bottom of my heart. You gave me another chance," Janice begins.

Patty nods and dabs at her eyes with a tissue. "Janice, honestly, it was a really hard decision for me, but in the end, I realized it's the least I could do. That's what I wanted to come over here and say. You entrusted Sol to us and gave me and Patrick a new chance. Who's to say what could have happened if you had made different decisions or been a different person?"

Patty looks down and plays with the tissue in her hands. "I really owe everything to you. I should have gotten in touch years ago. I think Sol would agree. You missed out on her for so long. I was selfish. And scared. I didn't want to lose her. And thinking about this surgery scared me about half to death. Anyone who knows me knows that I don't do doctors, needles, pills, much less go under anesthesia and have surgery. But I knew I had to do it. At least to try to give you more time together."

Janice looks at her with tears starting to form in her eyes. Now she nods. "Well, leave it to Jackie to push the boundaries. But I'm so glad she did. Or we wouldn't be having this conversation. And I'm so happy I finally got to meet Sol too. You know, Jackie has been keeping up with her, but I tried not to think too much about her and focused on what I could control. Did she tell you that I put her in my will? I hope you don't mind. It's nothing big, but it feels good after all these years of being apart. Of course, we never expected or even thought about you getting tested, much less matching me and donating. I know it's been so long, but I also wanted to tell you that I'm sorry about Patrick."

Patty reaches up and squeezes Janice's hand.

"Thank you. I'm sorry about him for you too. Even though your relationship was short, you'll forever be connected to him because of Sol. I was in such shock when that accident happened. I wasn't in any place to talk with you then. I was a mess. But I'm glad Jackie connected us after all these years. I guess it would have come out sooner or later with all the DNA testing and everything, but I think this is a happier ending." Patty pushes herself up out of the wheelchair and gives Janice a hug.

Janice holds her tightly. "Yes, we're really family now. A part of you lives in me. And a part of me was already in your life. Let's pray that my body doesn't reject this one."

"No way that it will! That would mess up the story!" Patty replies, laughing.

"We agree!" Sol and Shyla cry out, then come over and join in the hug. Willow appears in the doorway. "Come on over here, Willow," Patty says, and Willow joins the hug too.

- 70 -

Jericho puts one paw up on his grandmother's bed to say hello. Sol follows closely behind into her mother's room back in Baltimore. "Fresh-squeezed lemonade, just the way you like it!" Sol calls out with a tray in her hands.

"Thanks, hon, you really don't have to baby me like this. I'm fine, just need to get a little extra rest. The kids at the store have been doing so well while I was gone, I don't feel like I need to rush back. I'm so proud of them. Small World Imports will live on!" Her mom has one of her colorful imported blankets arranged over her legs, and the ceiling fan above keeps the summer air moving through the room.

"Of course it will live on! You're not dying yet! But I'm glad they're doing so well. It's been long overdue for you to let them take some of the load off of you. Shyla texted me earlier to say that Janice is doing well so far. She's still in the hospital, but all signs point to her getting out next week. They are going to try to do that party that they started planning during her first surgery next month. Thea says she wants to go with me. I'm becoming quite a regular on those flights to Boston!" Sol puts the tray down on her mother's side table, then perches on the edge of the bed and pets Jericho's head with one hand.

"That's good. I'm glad you're getting to know all of them. Your father... I'm sorry he missed all this. But most of all I'm sorry he missed out on you and your sisters. I have been so blessed to have you all these years, and now I guess I can share you a little." Patty takes a long sip of lemonade and smiles up at Sol. "Delicious!"

"Thanks, Mom, I appreciate everything. I wish I could have known Dad, but I'm so thankful to have Mickey in our family too. I guess we couldn't really have both. Just like you couldn't have me without that time of you being separated. It reminds me of that verse that talks about God giving beauty for ashes. I never would have planned my life out like this, but God definitely has the most creativity!" Sol looks out her mom's window at the tree bending in the wind. She thinks about what her mom said about Willow's name.

Her mom follows her gaze, then looks back at Sol and reaches out to move her hair back over her shoulder. "Yeah, you're right. It's a lot to mourn but a lot to be thankful for. When I'm feeling a little better, I'll go through some old boxes and tell you some more about your dad."

Sol looks back at Patty. "Thanks, Mom. Did I tell you I'll be starting therapy soon? I'll probably have some more questions for you."

"That's good, Sunshine. It will be nice to have someone outside of the family sort through all of this with you." Her mom smiles.

"Oh, guess what else!" Sol excitedly says. "Remember I told you Great-Aunt Tabitha was doing the dating app for me when you were in surgery? I have a date with one of the guys tomorrow! Turns out he works in the building down the street from me, so we're going to walk over to the brewery for a drink after work."

Her mom's smile gets even bigger. "Great! I hear that Great-Aunt Tabitha has a lot of admirers herself. Well, you know I want the very best for you. You'll keep on writing your own story now."

Sol leans over and gives her mom a hug. "I'll let you know how it goes! Love you, Mom!"

"Love you, daughter."

Notes

I'd love to hear what you thought about this book! Email me at read@chavosabooks.com or message me on social media @chavosabooks.

The reading program that Sol works for is inspired by a real literacy organization I've been volunteering with for many years. Check it out at readingpartners.org, and consider becoming a volunteer!

Nearly one million patients in the United States have kidney failure, requiring dialysis or kidney transplant for survival. Kidney transplant is the most effective long-term treatment for end-stage kidney disease. More than one hundred thousand patients in the United States are waiting for a kidney transplant, which far outnumbers the number of donor kidneys available for transplant (twenty-one thousand in 2019). The average waiting time for a kidney transplant can be three to five years and even longer in some geographical regions of the country. Live donor kidney transplant helps reduce the shortage of organs for transplant and offers patients with kidney failure the ability to receive a transplant sooner than on the waiting list. In some cases, kidney transplant can occur even before starting dialysis. Patients who receive a live donor kidney transplant report better quality of life, and kidneys from living donors last longer than kidneys from a deceased donor.

For more information about kidney transplantation and living donation, visit these sites:

- transplantliving.org
- kidneyregistry.org

Thea's Road Trip Playlist

The ultimate "meet-your-sister-you-didn't-know-you-had-because-your-biological-mom-you-didn't-know-you-had-needs-a-kidney playlist!"

Search for C. H. Avosa to listen to this playlist on Spotify.

#	Song	Artist
1	Family Affair	Sly & The Family Stone
2	We Are Family	Sister Sledge
3	Why Can't We Be Friends?	War
4	That's What Friends Are For	Dionne Warwick, Elton John, Gladys Knight, Stevie Wonder
5	Lean on Me	Club Nouveau
6	Who Can It Be Now?	Men At Work
7	Who's That Girl	Madonna
8	True Colors	Cyndi Lauper
9	Somewhere Out There	Linda Ronstadt, James Ingram
10	No Roots	Alice Merton

11	Home	Phillip Phillips
12	I'm Not a Girl, Not Yet a Woman	Britney Spears
13	Who I Am	Jessica Andrews
14	My Wish	Rascal Flatts
15	Live Like You Were Dying	Tim McGraw
16	Chasing Clouds	Marsha Ambrosius
17	Fault Lines	Fyfe
18	You Say	Lauren Daigle
19	Whatcha Lookin' 4	Kirk Franklin, The Family
20	Where Have You Been	Rihanna

Acknowledgments

Now I understand why the acknowledgments sections in books can be so long. You just can't write a book without support from so many people. And I had no idea what I was getting myself into!

First, to all the "Theas" in my life, I wouldn't be here without you. Thank you for all of your support and encouragement and belief in me. I hope you found a piece of your own story in this one. I couldn't write a story without including yours.

Thank you to all my family, by blood or love, for your role in my journey. A special thank-you to my mom for cultivating a love of reading in us from an early age and for all her editorial help and support in writing this.

Thank you to Natalie Mangrum for "going first" in writing a book and being such an inspiration with the #ownyourstory movement. I probably wouldn't be here today if you hadn't gotten me involved in your design and publishing process!

Thanks to Jason Hawkins, head of research services at the Thurgood Marshall Law Library, who helped me track down law school catalogs from the early 1980s. The website familyecho.com was so helpful for creating a fictional family tree that I could use to keep my characters straight. Thanks to Jim Hodgson for his workshop on fiction writing that really helped me with the practical side of writing a novel.

Thank you to those who helped me with character names—Ashley and Mary—and with song suggestions for Thea's playlist—Rachelle, Allie, Sarah, and Tolu.

To everyone who shared their personal stories with me, I appreciate your generosity and openness so much. To Tasha and Mary for sharing their experiences in the kidney transplant process. To the Facebook groups I Hate Dialysis, Living Donors Online!, and Late Discovery Adoptees & Family, and websites latediscoveryadoptees.com and npefellowship.org—thank you for graciously allowing me to listen to your experiences. I learned so much from you. To Crystal Lowery for sharing about her role as a senior program manager at Reading Partners. To Emily Hart of Sorrow Rejoicing for talking with me about her losses and hope. To Julie Stromberg, who opened my eyes to issues of adoptee rights many years ago. To Libby Copeland for her book, *The Lost Family*.

A huge thank-you to all my readers for your time, attention, encouragement, and commitment to making this book the best it can be: Ashley Timsuren, Jeneil Russell, Rev. Johnny Kurcina, Dr. Desirée de Jesus, Gail Newman, and Nicole James. Your thoughtful feedback made it a thousand times better. And extra thanks to Nicole for help with the discussion questions!

Thank you to Dr. Virginia Wang, my dear friend, healthcare researcher (including kidney care), one of my first readers, and the one who connected me with Lisa!

To Dr. Lisa McElroy, assistant professor of abdominal transplant surgery at the Duke University School of Medicine, thank you for taking the time to carefully review my manuscript, read and reread chapters, and give me so much valuable feedback to make this book as accurate as possible. It's been a pleasure working with you, and I look forward to partnering with you on increasing equity in the transplant process. Any and all mistakes are my own.

To my editor, Jenny, yay, we finally get to work together! To amazing fiber artist Julie Shackson, I'm so privileged to get to use your work on my cover.

To Jonas Nascimento and to the Charles Village D-group, thank you for all your prayers for this book! To Tracy S., thank you for your support and encouragement on my journey.

To my adopted city of Baltimore and all my Baltimore friends and neighbors, I hope I have done you proud.

To all the amazing single women out there, I see you! Keep being amazing!

And to Jesus, the author and perfecter of our faith, I owe you everything.

Discussion Questions

There are many different themes woven throughout the book, which should lead to lots of good discussion. Here are some potential questions to get you started! You can also download a printable copy of these questions at chavosabooks.com.

I'd love to hear about what you discuss. Email me at read@chavosabooks.com or message me on social media @chavosabooks.com.

1. Has anyone from your past ever contacted you with unexpected, life-changing news? Or have you ever been the one to contact someone? How was your life changed by this experience?

2. Sol's experience of nontraditional adoption is reflected in many cultures. In your culture, how is adoption viewed and experienced? Do you have a personal experience of adoption, and if so, how does it compare with Sol's?

3. What do you think about Sol's dating experiences? What experiences have you had with online dating? If you're not a single person, has this book changed your understanding of single people at all?

4. Considering the marriages in the novel, choose one couple that you found most interesting, and describe how the marital dynamics showed up in the overall story line.

5. The novel explores some of the issues surrounding organ donorship. What do you think would be the most pressing concern for you if you were to consider donating an organ? Are you registered as an organ donor? Why or why not?

6. How do you think you would feel if you found out you were a different ethnicity? Would it make a difference which ethnicity? Have you ever/would you ever take a DNA test? How do you think Sol handled it?

7. What do you think about the representations of black and white characters in the book?

8. Describe the role that forgiveness played in this novel. How does it compare to the role that forgiveness plays in society? In your family of origin? Your own life?

9. We get to read Sol's journal as we go through the story. How does that affect your experience as a reader? Describe any ways that you use journaling personally and what it means to you.

10. What do you think about the role of faith in Sol's story? How do you think the story line would have been different without it?

11. Describe some of the ideas of family as seen through the eyes of different characters. What, if anything, surprised you about the family relationships in this book?

12. What does family mean to you? How does biology affect our willingness to make sacrifices for others?

13. What do you think about Janice's decision to ask Patrick and Patty to raise Sol?

14. What character do you most relate to or like? Why?

15. How would you characterize the relationships between Willow, Dove, and Sol? Did you find their responses to be believable throughout the story? Describe what you think your response may have been as a sibling in that situation.

16. How did the particular settings of Baltimore and Boston affect the story? How might the story have been different if set in another US city, or another region, such as the Deep South or the Midwest?

17. Are there any other themes that stand out to you?

ABOUT THE AUTHOR

C. H. Avosa is an author, designer, and owner of several businesses, including Avosa Books. She's dedicated to helping increase childhood literacy and getting new stories for all ages out into the world. When she's not traveling, she lives in her adopted city of Baltimore, Maryland, with a multitude of dogs.

Visit her website at chavosabooks.com.

CPSIA information can be obtained
at www.ICGtesting.com
Printed in the USA
BVHW040219220421
605623BV00013B/593